SHERLOCK HOLMES
CONSULTING DETECTIVE

CORNERSTONE BOOK PUBLISHERS

"Dedicated to the loving memory of Sharon Bland, a true Sherlock Holmes fan, from her son-in-law, with affection always, Mark Maddox."

Sherlock Holmes: Consulting Detective
An Airship 27 Production
www.airship27.com

Published by
Cornerstone Book Publishers
New Orleans, LA
www.cornerstonepublishers.com

Editor: Ron Fortier
Associate Editor: Charles Saunders
Production and design: Rob Davis.

ISBN   1-934935-50-6
        978-1-934935-50-7

Printed in the United States of America

10 9 8 7 6 5 4 3 2 1

SHERLOCK HOLMES
CONSULTING DETECTIVE

Contents

"The Massachusetts Affair"
Aaron Smith...4

"The Problem at Stamford Bridge"
Van Allen Plexico...44

"The Adventure of the Locked Room"
Andrew Salmon..67

"The Adventure of the Tuvan Delegate"
Van Allen Plexico..111

"Dead Man's Manuscript"
I. A. Watson..135

The Game is Afoot
Ron Fortier...180

SHERLOCK HOLMES
CONSULTING DETECTIVE

"The Massachusetts Affair"

by Aaron Smith

T here have been more than a few occasions on which the events in which Sherlock Holmes and I have found ourselves to be involved have been of such a nature that I have been unable to publish accounts of them for reasons either political or personal. In these cases, I still find myself hoping that some record of Holmes's amazing talents and skills can be preserved for future generations to examine, so I have sometimes written accounts of these events and then deposited them safely in a place where they can be hidden away until such time that it is indeed proper for them to be made available. Having said this, it is clear to me as I write this that if anyone is reading this account, it must be many years in the future. If this is the case, then I find it very gratifying that even many years from now, there are those who can appreciate the unique mind and astounding abilities of the most fascinating individual it has ever been my privilege to know: Mister Sherlock Holmes.

I t was the most bitterly cold winter I can recall. The weather was brutal that year in London and the surrounding area. If my experiences as a young man in Afghanistan had shown me heat of a level almost intolerable to the human body, then that winter demonstrated the opposite, such a chill it was that hung in the air for what seemed like a terribly long season.

By the time the hansom cab deposited me on Baker Street, I could scarcely keep my teeth from chattering against each other as I paid the driver for his services. I rushed inside as quickly as I could and hastily asked Mrs. Hudson to brew a pot of tea. As I made my way upstairs I could hear the final strains of one of Sherlock Holmes's rather unique violin compositions. As I flung open the door and entered the room, he was placing the instrument in its case, apparently finished playing for the evening. He turned to acknowledge my presence as I began to shed my coat.

"Did your excursion reach a satisfactory conclusion, Watson?" he inquired.

I shook my head as I responded, "Unfortunately, Holmes, the patient died not long after my arrival. There was nothing I could do. His illness had progressed too quickly."

"I see." muttered Holmes uncaringly, and turned away to stare out the window. He apparently had some puzzling matter on his mind, as was usually indicated when he had been scraping on his violin. For twenty or thirty minutes he silently gazed out the window, during which time I went about the business of trying to warm myself now that I was safely inside again. Mrs. Hudson promptly brought in the tea I had requested and I soon sat down with a steaming cup and began to light my pipe. I intended to retire for the evening as soon as the chill had left my body.

Rest, however, was not to come as soon as I had hoped, for we soon heard Mrs. Hudson making her way up the stairs again, followed by the sound of another, heavier set of footsteps. The door opened and Mrs. Hudson appeared in the threshold to announce that a gentleman had arrived and had asked to see Holmes. Mrs. Hudson stepped aside and the visitor entered. He was so tightly bundled against the winter wind that only his two blue eyes were visible among the thick layers of clothing in which he was clad. He had on a large wool hat, a heavy overcoat and a scarf wrapped tightly around his neck. His pants looked several sizes too large for his build and I realized that he had put a larger pair of trousers on over whatever he wore beneath them. Leather gloves covered his hands. This man had done all he could to prepare himself for the trip to Baker Street.

As the man entered our rooms, Holmes turned from the window to see who had entered, and without a single second's hesitation exclaimed, "Well, Watson, it seems that an American Naval officer has seen fit to visit us this evening."

Shocked by Holmes's abrupt announcement, the visitor tore off his scarf and with an expression of amazement inquired, "How the devil

"Did your excursion reach a satisfactory conclusion, Watson?"

could you know that? I just walked in and I'm covered head to foot against this ungodly cold!"

Holmes sat himself down in his usual chair and responded to our guest's shock. "Covered from head to foot perhaps, but your usual clothing is covered only from head to ankle. The trained eye can tell more about a man from his shoes and his posture than the untrained eye can discover by reading an entire biographical volume."

As Holmes spoke, our visitor removed his hat, gloves, and overcoat. He was now clad in the shirt and jacket of, indeed, an officer of the American navy. Only his uniform pants were now obscured by the oversized second pair of trousers he had donned. When visible, he proved to be a man of twenty-five to thirty years old, with somewhat curly brown hair and a cheerful face, a bit softer than one might expect from a military man. Once he had finished uncovering himself sufficiently for an indoor climate, he stood before Holmes and introduced himself. "I am Lieutenant David Sutherland, and you, Sir, I would presume to be Mister Sherlock Holmes!"

Holmes shook the young officer's outstretched hand and confirmed his assumption. "Indeed I am, Lieutenant, and this is my associate, Doctor John Watson. I assure you that whatever business has brought you to our door tonight may be freely discussed in the doctor's presence. He has assisted me in many matters in recent years."

Once introductions had been made, Holmes inquired as to what had prompted the young lieutenant to seek us out. I motioned for Sutherland to sit, and as he did so he began to explain his reasons for coming to us.

"I'm the third officer on the United States Navy's battleship, the *Massachusetts*. We arrived and docked several days ago, having been assigned to deliver some documents to some officials here in London. I'm afraid my duty forbids me from revealing to anyone exactly who the documents were being delivered to or what information they may have contained, but thus far I believe that to be irrelevant to the reasons I have for coming here tonight."

As Lieutenant Sutherland was thus beginning his narrative, Mrs. Hudson returned with another pot of tea so that we could now offer some refreshment to our guest, who gladly accepted. Once Mrs. Hudson had poured a cup for the young officer, she departed and he was able to continue his story.

"It was the ship's captain, Abraham Holt, who dispatched me to come and visit you, Mr. Holmes. He ordered me to come ashore, telling no one else onboard, whether officer or enlisted sailor, where I was going. I was to come straight here, making no stops upon the way, and speaking to no one save the driver who would deliver me. That is precisely what I did."

Holmes raised a hand to halt the lieutenant's tale. "Might I ask, Lieutenant, why the captain chose to send his third officer? I would assume that the first officer would be the one most trusted and confided in by the ship's commander."

Sutherland, who did not seem surprised to be questioned thus, patiently answered Holmes's question. "Well, Mr. Holmes, Captain Holt is quick to confide in me because I happen to be his nephew. My mother is his younger sister and my uncle and I have always been quite close. He's been like a father to me since my own father died when I was just a boy. He asked that I be posted on his ship when I received my commission."

"Thank you. You may continue, and hopefully tell us precisely why you have come here this evening." said Holmes, gently indicating that Sutherland should make the point he was struggling towards with his speech.

Lieutenant Sutherland fidgeted in his chair a bit, seeming to grow more nervous as it grew time to reveal the reasons for his visit. "Well, Mr. Holmes, we found a dead man on board the *Massachusetts* an hour before I got here!"

Holmes straightened up in his seat, as did I, now truly anticipating the next details to come from Sutherland's mouth. His slow, plodding narrative had just become more interesting. Perhaps, I thought, this would indeed be worth delaying my night's sleep for.

I couldn't help myself and interjected, "A dead man? Was it a member of the ship's crew?"

"No, Doctor," responded Sutherland, "We have no idea who he is...or was. There's a cabin on the ship that rarely gets used. It's a pretty large room, about the same size as the captain's quarters, but it's reserved for special passengers, like admirals or maybe a senator or some such dignitary. Now, even though nobody ever sleeps in there more than once or twice a year, it still has to be kept as well maintained as the rest of the ship, so the crew still cleans it. Well, tonight one of the crew went in to sweep the place out, right on schedule, and found a dead body right in the middle of the floor, just laying there. It wasn't a sailor and it wasn't an officer. He was just dressed in ordinary clothes. The crewman who found him called for one of the petty officers, and he called for the chief surgeon, and he called for the first officer, and he called for the captain, and next thing we knew, almost all the officers and a few of the enlisted sailors were crowded in that little room with a dead man that nobody had ever seen before!"

Poor young Sutherland had gotten himself so excited relating the discovery of the corpse that he had to stop for a moment to catch his breath. As the lieutenant paused, Sherlock Holmes leaned back in his chair drew in a deep breath, placed a finger against his upper lip, and closed his eyes for a moment. Over the course of our time together, I had seen Holmes do this many times. I knew that it indicated that something interesting was happening within his sharp analytical mind, but I would never be so bold as to guess exactly what those processes might include.

After a moment had passed, Holmes opened his eyes and spoke. "Have the police been notified? Are they involved at all yet?"

Sutherland, who had caught his breath by now, answered. "No, Sir. My uncle, umm…I meant the captain, wouldn't allow it. As far as he's concerned, his ship is part of the United States and whatever happens on board is not the business of any other nation. No offense intended towards the English of course, gentlemen."

"It relieves me to hear that, Lieutenant. Perhaps the scene and the body within it will not have been terribly disturbed then." said Holmes.

Sutherland nodded in agreement, "It hasn't been disturbed at all, Mr. Holmes. The captain wouldn't let anyone move it or even touch it. He said he had read about your work and he wanted you to see the dead fellow exactly as we had found him. He's probably had the body locked in that room with armed guards outside since I left the ship."

Holmes clapped his hands together loudly and suddenly stood straight up. His rapid springing into a standing position slightly startled the young lieutenant. I, however, was used to Holmes's sudden changes in mood and the quick shifts in physical position that accompanied them.

"Well, Lieutenant Sutherland, you have brought me news of an unidentified corpse in a carefully guarded room, which has been largely, at least, unaltered in any way! You may relate any other details that come to mind on the way to this battleship of yours! Come, Watson!"

Sutherland, Holmes and I quickly dressed ourselves for the winter weather and prepared to leave at once. With Holmes of a mind to inspect the scene immediately, he was like a force of nature, his analytical mind clearly anticipating the exercise it was about to get. Once dressed to guard ourselves against the cold, we headed down the stairs and out the front door. As we descended the seventeen steps, Sutherland remembered the financial part of hiring a consulting detective and felt the need to explain, "Oh, Mr. Holmes, I was told to assure you that any fees owed you once this business is concluded will come from Captain Holt himself."

We were able to hire a coach to take us to the docks quickly enough and while we could still feel the cold inside the cab, at least we were somewhat sheltered from the strong winds that added to the painful chill. As we rode, Holmes was mostly silent, alternating between staring out the window and closing his eyes for short periods of time. I myself felt more like talking and I engaged Lieutenant Sutherland in some conversation about his naval career in general and his ship, the *Massachusetts*, in particular.

The *Massachusetts*, Sutherland explained to me, was one of several Indiana-class battleships. It had been commissioned in 1895, had a crew of approximately 600 officers and men, travelled at a speed of about 15 knots, and was armed with 4 thirteen inch guns, 8 eight inch guns, and 4 more guns of 4 inches each.

David Sutherland himself had decided upon a navy career in order to fulfill what he assumed would have been the wishes of his deceased father and also in order to please his uncle, Holt, who had been, as he had told us earlier, like a second father to him. His real father had also been a sailing man, having been lost at sea when young David was a lad of only nine years old. Judging by the way the young officer spoke of his work, he quite enjoyed what he did, and retained a boyish enthusiasm about his duties and the potential future he might have. He confided in me that he had high hopes of one day following in the footsteps of his uncle Abraham and captaining a vessel of his own.

The pleasant conversation with Lieutenant Sutherland made the trip seem shorter for me at least and we soon reached our destination, the docks. Sutherland paid the coach driver with some money that had been given to him by his uncle and captain and we exited the carriage. As we did so, I at least momentarily, forgot how bitterly cold it was as I saw, for the first time, an American battleship. I had been to sea, and even spent a short period of time aboard military vessels during my service in Her Majesty's army, but my memories of the warships that I had been aboard were quickly swept aside by the sight of the *Massachusetts*. It was a monstrous looking vessel, a ship that one could tell, by sight alone, was obviously designed as a bringer of destruction to any people unfortunate enough to become the target of its guns. Were the gods of the ancient Romans to come to the world of the late 19th century, this battleship would surely make a fitting chariot for Mars. I was most impressed and for a moment was lost in thoughts of how far naval warfare had progressed since the wind-carried sailing ships of Lord Nelson's era.

My thoughts returned to the present as Holmes, boiling over with the enthusiasm that inevitably came to the surface when a new case awaited his attention, suddenly shouted, "Take us aboard, Lieutenant! We won't get to the bottom of this business by loitering on the docks!"

Sutherland led us towards his ship, removing the scarf that covered the lower half of his face so that the guard would allow us to board the *Massachusetts*. We moved at a brisk pace up the long metal walkway that had been placed so as to allow one entrance to the ship.

We made it on board the battleship and found ourselves in one of her narrow corridors. It had little room to maneuver, but looked impressive all the same. Lieutenant Sutherland of course went first, followed by Sherlock Holmes who seemed ready to plow ahead and overtake the young officer's somewhat leisurely pace. I followed behind them. The interior of the ship was quite clean and very Spartan. This was clearly a vessel on which function far outranked form. Still, it was plain to see that warships had evolved in a way to be much more comfortable than they had been only a few short decades earlier. Most notably, the hallways of the ship were well heated enough that we were able to shed our hats, gloves and scarves quite quickly, which allowed us to move more normally than we had when completely sheltered against winter's fury. We passed several sailors as we walked the corridors, some of whom saluted Sutherland, but all of whom seemed too busy going about their nautical duties to wonder who the two strangers who accompanied him were. After a few minutes and a climb up several ladders to a deck higher than the one upon which we had entered the ship, we reached our destination, the visiting dignitary's cabin. The door to the room was closed and two men, both in the uniforms of senior officers, stood in front with the postures that some men assume when waiting with great anticipation.

The lieutenant made introductions between Holmes and I and the two officers. We quickly shook hands with Captain Abraham Holt and the ship's chief surgeon, a fairly young doctor named MacFarlane. Abraham Holt was a broad-shouldered bulldog of a man, perhaps fifty years of age, with a neatly trimmed graying beard and the sort of toughened, experienced face that made one think he would be able to handle himself admirably in a barroom brawl as well as in a heated naval engagement. MacFarlane was at least a decade and a half younger, his face so clear of whiskers that one might suspect that he shaved more than once a day. He looked like a military man only because of his uniform, his neatness, and the straightness of his stance. Otherwise, he more strongly resembled a poet or a schoolteacher. This was no Old Salt, but a man of high intelligence and a gentle demeanor, if one were to judge by first impressions.

Captain Holt seemed boisterously excited to be making our acquaintance. He vigorously shook Holmes's hand, and then mine. "I'm very glad to meet you, Mr. Holmes! Even in America, there are those who have read of your knack for solving even the most perplexing puzzles. Being here in London when this strange event occurred, I naturally thought of consulting you. It's truly an honor to shake your hand, Sir!"

The three officers, unaccustomed to Sherlock Holmes's sometimes stern and abrupt manner appeared somewhat taken aback when the detective reprimanded the ship's commander. "Captain Holt, I realize that some people may think of my work as some grand romantic adventure, thanks in no small part to Dr. Watson's overly fanciful written accounts. But I assure you that the tools of my profession are cold, calculating observation and reason. Need I remind you that behind that very door," growled Holmes as he pointed to the closed dignitary's cabin, "lies a dead man of undetermined identity and origin? There will be time for pleasantries when this morbid business is concluded. I suggest we attend to the matter at hand."

Captain Holt's face went crimson with embarrassment, but the color quickly faded from his cheeks as his face resumed its previous authoritative demeanor. "Very well, Mr. Holmes," said the captain as he opened the cabin door.

The door swung open and we entered the cabin. Captain Holt entered first, with MacFarlane close behind. Holmes was next, and then I. Lieutenant Sutherland came in last. The room was fairly large as far as ship cabins go; approximately the same size as a typical captain's quarters. As it was currently unused, save as a place where unexpected corpses appear, it was mostly empty. Against one wall was a bed, obviously empty. A small desk and chair were on the other wall. There was enough space within the cabin for the five of us to stand comfortably while looking down at the body, but there was not enough room for much more maneuvering than that. As we had anticipated, there was indeed a dead man lying on the floor of the cabin. He was on his side, sprawled out and of course very still. At first glance, I judged him to be about 35 years old, dressed in a cheap suit and brown shoes. There was nothing unusual about his appearance. He had not shaved in several days and his hair was ruffled, although the state of his hair may have been due to the fact that he had fallen to the ground when he died. On his face was a blank, open-eyed expression. He had certainly not passed quietly away in his sleep. I could see no blood or other signs of violence, so I could not be sure of how he had died until such time that I had an opportunity to examine the body. I had observed the obvious facts of the matter, but I could not help wonder what Holmes was seeing at that moment. We were both viewing the same morbid scene, but he certainly saw far more than I could.

Sherlock Holmes in a room with a mysteriously dead body was very much like an animal in its perfect environment. This was Holmes's natural state, to which he was as perfectly suited as a fish to the sea or a lion to the wide plains and high grasses of the African continent.

While Holmes and I were taking our first look at the scene, Holt had turned to Sutherland and was dismissing the young man from the scene. "You did well, my boy, bringing Mr. Holmes and the doctor here. You missed your supper. Go and eat, Lieutenant." David Sutherland responded with a salute and quickly left the room.

Holmes, meanwhile, had gone into the state which I had seen him go into many times before. He flung off his coat and his hat and rolled up his shirtsleeves. He stared at the whole of the scene for a few moments, then sprang into motion, circling the body like a bird of prey, his hawk-like nose sniffing the air in search of any unusual odors which might give a hint of what had occurred here, his eyes moving over every inch of the deceased's body, rapidly examining every fold in the man's clothing, every detail of the position in which he had fallen, his relation to the walls and furniture of the cabin, and every other particular of the entire scene. Doubtlessly, Holmes had deduced many things already, and the body had not in any way been moved or touched by either of us as yet.

While Holmes prowled for indications of the facts of the matter at hand, Captain Holt almost attempted to interrupt. "What do you think, Mister..." the captain began, but I put a hand on his arm, indicating that he should not approach Holmes anymore than one should do anything to distract a surgeon with scalpel in hand. "Captain, it is better to wait until Holmes has examined the scene. When he is ready to speak, he most certainly will," I said to him.

I then turned to MacFarlane and questioned my fellow physician. "Have you examined the body at all?" The ship's surgeon replied that he had done nothing more than to check the man for a heartbeat or breathing. Once he had ascertained that the man was dead he had, as per the captain's orders, done nothing that might disturb the scene. Apparently, the captain had decided immediately upon the body's discovery to call upon Holmes rather than involve Scotland Yard. I found this a bit odd, despite Holmes's reputation, but I said nothing. I would wait until Holmes mentioned it, or at least until we had a chance to discuss things in privacy.

Some time passed and Holmes finally turned away from the body and back towards the rest of us. "Captain, would it be possible for the surgeon and yourself to leave the cabin for a short time? I should like to examine the corpse more closely now. Dr. Watson will of course assist me." Captain Holt hesitated for a moment, but nodded in agreement and left the room with MacFarlane following behind him.

The door closed with the two officers on the outside and Holmes and I in the cabin in the company of the dead man. Holmes knelt down and reached into the man's pockets. He produced a handkerchief, a small box of matches, a penknife, several coins, and several folded papers. He placed most of the objects on the floor in a small pile and began rifling through the papers. I, in the meantime, began to examine the body itself. I saw no signs of strangulation. I could find no obvious wounds. It was only when I felt the scalp that I could feel that the skull had indeed been struck, most likely by a large, heavy and blunt object. The skin had not been broken, so no blood had erupted, but the blow must have done enough damage to kill. Perhaps a fragment of the skull had been driven into the brain.

Holmes had finished looking through the man's pocket contents and looked up at me. "A hard blow to the head then, Watson?" he inquired.

"How did you know?" I asked, thinking that I should have been used to such occurrences by now.

"It was not the man's head that told me the story, Watson. It was your reaction as you examined it," Holmes explained.

"What was in those papers, Holmes? Anything of importance?" I asked.

Holmes waved the papers in the air with a satisfied look on his face. "Indeed there was. The victim's name for one thing! We are looking at the body of one Edmund Gibbs of the town of Mystic in the state of Connecticut in the United States of America."

"Excellent," I said. "At least we have identified him. What else have you learned from the body?"

Holmes began to speak. Even after observing many such scenes, I still marveled at Holmes's ability to derive so much from seemingly so little. "Gibbs was man of modest means, as evidenced by his inexpensive attire.

His shoes are worn, and if you were to examine his pants you would find that he has mended several small tears in the fabric. His sewing skill is sufficient to present a good appearance to a casual observer, but the flaws are evident upon close examination, indicating that it was he, and not a professional tailor, who sewed the splits. A tailor who sewed like that would not remain in the profession for very long. His clothes are, however, meticulously kept. This man was obviously concerned with making his appearance as presentable as possible, despite the cheapness of his attire. This indicates habits acquired in military service, which I will address further in a moment. The calluses on Gibbs's hands tell me that he does manual labor of some sort, but the condition of his fingernails would hint that he has not worked too much lately. Perhaps he has been unemployed in recent weeks. Note also that he had no money on his person when we arrived here, save for the few small coins I found in his pockets. This, however, does not mean that he was bankrupt, for whoever killed him may have taken it. But since we have already decided that he was not a wealthy man by anyone's definition, it is unlikely that robbery was the sole motive of the murderer. I have also decided that Gibbs was at one time in the American Navy himself. Notice the soles of his shoes. There is very little dirt on them, none of it very fresh. This tells me that he did not sneak aboard this vessel here in London. I believe this man stowed away in America and has been aboard for the entire voyage here. He somehow managed to remain undetected until he died here in this room, so he must have had some knowledge of where one might hide himself sufficiently well enough to keep from being found during a journey across the Atlantic Ocean. Not only would he have to hide himself well, but he would need to know the pace of a day's activities aboard a naval vessel in order to be able to move around without being caught. After all, he had to eat at some point. Such familiarity with the design and routines of a ship such as this would indicate experience in the American fleet."

As always, I was astounded by how much information Holmes was able to cull from such a short period of investigation. We now knew the man's name, which was the simplest part of it, having found identifying papers in his pockets. More importantly, we had some idea of what kind of a man he was. He was not wealthy by any means, but was careful about his appearance. He probably had served in the military at some point in his lifetime, specifically in the American navy. We had also determined how he had died. The unfortunate man had been killed by an impact to the head. The body did not appear to have been moved, so we could assume that his death had occurred in this cabin. Since there were no nearby objects upon which he could have struck his head accidentally, it was clear that someone else must have been present, and that other individual must have been the murderer. The killer had taken the object with which the deadly blow was struck with them when they left the cabin.

Having learned these things in the course of our time in the cabin, Holmes and I were now prepared to return to the company of the two senior officers who had allowed us the time to examine the room and its dead occupant. We left the cabin, closing the door behind us. Holt and MacFarlane were waiting in the hallway for us to emerge.

"Well, Mr. Holmes? How did the examination go? Have you learned much about our unexpected guest?" asked Captain Abraham Holt.

The detective replied, "We have learned all we could from our observations of the body and the room. If you wish you may now have the body moved to a place where it will not attract further attention."

Captain Holt called for two of his crewmen to take the corpse away. When the two burly sailors had lifted the remains of Edmund Gibbs, Dr. Macfarlane led them away to a place where the body would be stored should we wish to examine it further. When the ship's surgeon, the crewmen, and the body had left the area, the captain invited Holmes and me into his quarters. We accepted his invitation and his yeoman soon brought us chairs upon which to sit and hot coffee to drink. Once we were settled, Holt asked us to tell him anything we could about what had happened aboard the *Massachusetts*.

Holmes began with a question for Captain Holt. "Tell me, Captain, have you ever heard of the name Ed Gibbs?" inquired Holmes.

"No, Sir. Doesn't ring a bell," answered Holt. "Was that the dead man's name?"

"Indeed it was," said Holmes. "Mister Gibbs resided in a town called Mystic, in Connecticut, which I believe is on the East Coast of the United States."

"Yes, it certainly is," Holt replied. "I myself was born in that state. Mystic itself is a seafaring town, although its business mostly involves the whaling business, rather than naval affairs." Holt then tried to guide the subject back to the dead man. "Do you know how the poor fellow died?"

"He was killed by a blow to the skull from some heavy, but not sharpened, object," Holmes volunteered, "I do not believe the motive to have been robbery. I also do not believe it to have been self-defense, for if one of your men had happened upon an intruder and killed him; you would certainly have been informed immediately. This leaves us with two possibilities: either one of your sailors or officers had some reason to slay this man and is therefore hiding something from you and the rest of the crew…or there was or is a second intruder aboard this ship. There is a definite chance that danger still walks among us here on the *Massachusetts!*"

Captain Holt nearly jumped out of his seat upon hearing Holmes's words. "Then I'll have the ship searched at once! From bow to stern, deck by deck, top to bottom and inch by inch, no stone shall go unturned! Whoever killed this Edmund Gibbs will not escape this vessel unpunished! "

Holmes gestured for the captain to remain in his seat and spoke to keep him from calling for such a search. "Not yet, Captain Holt. Raising such an alarm will surely cause the murderer to try to flee the ship, should they still be aboard. If this person reaches the streets of London, we shall never find them. It is far better that we keep what we have spoken of to ourselves for now, and Watson and I will, with your permission of course, continue our investigation."

Holt agreed. He then offered us the option of spending the rest of the night on his ship, so that we might rest and continue with the matter in the morning. I expected Holmes to insist on continuing our task immediately, but he instead accepted the captain's offer. Holt asked if we would feel it to be too unsettling to sleep in the dignitary's cabin, which was of course the room where the corpse had lain until a short time before. Things like that did not disturb either of us, so we gladly agreed. We retired to the cabin. Holmes, whose sleeping habits were not those of the typical man, elected to sit in a chair and spend the night in one of his trances of analysis. I took to the bed and fell asleep after a brief conversation, during which Holmes revealed a very important piece of information to me.

"Captain Holt is lying to us," said Holmes.

When I asked how he had ascertained this, he explained, "While we drank our coffee, I asked if he had heard of Ed Gibbs. I was very careful to phrase the question in that way. When Holt was on the verge of ordering the ship searched, in his excitement he referred to the deceased as Edmund Gibbs. The nickname Ed can stand for Edmund, certainly, but it may also be Edwin or Edgar, or most frequently, Edward. Captain Abraham Holt had surely heard of Edmund Gibbs before! There is more happening here than this vessel's master has told us!"

Despite having the mystery of what was really happening aboard the *Massachusetts* on my mind, I slept soundly and comfortably that night, happy that we had taken the dignitary's cabin rather than choosing to sleep in the much more cramped crew's quarters. As far as I know, Holmes did not sleep, but sat in the cabin's chair all night, doubtlessly deep in thought, as was his custom when engaged in the contemplation of a new case. I awoke early, and Holmes and I joined the ship's officers for breakfast. Lieutenant Sutherland was minding the bridge that particular morning so he did not eat with us. Most of the other senior officers were present, including Captain Holt, Dr. MacFarlane, the first and second officers, the chief engineer, the gunnery officer, and several others. It was an enjoyable morning meal consisting of hot coffee, hotcakes, fried potatoes, bacon and sausages. The mood was a good one all around and the officers seemed to be content to avoid talking of the appearance of Gibbs's corpse and the mystery surrounding it. Instead, talk turned to life on the seas and the officers, all of whom were experienced seamen, took pride in sharing anecdotes of their seafaring memories with Holmes and me. Some spoke of narrow escapes in dangerous situations, while others related tales of great storms they had lived through at sea. Several spoke highly and with great respect of friends and comrades who had died at sea, and a few recollections of exotic women encountered at foreign ports made the rounds of the table that morning.

After breakfast, Captain Holt took us on a tour of most of the vessel. We were allowed to observe the sailors at work in many different parts of the ship. I found it fascinating myself, while Holmes's attention, I could tell, was more focused on memorizing the layout of the decks in order to piece together some theory about what had happened to lead to the demise of Edmund Gibbs. Despite being concerned with seeking out the truth, Holmes was entirely civil towards Holt, giving no hint that he suspected that the captain was concealing things from us.

As noon approached, Holmes and I decided it would be a good idea to spend a short period of time off the ship. In order to disembark, we made the excuse of some slight claustrophobia on my part. This was, of course, a ruse and the real reason was so that we would be able to discuss matters without either being overheard or arousing suspicion by retreating behind the door of the cabin in which we had spent the last night.

Before leaving the *Massachusetts*, Holmes took David Sutherland aside and implored him to discreetly stay close to the captain. He hinted that he had some suspicions of imminent danger to the lieutenant's uncle, but did not wish to alarm the captain or crew. Sutherland, noticeably concerned with Captain Holt's safety, immediately agreed.

Holmes and I spent three quarters of an hour walking along the docks.

The daylight had brought a temporary reprieve from the terrible winter winds of the night before. While it was still quite cold, it was not unbearable and we were able to wander about without completely restricting ourselves in multiple layers of heavy clothing.

As we walked, Sherlock Holmes began to talk about what he thought, in theory, might have brought Edmund Gibbs and his as yet unidentified companion (and killer) on board the battleship.

"Let us think this over, Watson. What would cause two people to sneak aboard this vessel and remain there, in hiding, for the entire duration of a cross-Atlantic voyage? What was the motivation behind the actions of our stowaways?"

I hazarded the first guess that came to mind, "Perhaps they simply wished to have free passage across the ocean."

Holmes shook his head. "No, Watson. There are many passenger ships that regularly travel from the East Coast of the United States to London. Would it not be far easier to conceal oneself on one of those ships? On a passenger ship of any class, the crew is far outnumbered by the passengers, a new batch of whom come aboard for every trip. One could easily slip aboard and blend in with the multitudes without being recognized as not belonging there. No, Watson, there must be some reason why they had to stow away on a specifically military vessel, perhaps specifically this one."

I guessed again. "Robbery then, Holmes? Perhaps there was something aboard which they hoped to steal."

Holmes again rejected my hypothesis, "Hoped to steal what?" asked Holmes. "There would be items of much more value on board a passenger ship, particularly one of the more luxurious ones. Many passengers carry large sums of cash or precious jewelry. There cannot have been much currency aboard our warship; certainly not enough to risk capture by the United States Navy and possible charges of treason! We may also strike from our list of ideas the potential motivation of trying to steal the documents that the ship was delivering to London. Were our unseen guests perhaps spies, or saboteurs, they surely would have realized that the documents would be delivered immediately upon arrival in England. This was done, and yet no attempt was made to interrupt or prevent their delivery. Simple passage from one place to the next was not the reason for stowing away, nor was any sort of theft. What does that leave?"

"Murder...of someone other than Edmund Gibbs himself?" I asked.

"Precisely," replied Sherlock Holmes, smirking just slightly as he sometimes did on the rare occasions when my theories came into the same

"Murder…of someone other than Edmund Gibbs himself?" I asked.
"Precisely," replied Sherlock Holmes.

line of reasoning as his, proving that I had learned at least something during my years as his chronicler and friend.

"The question then becomes: Who did they intend to murder?" I pointed out.

Holmes however, raised the stakes considerably by replying with, "Or who *do* they intend to murder? Remember, Watson, the second stowaway may still be on board, and since no one other than Edmund Gibbs has died, danger still lies in wait on the *Massachusetts*. We must assume that Gibbs and the other person came aboard together in order to kill their intended victim. Then for some reason, the second would-be-murderer became an actual murderer, but slew his partner rather than the original target. Why, I do not know as yet, but two possibilities come to mind. First, we may consider the idea that it was a sudden disagreement, culminating in a violent incident, which led to the death of Edmund Gibbs. The other possibility is that there was something of value to be gained from carrying out the originally intended killing, most likely money, as it often is in these cases. Perhaps the not yet deceased stowaway decided to take all of the payment for himself, and so disposed of Gibbs before the crime for hire was carried out."

"A sound theory, Holmes, but it leaves one more open question. Who was the intended victim? If all that you have just said is so, which member of the *Massachusetts* crew's life is in danger even as we speak?"

"I have an idea about that, Watson," Holmes said, "but I wish to confirm it before I decide whether or not I am correct in my assumptions. We shall return to the ship and have a private conversation with Captain Holt."

"So do you believe the captain himself to be the target of the potential assassin?" I guessed.

Holmes nearly shouted with surprise. He almost smiled. "Very good, Watson, very good indeed! I do suspect that the captain was the one whom the stowaways intended to dispose of. How did you come to this conclusion?"

It was rare that Holmes showed such joy, but I assumed it was because in moments like these he briefly felt a sort of kinship with whoever had made a statement that matched his own theories. To have the type of mind that a man like Sherlock Homes possesses can make for a lonely life, as one is constantly thinking and reasoning in ways that elude most common men. Happy to see him smile, however briefly, I admitted, "I'm afraid it was merely a guess, Holmes. The captain is the most prominent person on a naval vessel, and therefore would be considered by many to be the most important. The more important one's actions are, as history will demonstrate, the more likely they are to have angered someone enough to resort to murder. However, I assume you have a more sufficient reason to fear for Holt's safety."

"My thinking went like this, Watson," Holmes explained, "If I were to sneak aboard a ship and intended to remain hidden for an entire trans-Atlantic voyage; I would certainly take as few risks as possible. Yet it would certainly prove necessary to move from place to place aboard the ship at some point, particularly if I wanted to close in on my prey, on the target of my murderous desires. How then, I asked myself, would I be most likely to go about travelling from area to area of the ship? Assuming I knew the general landscape of the ship's interior, I would most likely have several or even many different hiding places in mind. I would then go into the open, risking being spotted, only for very brief periods. I would leave one place of concealment, move quickly, and conceal myself again in the next location. When preparing to strike down my victim, were I the shipboard assassin, I would be certain to find a hiding place as close as possible to where I intended to attack. Now we know that Edmund Gibbs's life ended in the dignitary's cabin. We might then call this the final hiding place of one of our assassins. He was in that room, and his partner was with him. Since hiding stowaways do not move about unnecessarily, they surely had a reason for being there. Hence, we assume they were hiding, waiting to go about completing their deadly task. So, Watson, what part of the ship is very close, almost immediately next to the cabin where the body of Edmund Gibbs was discovered?"

"The captain's quarters!" I exclaimed as I understood the logic behind Holmes's deductions.

"So now you see. That is why we must now speak once again with the captain," Holmes stated excitedly, "But, Watson, I assure you that this will not be the friendly banter over coffee that it was last night. I intend to demand the truth from Abraham Holt, and I will not stop until I get just that!"

With that small outburst of excitement, Holmes began to walk back towards the *Massachusetts* at a brisk pace. There was, however, enough time before we reached the battleship for Holmes to pose a rather unexpected question.

"What are your thoughts on the subject of dreams, Watson?" inquired my friend.

Surprised to be asked such a thing by one whom so rarely spoke of anything that could not be measured, verified, or analyzed scientifically, I tried to compose a suitable answer. "They are, I suppose, simply a bundle of fantasies, sometimes narrative and often surreal, that result when the sleeping mind jumbles together all the thoughts and images that accumulate when awake. Dreams lack logic and reason because the mind is floating freely through its thoughts, rather than in any ordered fashion or through any conscious effort."

Holmes thought for a moment about what I had said, then replied. "I think very much the same of the majority of dreams, especially the most dramatic of them. But I also believe that on some occasions, the less fantastic of what seem to be dreams may be indicators of events that actually occurred in reality, unrecognized by the waking mind. I am a firm believer that the senses of a human being detect more than the mind has the time or energy to perceive and categorize. If our talk with the captain goes as I hope it will, you may soon see what I mean."

With that statement, we reached our destination. Our stroll along the docks of London was at an end, and the sailor guarding the walkway onto the *Massachusetts* let us pass once more into the corridors of the American warship.

We were greeted by David Sutherland as we boarded the vessel. The young officer reported that nothing unusual had occurred while we had been away. He also assured us that he had followed Holmes's request and kept careful watch on his uncle. Holmes politely asked the lieutenant to find the captain and ask him to meet us for a private conversation. Sutherland walked off down the corridor at once after promising to have Captain Holt meet us in his quarters.

We reached the door of the captain's cabin long before Holt did. Apparently he was occupied with some ship's business. After about a quarter of an hour had gone by, Captain Holt finally appeared. He apologized for the delay, but offered no explanation. We did not ask for one. Although we suspected him of being less than truthful with us on the matter of Edmund Gibbs, I still had enough respect for his rank and position that I felt it would be uncouth to ask what he had been doing while we waited. Holmes, if I knew the man at all, probably thought it irrelevant which bit of petty nautical business had kept us waiting. When Holmes was fully engaged in one of his investigations, trivial details that did not directly relate to the matter at hand were the furthest thing from his mind.

Abraham Holt politely invited us in and we entered his quarters. The chairs that had been provided the previous night were still within. The captain sat and motioned for us to do the same. I took a chair and settled into it, but Sherlock Homes dismissed the idea with a wave of his hand and remained standing. He had a harsh, predatory look in his eyes.

Holmes began to speak. He paced back and forth in front of the captain as he talked. I simply sat back in my chair, observing Holmes at work, while keeping myself ready should I have to leap to Holmes's defense if Holt should become enraged. Sherlock Holmes in a calm pleasant mood was one thing. Holmes in a state of complete focus and thirst for truth was something else entirely. All social conventions and illusions of politeness vanished when Holmes was in such a mind-set, and I had, on more than one occasion, seen this mystify and then greatly upset the target of his interrogation.

"Captain Holt, I came here, to your ship, because my presence was requested by none other than yourself," he started, "When Dr. Watson and I arrived here, we did indeed discover the dead man whom Lieutenant Sutherland had told us of. We then proceeded to begin trying to determine how he had died and how he had come to be aboard your ship. When I am asked to take on a matter such as this, I place myself wholly at the disposal of my client, and in return I ask only that they demonstrate complete openness and honesty with me. My dear captain, I have strong reasons to believe that you have been untruthful with us."

An expression of indignation flashed across Abraham Holt's face, and he began to lift himself off the chair as if to stand and protest Holmes's accusation.

"Sit down, Captain!" shouted Sherlock Holmes, and Holt, a man who would normally have been the one bellowing orders, saw the intensity in the detective's eyes, and immediately fell back into a seated position.

"You insisted that you had not heard of Edmund Gibbs before his murdered corpse was found aboard this vessel," continued Holmes, "I have determined that this is not true. I demand, as I said a moment ago, honesty from my clients. Will you now reveal to us the actual truth of this matter, or shall Watson and I leave this ship and notify the British government of the presence of Gibbs's body on an American warship in London harbor?"

Holt's face actually quivered a bit and he sighed, "No, Mr. Holmes, I implore you not to do that. The resulting scandal would ruin my career. I fear that I have been somewhat dishonorable in my private affairs...but I am a good captain! I am an asset to my country's navy, and would not wish to be relieved of the duties which I feel I have performed most adequately for nearly thirty years."

"Then I suggest that you tell us the truth about your relationship with Mister Edmund Gibbs," demanded Holmes.

Captain Holt settled in his seat and admitted some facts that he had previously withheld, "Yes, I knew Gibbs. He and I were shipmates. I've known him for a good decade or more. We served together on several ships. I liked him, and we might have even been friends, if not for the fact that I was an officer and Gibbs was an enlisted sailor. He was a petty officer, and a damned good one, but never had the opportunity to seek a commission. He did his job, and did it well, and I often wished that all the sailors under my command were that proficient. He left the Navy several years ago and as far as I knew until last night, he was working on whaling ships as a navigator and first mate."

Having prompted honesty from the bearded seaman, Holmes's rage subsided and he finally sat down. He sat directly across from Holt and assumed a relaxed, unthreatening posture. "Thank you, Captain Holt. I hope that your display of truthfulness has lifted a great weight from your conscience. Now, let us turn the subject to something a bit more fanciful. Tell me, do you often remember your dreams?"

"Mr. Holmes, I fail to see what that has to do with the death of Ed Gibbs, but no, I very rarely recall having dreamt at all," said the captain.

"Do you recall any dreams in recent nights, even small fragments of a dream?" Holmes asked next.

"Well, now that you ask, perhaps I do. Two nights ago I awoke for a moment, having caught a hint of the scent of jasmine. I thought it quite odd that I might smell jasmine on a battleship, you see. Once I realized I had dreamt it, I fell asleep again. Other than that," recollected the ship's commander, "Nothing else springs to mind. Why do you ask that?"

Holmes ignored the captain's request for his reasons and simply kept the interrogation flowing. "If I may ask, Captain, are you a married man?"

"Yes Sir, Mr. Holmes. I've been married twice. My first wife died suddenly about a decade ago. It nearly broke my heart. We had spent thirteen years together, when I wasn't at sea, and I had planned to retire early, find a job on shore, and perhaps even have a child or two. When I lost her, I accepted command of my first battleship, content to be as far from land as possible. Since then, my only family has consisted of my sister, whom I rarely visit, and David, who I've tried to watch over as he follows in my footsteps as a naval man." The captain was visibly saddened as he spoke of his deceased wife.

"And your second wife?" inquired Holmes.

"Rebecca is her name, Mr. Holmes. I married her three years ago. It caused quite a stir among her social circle as I recall. You see, Rebecca is twenty-five years younger than me. She's much closer to my nephew's age, and people seemed to think I married her for her family fortune. Well, fortune may not be the right word. She has more money than any sea captain is ever likely to lay his hands on, though. But it wasn't greed that led to the marriage. I've no great use for money, Mr. Holmes. It was her companionship that I valued," explained Holt.

"You used the past tense in that last sentence. Do you no longer value her company?" asked Holmes upon noticing the captain's choice of phrasing.

"Sometimes women can grow cold," said Captain Holt, with a look of regret on his face. "Perhaps it was my fault. Not every woman is fit to be the wife of a sailing man. My long absences must have left her quite lonely. No woman as young as Rebecca should be left alone for months at a time. After a year or so, she seemed distant when I came home. The love and warmth had gone out of her eyes. She looked at me like she might look upon a stranger."

"That is most unfortunate," said Sherlock Holmes, "If I might ask another question, Captain, did your wife Rebecca ever come into contact with Edmund Gibbs?"

"Yes, Sir," answered Holt, "in fact, Gibbs tried to call on her before I did, but she rejected his attentions. It was odd enough that she might choose to enter into the company of an officer, considering her social and financial standing. Marriage to a common sailor was out of the question."

Holmes was silent for a moment, as if his sharp mind were busy digesting this latest revelation. He formed his fingers into a pointed steeple, sat back, and closed his eyes. When he opened them, he leaned forward and resumed speaking. "I am now going to ask you a rather delicate question, and I trust that you will continue to be completely honest with me. Please keep in mind that no one is present save for you and me and Dr. Watson, who I would trust with my very life."

Captain Holt sighed and replied, "All right, Mr. Holmes. I'll do my best to answer with the truth."

Holmes spoke softly and gently, knowing that he was asking a lot of Holt. "Has there, in recent times, been another woman in your life besides your current wife?"

"Indeed there has," admitted the captain, "Her name is Madeleine, and I may be in love with her."

"Will you tell us how this situation came to be?" asked Holmes.

"Yes. About a year ago, I brought the *Massachusetts* into port in New York City. She needed some minor repairs and restocking of supplies. We had a few days to relax, except the engineers and supply personnel, of course, so most of us went ashore and took a bit of leave we'd been delaying in the name of duty. I happen to have a fondness for old history books, so I visited some shops for a day. It was there that I met Madeleine. Only twenty years old, and so beautiful and full of life, I couldn't look away from her. She's the type of girl that has an imagination, Sir, a potent imagination, and I think she got caught up in the idea of the romance of the high seas and all the gibberish that land-living people associate with sailors. The idea of reeling in a captain, of all things, must have tempted her, and I gave in to the temptation of it all. I wasn't proud of it, but I have to admit that it was a wonderful time. I felt wanted, I felt alive, and I felt young like I hadn't felt in a very long time."

Holt couldn't help but smile slightly as his memory brought him back to that time spent in New York.

Holmes stood up and placed his hand on Holt's shoulder in a reassuring manner. "Thank you for sharing these facts with us, Captain Holt. Rest assured that none of this shall be related to any other person, either aboard this ship or ashore. If you don't mind, I should like to have a word in private with Dr. Watson. May we have use of the dignitary's cabin for half an hour?"

Captain Holt answered in the affirmative and Holmes and I left his quarters. The captain returned to his duties and we went to the neighboring cabin and closed the door behind us.

"I am always amazed by your ability to pull the truth from even the most obstinate individuals," I complimented my friend.

"It was an enlightening conversation, Watson, and it confirmed my ideas. Captain Holt is indeed the target of the assassination plans, and I believe our second stowaway is of the female gender."

"How do you know that?" I asked in my eagerness to hear the reasoning behind yet another of Holmes's discoveries.

"If you recall," replied Holmes, "I first established that Abraham Holt is, like many people, the sort of man who rarely recalls his dreams. Knowing this, I thought it reasonable to assume that his recollection of the smell of jasmine, which he attributed to dreaming, was in actuality something that his senses detected while in a half-sleeping state. The ventilation and flow of air on an ironclad ship is a very interesting thing. The passage of air is determined by the design of the walls and ceilings. Looking around the captain's quarters and also the dignitary's cabin, one might see that it is quite possible that an unusual aroma in one compartment might be detected by the nose of the other compartment's occupant. Captain Holt did not dream of the scent of jasmine. He smelled a woman's perfume! Since his mind, half awake, could not reason why he would smell such a thing on board a military ship, he naturally attributed it to a dream."

"So the murderer of Edmund Gibbs is a woman!" I excitedly stated, seeing clearly how Holmes had reached his conclusion.

"Yes, Watson, indeed she is! If my other assumptions are correct, she is still concealed somewhere on this ship, still awaiting her chance to spill the blood of Captain Holt. Would you be so kind as to go and find Lieutenant Sutherland and bring him to me?" Holmes requested.

I was off at once. Luckily, Sutherland had no pressing matters of duty to attend to at that moment and I was able to deliver him to Holmes without delay.

David Sutherland entered the cabin with me and Holmes immediately posed a question to him. "Lieutenant, is there a place on board this ship where anything of a soft material is stored when not in use? I mean bed linens, blankets, spare uniforms and that sort of thing."

"One of the storage compartments down in the ship's belly, Sir. Why?" said the youthful third officer.

"An experienced military man would be able to fall asleep anywhere, but a woman finding herself on a naval vessel would be most likely to bed down in the closest thing to an actual bed she could find," answered Holmes.

Sutherland was surprised to hear Holmes's answer and continued his curious inquiries, "A woman? What woman? Why would a woman be on the *Massachusetts*?"

"To kill your uncle, of course," Holmes revealed without a second's hesitation. "Now call for two armed men, and we'll all go to this storage compartment of which you speak."

Sutherland had two sailors summoned and the five of us travelled into the bowels of the battleship. The lieutenant and his two men carried a pistol each. I missed my old revolver at that moment, but had thought it unwise to bring a weapon onto a warship belonging to a nation that was not my own. As we walked, Holmes declared that should we find the person we sought, violence and gunfire should be used only as a last resort. He wished to take her alive, as a prisoner if possible. As we neared our destination, Sutherland wisely held up a hand to indicate that we should proceed in as close to silence as possible and we crept close to the door of the small closet on the lower decks. David Sutherland, taking advantage of the opportunity to act courageously, led the procession, followed by the two gun-wielding crewmen. Holmes went next, and I came up last in our little search party. We stopped in front of the door and I took in a deep breath as I knew the next moment could potentially be a dangerous one. If Holmes's ideas were correct, as they often were, we might be cornering a dangerous individual. Even a woman could be a cold-blooded killer and a trapped one was likely to resort to desperate measures when trapped. Hiding behind that door might be a woman who had already slain one man, and so would probably not hesitate to defend herself, violently if need be.

Lieutenant Sutherland tore open the door of the small storage room. We held our breath as the hatch flew open to reveal the interior of the room, but at first glance it appeared that Holmes had been mistaken. All we saw for that first second were several shelves upon which rested folded uniforms and sheets, and a heap of heavy woolen blankets on the floor. It truly looked as though no one were inside the closet, until David Sutherland stepped forward and bent down to look in the pile of blankets.

As he lifted the topmost blanket, a shrill scream cut through the air and a slim, disheveled young woman suddenly sat up! Before any of us could properly or decisively react, the terrible booming sound of a close-range gunshot exploded in our ears. Lieutenant Sutherland fell backwards, landing on top of one of the two sailors. The second sailor rather stupidly decided to kneel down and assist the fallen officer and took his eyes off the gun-wielding woman. She aimed at me, about to fire a second shot, when Holmes leapt, throwing himself between me and the would-be assassin, knocking her down, and landing atop her. Her pistol fell from her grasp and her wild shrieking grew louder, sounding like a banshee out of an Irish folk tale.

"Watson, grab her gun!" barked Holmes, and I immediately did as he said. He had turned himself around on the floor so that he was now seated against the storage compartment wall with the screaming girl on his lap, his arms holding her still, despite her struggles. Although Holmes was long and lean of frame, he was in excellent physical condition and I had, on numerous occasions, seen him exhibit remarkable strength. Holmes shouted another order at me, "See to Sutherland! He's been wounded!" then yelled to the two sailors, "Get up, you two! Take this wild woman from me, and use caution or she'll claw your eyes out!"

Having heard the commotion, other crewman had come running. Holmes was quickly taking control of the whole situation, as his authoritative demeanor could compel men to obey him despite his lack of uniform or insignia of rank. Meanwhile, I was kneeling next to David Sutherland, who had taken a bullet to the upper chest, just below the shoulder. It had missed his heart or he'd have been dead already, but he was losing a great deal of blood. I shouted to two sailors who had just come running towards the sounds of the chaos, "You men, help me get this man to Dr. MacFarlane!"

Holmes and I temporarily separated at that point. He followed the two sailors and their captive girl as they headed off to find Captain Holt and the first officer. I of course went with Sutherland and the two sailors who bore his bleeding, unconscious body to the sickbay.

The two crewmen who carried Sutherland must be commended for both their speed and the care which they took in maneuvering the injured young lieutenant through the narrow spaces of the ship. Had he been jostled or bumped against the walls, his injury might have been aggravated to an even greater degree. We rushed to the sickbay and the sailors placed Sutherland on the table. MacFarlane and I got to work immediately, desperately trying to save the heroic youth's life.

My presence on the *Massachusetts* turned out to be a fortunate thing for the lieutenant. It is not as though my skill as a physician was greater than that of Ship's Surgeon MacFarlane, for he proved, by his actions during that time, that he was a first-rate medical man, even under the stress of such a sudden emergency. I must, however, give myself a certain amount of credit simply because circumstance placed me on that ship at that moment. Were there not two skilled physicians instead of the usual single doctor on board when Sutherland was shot, the lieutenant might very well have died. But two of us there were, and the combined efforts of MacFarlane and I were sufficient to save David Sutherland's life. We were able to stop the bleeding, remove the bullet, clean the wound to a degree that we hoped would prevent any major infection, and bandage the area. We believed him likely to survive, although it would probably be several hours before he regained full consciousness and he would need several weeks to fully recuperate. Had Sutherland been an older or weaker man, the loss of so much blood alone would have been enough to kill him, but he was healthy, young, and strong. Once MacFarlane and I agreed that the lieutenant's condition was stabilized and his life was no longer in imminent danger, I left that area of the ship and went to find Holmes.

I quickly journeyed to the deck with which we had become the most familiar and found Captain Holt and several armed guards standing outside the door to the dignitary's cabin, which was closed. I asked about the location of Sherlock Holmes.

"He had the men take Madeleine inside, and then insisted that we wait outside," answered the captain as he pointed to the door. "He said we could let you in when you arrived. But first, Doctor, please…how is David? Is he…?"

The worried look on the captain's face told me that the life of his beloved nephew was most important to him, far overshadowing the potential embarrassment of his illicit lover having been found on board his ship. I truly felt sorry for the man.

"With a little luck, he'll pull through this and be fine. He's young and strong. His actions today were truly courageous. You should be proud of him," I said. A look of great relief washed over Holt's face and he let out a deep sigh.

One of the sailors opened the door long enough for me to enter the dignitary's cabin, and then closed it behind me. Inside, I found Holmes seated on a chair, directly across from the young woman, who was sitting on the bed. In the time between the incident in the storage compartment and my arrival at the cabin, Holmes and the others had come to the cabin and placed the girl inside. Holmes had then asked the others, including the captain, to leave him alone with her. The captain suggested that she at least be tied up, so as to prevent her from becoming violent again, but Holmes had decided that such an action was unnecessary. "You may sit on the bed," Holmes had told her. "Any attempt to attack me or try to escape will result in my shouting for the guards. Such a cry will most likely result in you either being shot or forcibly restrained. I have no desire to witness further bloodshed today, so I suggest you behave. We are simply going to talk."

Holmes, ever the civilized man when he wanted to be, had even provided her with a damp cloth with which to wipe away the grime that had accumulated on her face during days of hiding in the ship, and a brush to tame her disheveled mane of long brown hair. Having made herself somewhat presentable again, she was actually a very attractive young woman, now calm and appearing small and vulnerable. This illusion of gentleness and vulnerability was far from the wild, shrieking animal we had been confronted by in the lower decks. I found it hard to believe that this delicate creature had murdered Edmund Gibbs and nearly killed David Sutherland.

I leaned against the wall behind Holmes and simply watched and listened as he conversed with her. His voice, which could vary greatly depending upon the needs of the situation, was now in its softer, more reassuring mode, much like the one he had used with Captain Holt when the questions about his wife were asked.

"Your name is Madeleine, I am told," stated Holmes.

"Yes, Sir," the girl replied. "Madeleine Dale. Who are you?"

"My name is Sherlock Holmes. I was asked to come here when the body of Edmund Gibbs was discovered in this very room. I have a very good idea of how that body came to lie lifelessly in this very room, Madeleine, but now I wish to hear the story told in your words."

The young lady shook and looked ready to burst into tears, but she quickly gained control of her emotions and started to speak. "I suppose it can do no more harm to speak of it now. You've been kind to me, Mr. Holmes. You could have killed me after I shot that man before. I didn't mean to hurt him, but I was afraid. You didn't kill me. You let me wash my face and didn't tie me up. I'm grateful, Sir; I really am. I'll tell you my story and then I suppose I'll go to prison...or be hanged.

"I'm from New York. I grew up poor, but I studied hard in school. I loved to read and I suppose I often let my romantic notions and my silly imagination get the best of me. I've always had a terrible habit of chasing after silly, stupid fantasies until my heart winds up shattered! I don't know why. I can't help myself!"

As I watched Madeleine Dale talk to Holmes, I could see why Holt had been attracted to her. Even under the circumstances, a certain waifish, innocent quality shone through in the way she talked. If she had channeled her imagination into storytelling instead of chasing much older sea captains, she'd have made a fine writer. After making that rather sad observation, I continued listening to her tale.

"I managed to get a job as a clerk in a small bookshop in New York. I enjoyed the work. What could be better than spending one's days surrounded by books? Life was good, but I was lonely, until one day a handsome, rugged and distinguished sea captain walked into the shop. He was older than me and that made him even more appealing to me. I felt a rare fit of bravery come over me and I smiled in a manner that I knew he could not ignore. He did notice, and we began to talk. First we were a clerk and a customer, and then I became flirtatious, I admit. As coincidence would have it, my scheduled hours were nearly over when he came into the shop and my smiles and attention made him ask me to dinner. I was flattered and delighted that a naval officer should take an interest in me, so I accepted. It was a wonderful evening and we talked for hours. What happened next was somewhat…intimate. I would be very grateful if you did not ask me to divulge the details of the rest of the night, Mr. Holmes."

Holmes nodded and assured her that she need not reveal information of such a personal nature to him. He then asked that she continue with the narrative of what had occurred after she had met Abraham Holt.

"The two days during which Abraham was in New York were the best days of my life, Sir. I was happy. For once, the events in my life were the equal of all my fondest daydreams. Then he had to return to his ship. He promised to return to visit me at the next possible opportunity, but we both knew it could be months before we saw each other again. We said our farewells just before he went back to his duties and sailed away. I didn't see him again until I boarded this ship in Connecticut. I thought of him often though. I hoped he would come back for me. I was under the impression that he had been honest in his affections towards me, and I did not know that he had a wife until she contacted me herself!"

Holmes then interrupted her story, "Do you happen to know how Mrs. Holt came to know of your existence, Miss Dale?"

"I couldn't figure that out myself at first, Mr. Holmes, but then one day the answer came to me. When we were walking along the streets after we met, we happened to pass one of Abraham's men. It was just a chance passing and the sailor simply saluted his captain and kept going, but he must have thought it a good idea to report the incident to Abraham's wife. I don't know why. Perhaps he thought she would pay him for such information. From my experience, she seems glad to pay handsomely when she wants something."

Holmes questioned her again. "When and how did you first become aware that there was a Mrs. Holt?"

Madeleine's face was suddenly crossed by a look of momentary sadness, as if Holmes's inquiry had brought a terribly bitter memory to the surface, but it quickly passed and she went back to telling her story.

"It was months after I met Abraham. A letter arrived one day. Mrs. Holt came right out and told me that she knew about Abraham and me. She told me right then and there in that letter that she held no ill will towards me, assuming that he hadn't told me that he was a married man, which he hadn't of course. I was shocked, I was angry, and I thought I would die from the ache in my heart, but I was intrigued as well. The strength and will of this Rebecca Holt showed in the way she wrote to me, in the way she seemed to want to take command of the situation, and it impressed me. I wrote back to her. I said I hated Abraham for what he had done to me, and also for what he had done to her. A few weeks later, I got another letter from her. There was money inside the envelope. She wanted me to come to Connecticut. It didn't say why, but I took it and I got on a train as soon as I could. I wanted to travel to someplace I hadn't been before, see new places, and I especially wanted to meet Rebecca."

"And what happened when you got to Connecticut, Madeleine?" Holmes asked.

"She invited me to stay with her. She told me that she knew that the *Massachusetts* was in port again, and not far away, but that Abraham hadn't even come home to see her this time, so cold had their love grown by now. Then, Mr. Holmes, she offered me something: a bargain of sorts; which I accepted. May God have mercy on my soul!"

At that moment, Miss Dale could contain her tears no longer and they burst forth like water from an overfilled well. Holmes produced a handkerchief from his pocket and gave it to her (I had used mine earlier to staunch the flow of Sutherland's blood). He opened the door momentarily and asked a yeoman to bring the weeping girl a glass of water. When Madeleine had composed herself again, she resumed her tale, which grew more morbid as she proceeded.

"She stoked my anger. I see now that she did that intentionally, and I shall never forgive her for that. She made it so that my madness, my heartbreak, and my lust for revenge on Abraham threatened to consume me. Then she tempted me with money, a lot of money, enough money that I could buy the bookshop if I wanted to! All I had to do to get it was to kill Abraham! I wanted, at least in my confused and bitter state, to do that anyway, so I agreed. But I didn't know how to go about planning a murder! That was when she decided to solve several problems at once. She contacted a man called Edmund Gibbs. He had been a friend, a shipmate of Abraham's, but he had also wanted to be with Rebecca. She had refused him and married Abraham instead, and some people she knew had told her that Gibbs, drunk in a tavern one night, had stood on a table and swore he'd steal her away from Captain Holt one day. She used that information to complete her scheme."

"Rebecca, being somewhat wealthy, was able to purchase information from some rather shady individuals; spies even. She learned that the

Massachusetts would soon be delivering something here to London. She introduced me to Edmund and made some arrangements. She promised her affections to him, just as she had promised money to me, if we would sneak onto the ship and murder Abraham. Edmund would use his knowledge of seafaring to conceal us onboard, and I would have the satisfaction of delivering the fatal blow to the man who had wronged me. Oh, Mr. Holmes, what a foolish child I've been! The idea in Rebecca's mind was that with the secret papers on the ship, the killing would be attributed to spies or traitors if we were not apprehended. She refused to give me the money up front and said she had sent it to an associate in England. I had no choice. If I wanted it, I would have to make the trip to London. Edmund and I both agreed to the wretched scheme, God help us."

"We snuck onto the ship in the dead of night on the evening prior to the departure. Edmund truly knew how to hide on a vessel at sea. It was uncomfortable and frightening, but my lust for money and vengeance blinded me to how foolish I was being. He began to show me how to move about unseen in the night and how to hide my presence from the crew during the day. We came up with a plan to move from place to place until we got close enough to Abraham to strike. We would go to the empty cabin near his room and wait until we had the best possible chance to catch him asleep. Edmund stole a heavy wrench from the engineers, which I would use to hit Abraham over the head. If the blow didn't kill him, Edmund would then use a knife to finish the task. We waited until the ship docked in London so that we could escape immediately when Abraham was dead and find the man who was keeping my money. We made it to the cabin and hid until the corridors were clear of any men. It was then, in that cabin, that Edmund decided to tell me that he wanted half of the money. He didn't trust Rebecca to love him as she had promised and he felt that the safer bet was for him to have some of the monetary reward. We argued and I…I hit him with the wrench! He fell to the ground, he stopped breathing, and he was dead! I murdered him, Mr. Holmes! I lost control of my wits then, and I ran out of the cabin and into the halls of the ship. It was only blind, stupid luck that kept anyone from seeing me. I could barely see through my tears as I ran up onto the upper, outer deck and threw that wrench into the water. Then I went back to the storage closet where I had been sleeping the days away since we left Connecticut. I stayed there, terrified and ashamed until you found me there. Oh, Mr. Holmes, this nightmare will never end! I feel so lost! I shall surely be hanged for what I've done!"

With that, the exhausted girl fainted dead away. I checked her pulse, making certain that she was not seriously ill. Holmes and I left her to rest and rejoined Captain Holt in the corridor.

MacFarlane has come up from sickbay to report that Sutherland was doing as well as could be expected. He agreed to watch over Miss Dale while we discussed matters with the captain. When we left the passageway, MacFarlane was seated in the chair by the bed where the young murderess lay, while two guards stood in the doorway. Holmes and I joined the captain in his quarters and drank coffee while Holmes related the tale that had just been told. When it was all told, Abraham Holt let out a worried groan and asked what would happen next.

"Do you intend to take any further action in this matter, Mr. Holmes?" said the now nervous captain.

"Only one action," replied Holmes. "Mrs. Holt's associate, the man who was going to pay your assassin, must be apprehended. However, I shall not involve the regular police. My brother has connections to some very discreet individuals within the British government and will be willing to handle the matter in a way that will attract no unwanted attention. Of this, you have my word."

Now Holmes turned to the matter of the conclusion of the case. "You will transport Miss Dale back to America, where she will be turned over to the authorities to face trial for the murder of Edmund Gibbs. I have no doubt that she will give a full confession. As I gave you my word on the matter of the London-based accessory to the crime, I now ask for your word that no harm will come to Miss Dale during the voyage to the United States. I trust that her testimony will go a long way towards seeing that justice is also delivered to your scheming wife. While I most assuredly do not approve of your marital misconduct, Captain Holt, it is no valid reason to have you killed. All parties in this matter bear some guilt, but the least of it is yours. Should you become embroiled in the trial and your reputation as an officer put at risk, you may write me and I will send a statement on your behalf to prevent you from facing excessive discipline should it come to that."

Captain Holt seemed shocked by Holmes's last sentence. "You would do that for me, Mr. Holmes, after all I've done to bring this danger down upon us?" he asked.

Holmes's eyes grew intense as he responded. "No, Captain, I would not do that for you. I would do it for your men, upon whom none of the blame for this lies. As far as I can see, for all your faults as a man, you are a competent officer and a fair captain. It would be a great loss to your nation and its navy if you were to be stripped of your commission. It is for the good of those under your authority that I would defend your career."

With those words, Sherlock Holmes put down his coffee cup, stood up and turned away from the captain. "Come Watson; we have spent enough time on the *Massachusetts*," he said, and we quickly disembarked.

Evening was arriving as we made our way home to our rooms at Baker Street and the harsh winter winds had resumed. Our time on the American warship had been interesting enough and I was thankful that no one else had been killed after our arrival. Holmes sat silently as the hansom made its way to our destination and I thought little of the now concluded case, thinking instead of Mrs. Hudson's tea and the warmth of a freshly lit fire. I was grateful, as always, for the comforts of our small apartment, and on that night I was especially happy that I had never chosen the life of a seafaring man.

++++

During the many years I resided in London, one of my occasional pleasures was the chance to peruse the American newspapers that sometimes arrived in our local libraries several weeks after their publication. I found it interesting to gain an occasional insight into the politics and culture of a nation to which we, the British, had played a large part in giving birth. Those imported newspapers were of particular interest in the months that followed our adventure on the *Massachusetts*. Madeleine Dale was shown some mercy by the courts, due partly to her willingness to confess to her crime, partly to the fact that her only victim had been a potential murderer himself, and party to the fact that much of the blame was placed on Rebecca Holt, as perhaps it should have been. Miss Dale was sent to prison, but not for such a long period as would prevent her from eventually having a chance at a happy life. Rebecca Holt was given a much harsher sentence, but elected to commit suicide rather than spend most of her life incarcerated. Captain Abraham Holt was not severely punished by the American government since his mission to deliver the documents to London had been completed and the incident on board the ship had caused no great delay in his duties. Holt eventually reached the rank of Admiral and finally retired to a life as a fisherman. He never married again. Lieutenant David Sutherland recovered from his injuries and remained in the navy. He realized his dream of commanding a ship of his own. It was with great sadness that I read of his demise years

"It is for the good of those under your authority that I would defend your career."

later, during the Great War, when he went down with his ship as many a heroic captain had done before him. Of all the officers and men of the *U.S.S. Massachusetts*, the only one whom I would ever see again was Dr. Christopher MacFarlane. He left the navy not long after he and I saved Sutherland from his bullet wound, and settled in New York City, where he opened a private medical practice and occasionally did some work for his government. Holmes and I happened to meet him again several years later when he travelled to London in the midst of a series of events that I have often referred to as "The Adventure of the Mummy's Rib."

The End

"Starting Out At Baker Street"

Like a rookie ballplayer walking into Yankee Stadium and being handed a bat! That's how I felt when Ron Fortier asked me to write a Sherlock Holmes story for this collection. If you don't believe me, if you think I'm exaggerating, just ask my wife. I was giddy, I was overjoyed, and I had to get out of the house for awhile and get some air, drive around, try to relax. It was almost overwhelming!

Writers fantasize a lot. Its part of what makes us writers. Sometimes we're lucky enough to get those daydreams and fantasies to materialize on a computer screen or a piece of paper. Other times they just remain fantasies. This story, my Sherlock Holmes mystery, was one of the former; one of those wonderful examples of things falling into place, actually coming to fruition, and being born as a mass of words and sentences, rather than just being a handful of gibberish that stays trapped in the cluttered attic that is the writer's mind.

Holmes, of all things! That was what made me more excited than I usually am over a writing job. I tend to have a methodical way of writing. I learned when I began to seriously write that the best way to approach a writing job is to treat it like a job, whether you're getting paid or not, or even whether it's guaranteed to be published or not. I don't mess around. If I set out to write it, it gets written, as quickly and as well as possible. I don't miss deadlines. I don't dilly-dally. It's a pleasure to sit and think

41

of stories, but it's work once they begin to be written. It's a serious task, and I tend to approach it seriously, so it was all the more unusual that I spent several hours with a silly boyish grin on my face when the subject of Sherlock Holmes came up!

I first "met" the great detective in the form of the actor Jeremy Brett back when the Granada television series was first being aired in the 1980s and '90s. I was fascinated by the character. Actually, I should say that I was fascinated by both characters, for Dr. John Watson held just as much appeal for me as Holmes did. One without the other just isn't the same.

Shortly after my introduction to the television Holmes, my grandfather gave me one of the best Christmas gifts I've ever received; a massive hardcover edition of The Complete Sherlock Holmes. It was, in fact, his personal copy, the one he had been given by his own father back in the '30s. I read it cover to cover, the entire thing, all four Holmes novels and all fifty-six short stories, and I wanted more. I still have that book. Thanks, Grandpa!

Of course, when a kid encounters a character like Sherlock Holmes, he just has to let his imagination run wild and he naturally makes up new tales for the character in his mind. I did it, and I'm sure many other kids have done the same in the century and change since A. Conan Doyle first gave the greatest of all sleuths to the world's readers.

As much fun as it is to imagine writing Holmes, being asked to write a Holmes tale that will actually be published is an entirely different thing! To be asked to contribute to the literary life of such an influential character, even if one's contribution will never be considered "canonical," is an honor and a privilege for which I will always be grateful. Thanks, Ron!

Having gone through the thrill of being asked to do a Holmes story, I then had to actually write the thing. I was nervous, I'll admit. Could I do the Great Detective justice? I had been reading a book about the history of naval warfare, so ships came to mind and I decided to set the story on a battleship. Once I had decided to do that, I simply began to write.

I started at the natural starting point. Where else would one start than at Baker Street? It felt like a visit to an old friend. I fell into the proper mood very, very easily. A cold London winter, Watson returning from the bedside of a patient, Holmes scraping out his own unique brand of music on his violin, Mrs. Hudson brewing a fresh pot of tea; all great archetypal symbols from this particular piece of literary mythology, all so familiar, but still so potent and endearing. Baker Street, to the Holmes fan, is home; a good place to start.

I sincerely hope that you, the reader, will have as much fun reading my Sherlock Holmes story as I have had writing it. I also hope that I have written a story that would have earned the approval of Holmes's "father." Thanks, Mr. Doyle!

Lastly, I hope that I have done justice to a character who has far too often been maligned and misinterpreted by those who have not actually bothered to read the original Holmes stories. Our narrator, John Watson, was not a stupid man. He was a medical doctor, a brave soldier, and a faithful friend. Most importantly, the good doctor was us! His were the eyes through which we got to observe the Great Detective at work. Let's forget the silly depictions in some films of Watson as a bumbling idiot or a dim-witted buffoon who just gets in the way. Men like Sherlock Holmes do not keep fools like that around. Watson was as important to Holmes as Holmes was to Watson; perhaps even more so. There is a definite reason why Doyle chose to use Watson's voice to tell the stories of Holmes, and the entire experience of Holmes's adventures would not be what they are without Watson's presence. Thanks, Doctor!

Aaron Smith

Aaron Smith has been writing something or other for as long as he can remember. He's written scraps and pieces of all sorts of things, from comic books, to rants about the people he interacts with and observes, to philosophical essays on religion, and most recently, pulp stories.

He currently has several projects in the works for Airship 27, including a western, a jungle adventure, a handful of crime stories, a World War I aviation tale, and the upcoming mystery novel, *Season of Madness.*

SHERLOCK HOLMES
CONSULTING DETECTIVE

"The Problem at Stamford Bridge"

by Van Allen Plexico

I had not encountered Sherlock Holmes in a matter of several weeks at the very least, my private medical practice being back in full swing again, when a rather unexpected document arrived in the post, addressed to me. It came not from Holmes himself—indeed, it bore no indication whatsoever that accepting it would lead me into one of the more remarkable adventures that he and I shared. Thus it was in a state of profound ignorance that I tore open the letter and studied its contents.

It was, in short, an invitation to attend a football match on the following Sunday afternoon at the recently opened stadium in West London—in the Borough of Hammersmith and Fulham, to be precise. It had come to me by way of Sir Stephen Wyatt, a gentleman of some means who had once been a patient of mine. I had diagnosed his ailment where a variety of other medical men had failed, and he had gone on to make a full recovery. Being a conscientious sort as well as a man of no small wealth, he'd previously expressed his appreciation with a fine turkey at Christmas time and a package of top-shelf tobacco (this Holmes had smoked the greater part of, unfortunately, before I was able to avail myself of it).

Now had come this invitation and ticket to a football match. Being no great fan of football or of most sports in general—and, honestly, believing whatever debt the gentleman imagined he owed me long since settled—I at first set the invitation aside and considered discarding it altogether. Perhaps only a vague curiosity kept me from doing so. Finally, however, I decided that, the weather being relatively pleasant outside and my wife being away on family business, I would undertake the short journey to West London and meet Sir Stephen at the match.

And so it was that I, Dr. John Watson, was in attendance at the sparkling new stadium called Stamford Bridge on that cool April afternoon when two famous players most literally collided on the field of play—and when an occasionally violent sport became the vehicle for outright murder.

The two celebrated players indeed collided, and not twenty yards from where I stood, near the center of one sideline. As the ball they had both gone for bounced away and into the possession of others, the two shoved one another back and forth, and then fisticuffs ensued. Each had given and received substantial blows before the referee managed to interpose himself between the two hulking men and separate them. Quickly he produced a red card from his pocket and waved it at each of them—I later learned this meant they both were being "sent off," or disqualified from play. The two sulked to their respective dressing rooms, exchanging hostile glances the entire way.

I was shocked by this display, though not nearly as thoroughly as Sir Stephen, who apologized profusely on behalf of his organization. It had turned out that he was part owner and member of the board of directors of the new club team that had been created to utilize this Stamford Bridge stadium—Chelsea Football Club. He expressed to me his profound concern that such an incident would damage the reputation of his team and the club itself. I could tell him little by way of comfort, such things being outside of my area of expertise. At any rate, I remained at the stadium for the rest of the match and did my best to encourage him.

Once the match had ended—it had been won by the visitors, called Fulham Football Club, by a score of 2-1—I bid my acquaintance a farewell, thanking him for the invitation, and started for home. But I had scarcely gotten to the coach that had been called for me before Sir Stephen came running out of the clubhouse and yelled for me to wait.

"Doctor! Doctor! Please—you must come quickly!"

Puzzled, I followed him back through the private exterior entrance and into the dressing room area, where I found a number of players and support staff gathered around in a scrum. Sir Stephen pushed several of them aside, pulling me along behind him. There, at the center of the crowd, I found two players, still in their uniforms, lying motionless on tables. One wore the white shirt and black trousers of the Fulham side, the other the royal blue of Chelsea. As I studied their faces, I realized that they were the same two men who had earlier been ejected from the match.

"We found them lying on the floor here," one of the Chelsea players breathlessly told me. "Both of 'em."

I performed a quick check on the Chelsea player first.

"Is he hurt, Doctor?" Sir Stephen asked desperately—and I recalled then that he'd told me earlier this man was his most valuable player, the highest-paid and most vital for their chances of a successful season.

"He is unconscious," I reported, "but should recover quickly." Then I turned my attention to the player in the Fulham uniform.

"Thank God," Sir Stephen was saying. "And is that one hurt?"

"Hurt?" I looked at him in surprise and with grim realization. "This man is dead!"

+ + +

"Watson! How good to see you."

It was two hours later and I stood in the doorway of my old lodgings at 221-B Baker Street, an address I had not visited in some time. The apartment was as untidy as ever, with stacks of paper occupying every available space, dirty dishes from both breakfast and lunch perched precariously atop some of them. Seated in a comfortable reclining chair on the far side of the room sat my longtime friend and crime-solving associate, Sherlock Holmes. His legs were propped up on yet another stack of his files, and he was in the act of filling his pipe with shag he kept in an old Persian slipper.

"I apologize for the intrusion, Holmes—" I began.

"Not at all," he replied instantly. "I know you will take it as no slight when I tell you the only visitor I welcome with greater anticipation is a client with a particularly challenging case."

"Then perhaps I might be able to kill two birds with one stone," I told him as I turned to hang my hat and coat. When I turned back, he was gazing at me keenly.

"I had not taken you for a football enthusiast, Watson," he stated matter-of-factly, "so I am curious as to why you should have attended a football match at Stamford Bridge today—and who was murdered there."

"What! But—how could you possibly have known that—"

I caught myself before proceeding further with that line of questioning, seeing as how I had, on far too many occasions, been the object of my friend's singularly remarkable powers of insight and observation. Still, in this case, I could scarcely think of how he had divined such knowledge.

Word of the player's death could not possibly have leaked out and reached him so quickly, not to mention how he could have known that I was present at the event. I said as much to him.

"Why, it is simplicity itself, my old friend," he replied with a tiny, wry smile. "Your nose is red, as from having spent some time outdoors very recently, in the cool air. Three strands of yarn lie upon your coat, there to the back, where you had not noticed them. They are of blue and white, clearly from a scarf of some sort, as with the type carried by sporting enthusiasts to celebrate their teams—but far too bright in color for most standard scarves. The coat is rumpled at the elbows, as from a crowd of people pressing in against you from both sides. Your shoes still carry a bit of dirt and grass about the edges. All of this indicates a likelihood of you having attended a football match. Judging by the colors of the yarn, I can rule out most of the sides in this area—but I do believe the new team, the one located in Hammersmith and Fulham, at the new Stamford Bridge venue, has adopted those exact colours."

He gestured to the newspaper that lay open before him.

"A quick glance reveals that indeed that very side—Chelsea—was scheduled to play a match earlier today, at their home grounds. A trip from that location to Baker Street just after the match should have put you here approximately a half-hour to an hour ago, give or take a variable or two—so something must have delayed you. Since you have come from there to here, unexpectedly, I surmise it was something of a criminal nature, prompting you to seek my assistance. Generally only a murder— and a prominent one—would be sufficient to send you in such haste to my door. But, in any case, I conclude you were in attendance at Stamford Bridge today—though what originally brought you to be there, as I said, I cannot guess."

Once I had metaphorically lifted my jaw from the floor and could speak again, I nodded in agreement.

"Just so, Holmes. Just so."

I laid out for him what was known thus far: that Fulham's most prominent player, John Cole, was dead and that Chelsea's most important player, Brian Dempsey, stood accused of the crime. Dempsey was resolute in his denial of any knowledge of or involvement in the slaying, though certainly all signs pointed to him being the culprit—not least of which the fact that several thousand people had witnessed his altercation with Cole on the pitch. In addition, I had learned that both players had wide reputations for being quick-tempered and violent men—a fact that did not help Dempsey's cause with the police.

"So you see," I said to my friend then, "this may be just as clear-cut a case as it first seems."

"And yet you hurried here at first opportunity, Watson, to put the matter before me. That indicates you do harbour certain doubts as to Dempsey's guilt."

"Well, perhaps," I conceded. "The man certainly protests strenuously enough of his innocence. And he seems, I daresay, believable."

Holmes nodded.

"I believe you did not err in coming to me, Watson."

He gathered up his coat and hat.

"While I would have preferred to share a pleasant dinner with you before heading out into the West London night, I believe time is of the essence—we must visit the scene of the crime and see what may be seen before it has become too terribly disrupted."

"Yes, of course."

I followed Holmes out the door and down the stairs and we raced for the nearest hansom.

+ + +

"Interesting that they should call the club 'Chelsea,' isn't it, Watson?" I looked up from my reverie as the hansom rolled to a stop at the Stamford Bridge grounds.

"How is that, Holmes?"

"We are not actually in the Royal Borough of Kensington and Chelsea, here," he pointed out, "but in the London Borough of Hammersmith and Fulham." He favored me with one of his enigmatic smiles. "Chelsea is actually somewhat to the east—we passed through it on our way here."

"Interesting, yes—but that couldn't possibly be relevant to the case, could it?"

"One can never be certain," he replied, before hopping down from the carriage and immediately looking about, his keen eye for detail clearly already at work.

The new stadium reared up just ahead of us, its bleachers and metal framework gleaming in the sun. A set of low buildings that served as its clubhouse and offices ran beneath one side of the bleachers, and we strolled in that direction.

Sir Stephen saw our approach and emerged from the clubhouse to greet us.

"Mr. Holmes, thank heavens you are here," he said, shaking my friend's hand enthusiastically. "Your reputation of course precedes you and if anyone will be able to sort this matter out properly, I know it will be you."

Holmes thanked him and immediately asked to inspect the area where the two men were found. Sir Stephen led us back into the dressing room I had attended some hours earlier, and Holmes wasted no time in whipping out his glass and studying everything from the tabletops to the floor to the grounds just outside, leading out onto the pitch itself.

"Finding anything of note?" Sir Stephen asked him at one point. Holmes, of course, ignored him and continued with his work, leaving the gentleman frowning and reddening. For my part, I could only laugh to myself, having been acquainted with Holmes and his manner for so long that I knew he would scarcely volunteer any details to anyone until he had sorted matters out for himself. Sir Stephen, like most everyone else who had ever found himself on the receiving end of my friend's silent treatment, appeared miffed at first, but I managed to mollify him somewhat with a few kind and encouraging words while Holmes continued his investigations un-interrupted.

"The accused—this Brian Dempsey," Holmes said after he'd gone over every inch of the dressing rooms and the surrounding areas. "I assume he has long since been taken into custody."

"Yes—Inspector Lestrade took him in just after Dr. Watson left to retrieve you."

"Lestrade. Ah. Well." Holmes made an unreadable expression—though I suspected I knew what it meant, given his history with the Inspector. "Come, Watson," he said to me then, an energy seeming to flow through him. "We must speak with this Dempsey presently."

+ + +

A short while later, with only a few scant hours of daylight re-maining, we arrived at the local station house. Holmes swept through the front door and past a small congregation of offi-cers loitering in the lobby, and I followed in his wake. Together we nearly collided with the exiting Inspector Lestrade. The Inspector appeared star-tled at first, but then his face settled into his customarily cynical expression as he realized just whom he had encountered.

"Good evening, Inspector," Holmes said with a slight bow.

Before he could go further, Lestrade sighed and motioned for us to follow him back.

"Save your breath, Mr. Holmes," he muttered. "I know why you're here. He's this way."

Lestrade led us into a small, tight room with rough, gray walls. Seated at a wooden table in the center was the accused Chelsea player—Brian Dempsey. The man was just under six feet tall, with shaggy dark hair and a pale complexion. His large hands were clasped in front of him on the tabletop, handcuffs binding his wrists. He appeared ashen.

Holmes introduced himself and immediately began his inquiry as Lestrade looked on, bemused.

"How did the deceased—the Fulham player, Mr. Cole—come to be in your company in the dressing room, Mr. Dempsey?"

The Chelsea man frowned.

"We'd had a run-in on the pitch," he replied slowly, cautiously. "He said some things I didn't appreciate. We both were sent off."

"They were ejected from the match," Sir Stephen explained from behind Holmes.

"So I went to the dressing room to change and to wait for the match to end," he continued. "But then Cole, he sends a note over from his dressing room, saying he wants to meet me afterward—to 'settle things between us for good,' as he put it."

Holmes's eyes lit up.

"And what became of this note, Mr. Dempsey?"

He looked up at Lestrade, who nodded and held a piece of paper out in one hand. "I have it here, Mr. Holmes."

"May I, Inspector?"

"Certainly."

Holmes took the folded paper and studied it closely for a few moments. Then, "And what did you think Mr. Cole meant by this note?"

Dempsey shrugged.

"Whatever I might have thought, I surely never considered he meant to kill me!"

"So you have *not* considered a plea of self-defense, then?" Holmes asked. "With this note as evidence, a jury might well be convinced that Mr. Cole intended to harm you."

"I can't claim something like that, Mr. Holmes," Dempsey answered him, his face drawn. "It's just not true."

"And yet you did kill him, did you not?" Lestrade asked.

"No!" Dempsey was vehement. "No, I didn't."

"Then what precisely did happen next?" Holmes asked, ignoring Lestrade.

"Well, sir," the man went on, "For my part, I was ready to settle matters at that very moment. –Not, mind you, *permanently*, not like *that*, but…"

"Yes, I understand," Holmes told him in a soothing tone. "Do go on."

"So I stepped out into the hall that connects the two dressing rooms, and found Cole there. We exchanged a few words—nothing memorable, really. In fact, he seemed to me to be sort of apologetic about our scuffle."

Lestrade barely restrained a snort at that.

"You're saying that Cole was calm—that he was not anxious to start up a fight once more, Dempsey?"

"That's right, Mr. Holmes. That's the God's truth!"

"Well then, sir—how did matters go from there to where they ended up?"

"I tell you, I don't know, Mr. Holmes. One second he and I were talking, the next I was waking up on the table with Dr. Watson standing over me."

Holmes considered this carefully, his eyes narrowing and his lips pursing.

"I have seen this sort of thing many times," Lestrade interjected at this point. "Particularly among violent, physically-oriented men. They black out and their natural instincts take over. Afterward they remember almost nothing of what has happened…" He gazed down at the accused with cold eyes. "…Of what they have done."

"Perhaps, perhaps," Holmes muttered, glancing from Lestrade back to Dempsey. "And yet…"

"I honestly think you're wasting your time here," Lestrade told Holmes after we'd exited the interrogation room and closed the door behind us. "This is as certain a case as I've ever seen." He shrugged. "Dempsey will hang before the month is out, mark my words."

"I have, as always, marked each of your words, Inspector," Holmes told him with a sparkle in his eyes. "As to the outcome of this case, however—I imagine we shall know the truth, one way or the other, in but a short time."

Lestrade frowned and started to say something in reply. Before he could, however, Holmes quickly requested for him to meet with us again at Stamford Bridge in two hours' time—a request Lestrade only reluctantly agreed to—and then bid him farewell. As he led me back out onto the street, I wondered where we were off to next, and asked him as much.

"Watson," he said then, in response to my inquiry, "I believe it would prove fruitful to pay a visit to the other club."

"To Fulham? You actually do believe there's more to this than a simple falling-out between two football players, then?"

"Nothing is certain as of yet," he replied quickly, forcefully. "But I must have more information before any conclusions can be drawn."

And so we caught a hansom and soon were drawing up to the curb before the stadium known as Craven Cottage.

Much larger than Stamford Bridge—as it was a good deal older—the Fulham stadium appeared dilapidated in spots, with rough areas missing their paint and sections of fencing rusted and torn. Overall it gave off the air of neglect and disrepair.

"I find I quite like the odd names of these facilities, Watson," my friend noted as we climbed out and paid the driver. "Craven Cottage indeed! Delightful. Perhaps there's more to this sport than I have previously believed."

The offices of the Fulham stadium, larger but not as nice in appearance as those of Chelsea, lay in a similar configuration to those of its neighbor, and we started toward them at a brisk walk. Then Holmes surprised me by pausing and fishing around in one of his coat pockets. He withdrew a small, square piece of paper—one I recognized immediately as being the threatening note from John Cole that Holmes had taken from Lestrade.

"You never gave that back to the Inspector," I observed pointlessly.

Holmes, to his credit, ignored my remark; he held the paper up to the setting sun and peered at it for a moment.

"Mmm…Just as I thought," he muttered. Then, "Watson, I have another task for you. While I speak to some of the interested parties here at the Cottage, I would like for you to pay a visit to the Victoria Stationery Shop." He pointed down a nearby side street and offered some quick directions—instructions that would lead me in the opposite direction from Stamford Bridge.

"Find me a match for this paper," he added, handing me the Cole note. "Bring back a sample."

"But how will I find such a match?"

"The watermark, Watson," he said with barely restrained impatience, holding the paper up to the light again. "You will note the stylized 'V' here, and the insignia below it."

"Yes—of course..."

"And ask the shopkeeper if he recalls selling any of this particular paper to a footballer in the past day or so."

"Certainly..."

He glanced up at the sun again, pursed his lips, and added, "It's not far—you should have plenty of time to pay the shop a visit and meet me back here before nightfall."

This all seemed rather puzzling to me but, having worked with Holmes for so many years, I knew better than to question him in such a matter. Instead I merely nodded, took the paper and set out on my way.

+ + +

When I returned from my excursion to the Victoria Stationery Shop, Holmes was just exiting the offices of Fulham Football Club.

"I trust your mission was a successful one," he said as we met on the street and he motioned for a hansom.

"Quite so," I replied. "They do sell this type of paper—it's made custom for them, and they're the only shop in West London to carry it—and the owner recalls selling a small package to a football player early this morning."

Holmes rubbed his hands together. "Excellent, Watson."

"He couldn't provide a good description of the customer, however, beyond his being a large man with short, dark hair, wearing a Fulham jersey. He recognized him somewhat, having attended a few games now and then, but could not name him."

"Disappointing," Holmes noted, "but not a critical failure to our efforts."

This surprised me, and I said as much.

"All will be apparent very soon," he replied. "We are very near solving this matter."

I blinked in surprise. "We are?"

"Absolutely."

A hansom pulled up and we boarded quickly. Out of the corner of my eye, I noticed a small man in humble clothes exiting the Fulham grounds behind us and hailing a cab of his own, but I thought nothing of it at the time.

"I, too, discovered some very useful information," Holmes volunteered as we set out for Stamford Bridge once more.

"Oh, yes?"

"Quite so, yes—but most of it came in my guise as funeral director, rather than consulting detective."

I gawked at Holmes in surprise and wonder.

He waved the matter away casually.

"There is one thing I require of you, Watson," he added almost as an afterthought. "Soon I believe we shall be once again at Craven Cottage. If this indeed turns out to be the case, I ask that you give Inspector Lestrade this list of questions he is to ask the club president."

Now at a total loss, I nonetheless accepted a small, folded piece of paper from Holmes and tucked it in my coat pocket. I hoped that he would be so good as to elucidate the matter a bit further. But, for the nonce, he would say no more.

+ + +

We met Lestrade at Stamford Bridge and were let into a meeting room by Sir Stephen, who then retired to allow us to converse in privacy.

Holmes wasted no time in laying out his thoughts for the Inspector.

"The note—the threatening note allegedly from Cole, sent to Dempsey. It was in fact neither written by nor sent by John Cole."

Lestrade stared dumbfounded at him.

"And you arrive at that conclusion *how*, Mr. Holmes?"

"It is elementary. Cole was a man of physical action and violence, to begin with—a footballer. Would he have gone to the trouble of traveling to a stationery shop—a shop far out of his way, no less—in order to purchase *high-quality paper* for his threatening note?" Holmes gave the Inspector a wry smile. "Hardly. A man in a rage, with violence or murder on his mind, would have grabbed the nearest scrap of paper at hand."

Holmes held up the note he'd taken from Lestrade in the interrogation room.

"Yet this paper was specifically purchased, some time prior to the match, at a fine stationery store—and, as my associate, Dr. Watson, has confirmed, a store on the far side of Fulham, nowhere near Stamford Bridge. The shop owner has confirmed it. Thus we can state with a high degree of confidence that the paper was acquired by someone who *intended* to write a note—who was planning to do so even before the match had begun—

and thus bought the paper prior to his coming to the stadium."

Lestrade considered this.

"It certainly does indicate premeditation on the part of Cole," he stated slowly, his mind working over what Holmes had said. "But I don't see how it clears Dempsey of killing him. Perhaps it would lend more evidence to a plea of self-defense on his part—but he's not claiming that!"

"There is more," Holmes went on. "The note—this premeditated note, as you put it, Inspector—was not written by Cole at all."

"Just because the paper was purchased at a shop across town, Mr. Holmes, doesn't mean—"

"How could Cole have written the note at all," Holmes continued on, ignoring Lestrade's comments, "when the man himself was illiterate?"

Lestrade stopped in his tracks and stared dumbfounded at Holmes.

"What? But—how can you be certain of that?"

Holmes drew a second piece of paper from his pocket and offered it to the Inspector, along with the threatening note allegedly from Cole.

"The handwriting on the two papers does not at all match, as you can plainly see," he stated, as if this explained all.

Lestrade glanced at the two papers just long enough to confirm Holmes's words, then stared back up at him dumbly.

"But—Mr. Holmes, you're not making sense! If the man was illiterate and could not write at all, how can you claim that this is a writing sample from him, to use for comparison?"

Now Holmes did smile, broadly.

"Because, Inspector—while Cole himself could not write, he had a trusted associate who did all of his writing for him. Everything from autographs to correspondence to contractual notes."

"Who—?"

Holmes nodded toward the short, stout man who stood just outside the doorway.

"Come in, if you please, Mr. Farnsworth."

The little man looked surprised, but then shuffled inside, hat in hand. With a shock, I realized he was the man I had noticed out of the corner of my eye as we had departed Craven Cottage.

"And who is this?" Lestrade demanded, now struggling to keep up with the flow of events.

"This is Mr. Abel Farnsworth, a very close associate and friend of the deceased," Holmes said. "I must admit that I was not entirely honest with him when I first met him, earlier this afternoon. I presented myself as an agent for the funeral home making arrangements for Cole's burial, and in that guise persuaded him to write up a short document delineating Cole's wishes as best he understood them in that regard."

Holmes indicated the second piece of paper.

"Afterward, I revealed my true identity and apologized to him for the quite necessary deception. You see, I had required from him a handwriting sample not tainted by any conscious or unconscious influences—by any knowledge of the true nature of my investigations."

"That's quite all right, Mr. Holmes," the man muttered softly. "I understand now what you were about."

Lestrade was frowning deeply even as Holmes smiled and nodded politely to the man.

"Mr. Farnsworth followed us here from Fulham because I explained to him that he might be invaluable in preventing the execution of an innocent man. He was nervous about accompanying us, but agreed to follow behind and to listen from a safe distance until he was needed."

"But just who is he, man?"

"He is the groundskeeper and caretaker at Craven Cottage," Holmes explained. He smiled to the shorter man. "And in addition to those regular duties, he has performed one other job there—he has been John Cole's able writing hand for several years now."

"Is this true?" Lestrade demanded.

"It is, sir," Farnsworth replied, gazing down at the floor. "I wouldn't normally have admitted it, o' course, in order to spare good Mr. Cole the embarrassment. But since he's passed on now..." He dabbed at the corner of one eye. "...and since Mr. Holmes has told me that the life of an innocent man depends on my admission..."

Lestrade held up the first paper. "And you did not write this note?"

"No, sir. I've never seen it before. And I wrote everythin' for the lad. Everythin'. He didn't want anyone else knowing he didn't have his letters, sir."

"And clearly the threatening note is not in Mr. Farnsworth's handwriting," Holmes added. "I submit to you, Inspector: Would an illiterate man, a man of no letters, with his usual confidante and note-writer far away at Craven Cottage, have gone to the trouble of asking someone else—someone he likely did not know—to write a threatening note? Would a man with such apparently bloody intentions have even bothered with a note at all?"

Lestrade took all of this in, then slowly nodded.

"Very well, then...I will accept—for the moment—that Cole could not have written the note, and that his confidante and helper in such matters didn't write it either. Someone else did."

"Someone planning *in advance* to write it," Holmes stated. "Someone who brought it, or at least the paper upon which it was written, to Stamford Bridge before the match, after having purchased the paper on the far side of Fulham."

"Very well—yes. So—have you also worked out exactly who *did* write it?" He regarded Holmes with skepticism and disdain. "And how that bit of information could *possibly* exonerate Mr. Dempsey and shed light on the true killer?"

"Perhaps," Holmes murmured softly, almost to himself. "Perhaps…"

Lestrade was frowning very deeply now, his eyes moving from Farnsworth to Holmes and back.

"Then I fail to see precisely what the use of all this was, Mr. Holmes."

Holmes nodded. Then, "Inspector, please accompany us back to Craven Cottage, where I believe we will be able to conclude this matter to your complete satisfaction."

+ + +

The sun had at last sunk below the London skyline as we all spilled out of the cab and stood before the offices of Fulham Football Club. The metal framework of the bleachers formed long, spidery shadows across the grounds as we followed the groundskeeper Farnsworth through the gate and into the offices.

We were met immediately by a man in his early sixties, immaculately dressed in full business attire. Farnsworth introduced us to him: Sir Adam Johnson, the Fulham Club Chairman.

Even as I was shaking hands with Sir Adam, I noted that Holmes had disappeared entirely—likely he had not even been seen by the Fulham man. My long years of association with Holmes and his methods of work caused me to realize that he was clearly up to something important and no doubt secret, and so I kept quiet on the matter. A second or two after that, I recalled the folded paper Holmes had given me earlier—the list of questions I was to hand to the Inspector, should we find ourselves at Craven Cottage again. Quickly I dug the paper from my pocket.

"So—why have I been summoned here at this hour?" demanded Sir Adam once we'd made introductions.

"Summoned here?" Lestrade glanced from Sir Adam to me with a puzzled expression. Then he looked down and saw the paper I was offering him. At that point doubtlessly he realized that Holmes was no longer in our company, and he opened his mouth to speak.

I cut him off as politely as possible under the circumstances.

"I, ah, believe the Inspector has a few questions for you," I told the man smoothly.

"I do?"

"Yes."

Lestrade appeared torn between astonishment, confusion, and outright anger, and could not decide which of those three reactions to choose—so he was combining all of them, to what I must say was a rather comical effect.

"Fine, fine," Sir Adam groused. "What would you like to know, Inspector?"

Lestrade was now staring at me—clearly he had decided to follow my lead, since he had no idea what was happening. I indicated the paper in his hand and nodded.

"Ah, yes," Lestrade began, having unfolded the note and read it. "Well. A few questions for you, Sir Adam, if you don't mind."

"Fine—do get on with it, then."

The questions were innocuous enough and scarcely worth repeating, and they dragged on for something like five or six minutes, with the Inspector making careful notes all the while. In the meantime, I kept a sharp eye out for Holmes—and was rewarded moments later when he rounded a corner just ahead of us and cleared his throat.

Everyone turned and saw him at once. Sir Adam's eyes widened.

"Mr. Holmes—you're back for another visit," he said.

Before anyone could speak, another man entered at the far end of the hallway, and Holmes dashed down past us to intercept him.

"Mr. Simon Lampard," Holmes said quickly.

"Yes?"

The man was tall and dark-haired, athletically built and wearing the uniform of Fulham Football Club—clearly a player on the team.

"Your game is up," Holmes announced grandly, his eyes meeting those of the footballer with great intensity. "All has been revealed. You can see that Inspector Lestrade has come to arrest your accomplice. Confess, for Sir Adam has already implicated you."

"Imp—implicated me?" Lampard's face twisted from surprise to anger. "Wha's he said, then?"

"Your game is up."

"He has told us that the entire plot was your idea—that you wished to murder your teammate and rival, John Cole, and that you blackmailed him into facilitating the crime and then helping to cover up your involvement!"

"What's all this—?" Sir Adam began, but before he could say more, I took the hint and coughed loudly, obscuring his remaining words.

"Yes," Holmes continued, "Sir Adam says it was all your idea—that you should be the only one to hang for it."

"That's not so," Lampard shouted angrily, his face now a deep red. "It was Sir Adam who proposed it—I went along, sure, but—"

"Quiet, you fool!" cried Sir Adam—but it was far too late for that now.

"You only handled the actual elimination of John Cole, then?" Holmes asked, his tone softening. "You weren't the actual mastermind?"

"No! It was Sir Adam! He talked me into doing it—and I wish I hadn't, now! I swear it!"

Holmes regarded the man with contempt.

"Inspector, you will wish to take this man into custody immediately, on the charge of the murder of John Cole."

Lestrade started forward, but Lampard had already whirled and started for the door. He had scarcely gone four steps, however, before he went sprawling to the floor. As I rushed forward to see what had happened, I became aware of another figure standing there, having deftly stepped from the shadows to trip Lampard.

"That's for you, you filth," Abel Farnsworth growled, and he kicked Lampard in the ribs. "John Cole was a good man, and he was my friend."

Lampard cried out in pain, then groaned as Lestrade handcuffed him.

I looked up then from Holmes and Lestrade to Sir Adam, who now stood alone at the other end of the hall. He nodded and clapped his hands, but I could see sweat trailing down the sides of his face.

"Good show, Inspector. Mr. Holmes. Good show. You've exposed the killer and revealed the depths of his perversity—that he would even attempt to implicate me in this business! Preposterous." He smiled. "I have to admit—you gave me quite a start there, Mr. Holmes, with your bluff to Lampard about my involvement and my confession—but I see now that it was just a trick to get him to confess."

"Indeed, it was intended to cause Lampard to confess his part in the crime," Holmes agreed with a narrow smile. "But what I said about your own involvement—well, Sir Adam, you and I both know that part was absolute truth."

Sir Adam blanched.

"What? How could you ever say that I—?"

Holmes held up a leather-bound book.

"I acquired this from your office some moments ago, Sir Adam," he stated. "Your ledger and records book. It reveals the sad state of your finances here at Fulham. From what you told me earlier today, together with this information, I was easily able to tell that your club is in serious financial difficulty. You confided in me your unhappiness with the opening of the new Chelsea club and their Stamford Bridge stadium so close to your own—such new competition could only cause you further financial troubles. Troubles you did not need, given that your most valuable player, John Cole, was entertaining an offer—a more lucrative offer—to leave Fulham for that selfsame new club, Chelsea."

"Well, that much is true, yes, but—"

"A simple solution presented itself to you, however," Holmes went on. "Remove Cole entirely—have him killed—and pin the murder on Chelsea's best player. By such an act you would remove a financial drain on your club, remove your rival's best player, as well—and make Chelsea out to be the haven of murderers, thus likely driving spectators who had begun straying to Chelsea back to Craven Cottage—and putting still more money in your pockets."

Sir Adam was now white as a ghost, staring dumbfounded at Holmes.

"But, Holmes," Lestrade said then, "why would Lampard go along with such a plot?"

"I spoke with him and with several other players during my visit here earlier today," Holmes replied. "A great rivalry existed between John Cole, universally regarded as Fulham's best player, and Simon Lampard, who toiled forever in his shadow, as it were."

"Ah," Lestrade gasped. "Lampard killed Cole out of jealousy!"

"Jealousy indeed," Holmes agreed, "together with the raise Sir Adam promised Lampard for doing the deed—a raise taken from a small portion of the money Sir Adam would be saving by no longer having to pay Cole's contracted salary."

"Diabolical," Lestrade muttered—then he moved quickly to grab Sir Adam before he, too, could attempt to flee.

+ + +

"Holmes," I said as we made our way home from West London at last, the hour having grown late indeed, "two things yet leave me curious."

"Indeed, Watson? Then ask away, by all means."

I frowned, considering the full body of remarkable events of the day and sorting through them in my mind.

"Of all the players on the Fulham side that could have been involved in the plot with Sir Adam, how did you come to be so certain that Lampard was the guilty party? Certain enough to spring your bluff on him in front of Sir Adam?"

"Simplicity, Watson," he answered. "Once I learned of the overall financial and personnel situation at the club, Lampard seemed the most likely suspect. To further confirm my suspicions, I met with the Fulham players separately for a few moments each, earlier today, while you were on your stationery store errand. To each I made a vague, veiled reference to the threatening note Dempsey had received. Of them all, only Simon Lampard reacted in the slightest as if he knew what I was talking about— and he is not a very convincing liar."

"Of course," I said. "None of the Fulham players could have known of the note's existence, as the note wasn't revealed until after Inspector Lestrade took Dempsey into custody—and by then, the Fulham players had all departed."

"Just so." He regarded me with a sidelong glance. "And your other question?"

"Farnsworth, the groundskeeper. How did you come to question him at all—or to feel him important enough to the case to require a false identity on your part while you did so?"

"I did not include that bit of information earlier for fear of embarrassing the man," Holmes admitted. "I must say, it was a bit of luck. Of course, we must occasionally rely upon chance to assist us; it is a capricious thing, a hindrance as often as not. But in this matter, it worked out in our favor."

"How so?"

"When I first encountered the good Mr. Farnsworth at the Fulham grounds, he was weeping, Watson—weeping bitterly over the news of Cole's death. That is what first raised my curiosity about him, and about his possibly important connections to the man and to the case. With Cole dead, a sympathetic ear was all that was required in order to gain from him the truth about the note."

"Ah," I managed by way of reply, then stared down at the floor of the carriage. We rode the rest of the way in somewhat awkward silence.

Our cab at last pulled up before 221-B Baker Street, and I saw my friend to the door. As he was about to enter, one thing more occurred to me and I cleared my throat.

"Yes, Watson? What is it?"

"Well, it occurs to me now, Holmes, that Sir Stephen at Chelsea will be quite delighted with the job you have done with this case. You have saved him and his organization no end of unjust embarrassment, as well as rescuing his best player from the gallows."

"Yes?"

"Well—it seems to me that he might well offer us something in return. Perhaps a season pass to the Chelsea matches?"

Holmes appeared to consider this for a moment, then wrinkled his nose and started inside once more.

"By all means, Watson, you should accept such a gift, were he to offer it. You have more than earned it with your work tonight." He snorted. "But as for me—I fear I have had quite enough of football for one lifetime."

The Making of "The Problem at Stamford Bridge"

by Van Allen Plexico

It was truly a fortuitous coincidence that Ron Fortier decided to put together a Sherlock Holmes anthology at the exact moment that I was reveling in all things "Holmes" myself. Primarily a reader and writer of science fiction and fantasy, I was drawn into British adventure literature via Patrick O'Brian's sea novels only in recent years, and had moved on to the realm of Sherlock Holmes within the past year. When the call came, I was in full Holmes immersion, working my way through the written stories in a big combined volume, listening to the audio books (free from Librivox.org), and avidly watching the marvelous Granada TV productions starring Jeremy Brett and Edward Hardwicke—all the while generally absorbing Sir Arthur

Conan Doyle's style and story approach as best I could, along with Brett's interpretation of the character's personality and dialogue.

Upon sitting down to write my first Holmes story, I asked myself what I loved most about England. Among any number of things the Premiership leapt to mind, as I have in the past few years become a fan of Chelsea Football Club in particular and the top flight of English soccer in general. So I knew my story had to involve soccer—and a murder, too, of course. A murder at a soccer match! So I had my premise. But what motivation for the killer, beyond simple thuggish brutality? A conspiracy by management and rival players, of course. All fell into place easily enough, and off I went.

As it turned out, the most difficult parts of the story for me were the two moments when Holmes deduces something about Watson (or someone else) via simple observation. It says all that needs to be said about Holmes's skills (and Doyle's) that it took me seemingly hours to come up with the things the detective spots in an instant.

Chelsea play at a stadium named "Stamford Bridge," and as it happened, one of the first Holmes stories I'd happened to encounter was Doyle's "The Problem at Thor Bridge." I thus chose the title for the story as a sort of nod to that Doyle adventure.

I'm not entirely sure English football was quite as organized and businesslike as early on as I make it out to be in my story. Certainly many of the clubs still around today were fielding teams in the late 19th Century. But I felt that any liberties with the timeline of the Premiership I might inadvertently be taking would be acceptable as long as all seemed plausible enough and the story was a decent one—one that strove to capture something of Doyle's classic approach to a Holmes tale. I hope this has been the case.

Sherlock Holmes Consulting Detective

"The Adventure of the Locked Room"

by Andrew Salmon

There were many cases in the inestimable career of Mr. Sherlock Holmes which I have documented but which, for a myriad of reason, have not seen the light of day. Most of these can be classified as being too injurious to the parties involved either due to their public stature and the delicate, personal nature of the events or the harm the resulting scandal of making them public would bring on those, whoever they may by, in the midst of them. The adventure of the locked room is one of the latter. As it involved Mrs. Hudson, however indirectly, and the woman had been so very, very good to myself and Holmes in those wonderful years at 221B Baker street, I decided at the time the investigation took place that I would not further darken the poor woman's door with a published account of the matter. However all these years later, with that splendid example of womanhood gone to her reward, I deem it safe to set the matter down for public consumption as it is one of the first cases in which I had the good fortune to observe my dear friend at work.

"You've not heard of the murder, then?"

This extraordinary interrogative began the matter and it was uttered by Mrs. Hudson herself shortly after Holmes and I had taken possession of the rooms she had to let at 221B Baker Street. On this particular Friday afternoon in late Summer 1881, Holmes and I, with the assistance of Mrs. Hudson, had been engaged in arranging our living quarters. In this comparative calm moment in the life of Holmes, we fell to and had undertaken the task of feathering our nest in a most handsome fashion. To wit we were awaiting delivery of a settee and the wagon was late, much to the chagrin of my esteemed colleague. Sherlock Holmes was not an individual who took inactivity lightly. In my brief exposure to him at this time, I had divined that his moods often fluctuated between great spurts of action and singular brooding. However, these seemingly inactive times were instances of the greatest mental musings which only appeared to resemble lethargy to the uninformed witness. Now as we awaited the new furnishings, he oscillated between sullen introspection in his large chair to the frantic pacing of a caged animal while Mrs. Hudson and I took to unpacking some of my things. I had urged my friend out of doors to take some exercise while I received the new furnishings, but he would not hear of it. That very morning, he had been hunched over his tiny lab table strewn with steaming potions and would not let them leave his sight while, as he put it, clumsy clods stomped about the place. And so he suffered like a convict at the start of a life sentence.

Mrs. Hudson, made exceedingly nervous by my friend's manner, felt compelled to say something which would occupy the capacious mind of Sherlock Holmes and her utterings had the desired effect. Holmes, upon hearing her query, sprang up out of his chair, for she had spoken during one of his sullen periods, and advanced upon the poor woman as if he meant her harm.

"What's that you say, madam?" he said.

Mrs. Hudson recoiled from his charge until she came up against the window sill and could withdraw no farther.

"Sir?" she managed.

"The murder, woman," insisted Holmes. "What of it? Speak plainly, now!"

"It was some four weeks before you entered into this present arrangement," Mr. Hudson began most timidly.

"So much time has passed!" muttered Holmes plaintively. "And this is the first I've heard of the matter!"

"Well, Mr. Holmes, I-I did not want it commonly known. Rooms to let under such a cloud as this... Surely you can understand. Yourself and Dr. Watson were the first, potential tenants who had not heard of the matter or recollected upon inspection of the rooms what had transpired. I let the rooms to you gladly, sir. Let us have an understanding on that. You and the doctor were not folks I simply settled on for want of better tenants to ensure the rooms were occupied. It was only the scandal which stilled my tongue. If you had only known what it was like."

Sherlock Holmes waved that away as if Mrs. Hudson's words were so much smoke from a brazier. "The tale, woman! Spare us nothing in the relating. Pray, quick as you please. I will assist you in the recounting by commencing with a question: the name of the individual who lost their life in these rooms, what was it?"

"Mr. Judson Farris."

"Excellent! Continue."

"Well, sir, he presented himself to me in a most correct manner one Sunday morning. He was tall, thin – something like yourself in appearance, Mr. Holmes. Although there was a sharpness to his carriage and manner, as if life had used him cruelly. Or, rather, that he used life cruelly. If you take my meaning. Now, please do not take me wrong, he held all the bearing of a gentleman. He glanced over the rooms and expressed his intention to rent them if I would allow him to have them."

"A further inquiry, if I may." Holmes held up a thin hand. "Glanced at the rooms, you say? He did not make a detailed inspection?"

"He did not. He paid me in advance and informed me that he would see to arranging the transfer of his things in the near future. This never took place as he was dead the next day."

I watched the eyelids of Sherlock Holmes adopt a hooded appearance as they half-closed over his probing orbs. At first I had concluded erroneously that this seemingly languid condition was brought on by his regular use of cocaine, but experience had taught met that when my friend adopted this posture he was deep in thought.

"Did he have any luggage with him at all?" asked Holmes quickly.

"No, sir."

"Nothing? A valise? Carpet bag? Sheaf or portfolio?"

"Why, yes, now that you mention it. There was a small portfolio crushed under his arm. He did not set it down during his inspection or while we concluded our arrangement."

Sherlock Holmes withdrew into a state of silent brooding. Until now, I was satisfied that my friend, in his desperation to engage his thoughts on something of substance, had seized upon Mrs. Hudson's tale merely as a means to this end. I was certain that this, ultimately, was an empty exercise, something to fill the minutes while we awaited the damnable delivery, for how could Holmes presume to solve an isolated case such as the death of Judson Farris with so little to go on? To say nothing of the passage of time. Enough time that the perpetrator might well have fled to any of the four corners of the globe. I would not begrudge my new companion his diversion, however, and did not give voice to these thoughts.

Suddenly Holmes sprang out of his chair by the fire and dashed to the heap of newspapers he had scattered about beside his chair. He began pawing through them frantically. I observed him in mute shock for a moment before my limited thought processes caught up to the steam locomotive that was the brain of Sherlock Holmes. My friend was in the habit of devouring each day's mound of newspapers and setting aside for future consideration those he was unable to get to on the day of their release due to his taking action in some line of inquiry. This was explained to me upon first moving into the rooms and being confronted by the stack of yellowing sheets. Holmes sought the papers covering the murder of Judson Farris all those weeks ago. He halted his search and turned to face me, a smile on his hawk-like features.

"Here it is at last!" He brandished a creased, dog-eared issue of the *Pall Mall* triumphantly and stepped lightly to my chair. "Read it aloud, Watson. I'm in such a state just now I cannot get past the headline."

As Holmes dropped into his chair beside me, I glanced at Mrs. Hudson whose eyes had the distant quality of one looking into the past for answers and finding none. I lowered my gaze to the paper and read:

"LOCKED ROOM MURDER BAFFLES POLICE! The small hours before dawn brought a calamitous uproar to quiet Baker Street. The deceased body of Judson Farris was discovered in the suite of rooms at 221B. Mr. Farris had only just moved into the suite some two days prior from his estate in Castleford, Yorkshire. His presence in London was something of a mystery in itself although police speculate that it was some business matter concerning his recently deceased wife that had brought him down to London. What has stymied police is how he came to his untimely end. The doors and outer windows of the rooms in which the body was found by the landlady, a Mrs. Hudson, were securely bolted from the inside, and no other means of entering or exiting was apparent. Added to that was the fact that Mr. Farris appears to have been suffocated by a gas leak yet all of the gas lines in the room were closed. The search itself has been hampered by a lack of witnesses. As the street lamp directly outside the edifice was out at the time, no one has stepped forward claiming to have seen anyone entering or leaving the building.

"Read it aloud, Watson. I'm in such a state just now I cannot get past the headline."

The article went on with some particulars of the investigation which, at the time of writing, had made no progress. I did not relate these passages to my audience because Holmes could barely contain his enthusiasm at the case that had, somewhat literally, been dropped in his lap. He bobbed his head excitedly at me and his eyes sparkled as I looked over the top of the paper at him. He rose up out of his seat, seized a cigarette and lit it. He turned to Mrs. Hudson, who seemed to have withered under my recounting of past events.

"Mrs. Hudson, I am well aware that returning to that fateful night might be unpleasant for you. However, as the matter has captured my imagination and I very much want to delve into the thing with the intention of solving the case — putting the matter to rest once and for all. Will you assist me in accomplishing this?"

Mrs. Hudson wrung her hands for a moment as she wrestled with past horrors in her mind. The outcome of said battle was never in doubt as she was a woman of strong, no-nonsense stock. She met the gaze of Sherlock Holmes and nodded her assent.

"Excellent! Let us see to the matter at once. Now, the papers say you discovered the body. May I ask you where in the room the body lay?"

"On the settee next to hearth, the very one I am having replaced today. I couldn't bear the notion of its continued use given what had transpired upon it."

Holmes strode to the centre of the room and stood to the left of the bearskin hearth rug and gazed down at the bare patch of floor where the old settee had rested until that morning when the moving van had carted it away. He looked left and right at the doors giving entry into the room. The one on the left led to the hallway and stairs leading to Baker Street, the door opposite gave entry to Holmes's bedroom. There was a door inside that room leading to a short flight of steps which communicated with another exit.

"It was pitch black, and I could barely see. I had not even the light from the fire to aid me as no fire had been prepared. The sun was just on the rise, but Mr. Farris had all of the drapes pulled. He was prone upon the settee," Mrs. Hudson went on with no prompting from Holmes. "The room reeked of a horrible poisonous cloud." A shudder passed over her sturdy frame. "Poor Mr. Farris, his lips blue, his face so swollen and congested, the protruding eyes..."

"What did you do when you found him?"

"I opened the drapes, flung up all the windows, then dashed from the room to find a constable. I could not spend another minute here."

"Quite understandable." Holmes nodded sympathetically. "The doors were locked?"

"Yes."

"The windows as well?"

"The outer windows were securely fastened, yes. The inner ones were up an inch or two."

"This includes the window in what is now my sleeping quarters?"

"It was bolted shut, sir."

"And what of the portfolio that was in Mr. Farris's possession?"

"I never saw it again."

"You were home when the murder took place?"

"I assume so, sir. It was late and I was sleeping. I did not discover the body until the following dawn when the smell of the gas reached me. I had been up preparing his breakfast at that time."

"You heard nothing in the night? No sound or disturbance?"

"I slept soundly, sir. It was the last sound sleep I had for quite some time afterwards."

"I can well imagine. You found no sign of forced entry anywhere?"

"I hardly took the time to look!" said Mrs. Hudson, terror in her eyes. "However the room appeared as it had when Mr. Farris had taken it. Nothing was out of place as far as I could determine."

"The article spoke of the street lamp being out. Were you aware of this?"

"Oh, that blasted lamp. It was defective in some way and had been going off and on for a fortnight prior to the dreadful event. Shortly before you and Dr. Watson moved in, a crew was out to make repairs. As you well know, it is working now."

"Indeed it is," said Holmes, nodding his assent. "The police, what did they do upon arriving at the scene?"

"They took possession of the body and I was glad to be rid of it. They asked questions which I answered to the best of my ability, although Mr. Farris had only been known to me for twenty-four hours and had received no visitors or mail. They prowled around, examined the hole in the roof, searched around the building."

"Hole in the roof?" asked Holmes, poignantly.

"Oh, yes, above the lumber room next to Dr. Watson's quarters."

Holmes gazed at me significantly.

"It's been fixed!" Mrs. Hudson said quickly. "Ten days before you came here, I had the entire roof re-tarred and the ceiling in the room re-plastered. It's tight as a drum, I assure you."

"I am certain it is," said Holmes, mildly.

Clearly shaken, Mrs. Hudson stood and faced us. "These horrors of the past are too much for me. If you have no further use for me I'll retire to my rooms until the delivery wagon rings."

"Please do so, my dear," said Holmes, taking her by the arm and leading her to the door. "I do apologize for dredging these things up, but I shall do my best to solve the murder and so dispel the dark cloud hanging over the rooms. Thank you for your assistance. Please do not trouble yourself further in the matter."

He closed the door behind her and faced me with intent anticipation colouring his features.

"Well, Watson, under normal conditions, I should think a look at the police file on the case would be the first order of business. However, as a last courtesy to the accursed, tardy deliveryman, we shall put that aside for the moment. As we happen to abide at the crime scene, perhaps we had best begin with an examination of it and uncover what secrets it may yield. What of it? Where do we begin?"

"The door, I should think," I replied. "Is that not how one usually gains entry into a room?"

"You are quite right. Though I'm certain the door was not used by the killer, we must be thorough and leave nothing to chance. Let the facts be our one and only guide." Next he stepped to the mantel and picked up a magnifying lens, and I thought he meant to begin the study of the crime scene at once. Yet with the lens in his fist, he turned to me and spoke instead. "What do you make of the affair?"

"As a physician, I can only state that it is possible that Mrs. Hudson is mistaken about gas asphyxiation. If the gas was turned off, then how was the man killed? Also, if the gas had been on and ended the man's life, then who turned it off, if we assume the room was sealed tight the entire time?"

"Your keen mind has plumbed the depths of one of the most interesting aspects of the case. Pray continue."

"This is only supposition on my part, however. I suppose that it is possible that Farris was strangled. The horrid, livid aspect of his features as Mrs. Hudson described could be brought about by choking."

"And the odour?"

"Upon death, a corpse emits various gases and fluids. It is possible Mrs.

Hudson detected these and assumed the gas had done him in."

"You are certain of this?"

"By no means. It is merely a possibility."

"Excellent, Watson! Excellent! I can most definitely use your assistance. Will you help me?"

"Certainly," I replied. Since returning from Afghanistan to recoup from my war wound, I had prescribed for myself a regimen of quiet and rest to which I had adhered to religiously for a long stretch of days. However in allying myself with Sherlock Holmes to secure lodgings, my quiet recuperative life seemed to have been thrust aside by adventure. Truth be told, I was not totally adverse to the swap.

"To the door, then, Watson," Holmes beckoned. "Let us see what we shall see."

The door was of solid oak bearing the common nicks and scratches of previous use. The lock was a heavy bolt of a kind to be found anywhere in the city. Sherlock Holmes bent and examined the lock with the lens on both sides of the door, a litany of non-committal grunts accompanying his action.

"The lock has not been picked," he observed.

"Perhaps an outsider," I offered.

"I think not. Even so fine a tool as an outsider would scratch the keyhole as the wielder attempted to turn the key from the other side."

"A screw?"

"Again, a skeleton key would leave noticeable marks. I see none."

"Shall we examine the street door?"

"We shall come to that presently. If we're to take the newspaper report at face value, it has been established that the inner door was bolted on the night of the murder. If the murderer had utilized any of the tools we mentioned on this one, we would have found the marks. Therefore, we must conclude that he did not and thus the door downstairs will also be free of such evidence. In the interest of complete thoroughness, the street door as well as its mate around side may have to be examined. For the moment, however, let us move on."

"The door to your chambers and the now repaired hole?"

"Watson, you have plucked the thoughts from my mind."

This inspection yielded the same results. The door to Holmes's sleeping quarters bore only the marks of casual use. He could detect no signs of tampering. As for the hole in his ceiling, Mrs. Hudson had implied much larger dimensions than were in actuality the case. Perhaps in her eagerness to put across that she in no way concealed damage or attempted to swindle us by its omission, it had taken on a larger size in her memory. The repairmen had done such an exceptional job filling in the hole that I had to stand right beneath it with a lamp held up to the ceiling to notice the faint shading in the plaster. My esteemed colleague concluded without so much as glancing at the repair work that it was possible the murderer had gained entry by this avenue on the night Judson Farris was murdered. However he deemed it unlikely, as the killer would have had to enter through the lumber room first where his footwear would have picked up considerable debris from the stacked cord wood and this would have been found on the carpet around the corpse, and none had been reported as found.

As all of the doors in the suite had been examined to my friend's satisfaction, this left only the windows and Sherlock Holmes went to them immediately. He chose the bow-window as the first one to explore. He tried the locks, confirming that they worked smoothly and sealed the windows from outside tampering. He opened the outer windows and the noise and clatter of Baker Street flooded in. Holmes leaned out, his eyes darting purposely this way and that. As the window was large and could accommodate both of us, I leaned out on the sill and joined him in taking the air. The stone sill felt rough and dried drops of black pitch from the roof repair dappled the surface and stung my palms. People strolled by oblivious to our inspection. A brougham swayed up the cobbled road.

"Well, Holmes, has the room yielded its secrets to you?" I prodded.

"It is in the process of doing so, I assure you," he replied his eyes roving around the street.

"All I see is a typical London street on a Friday afternoon," I replied. "We have seen doors and windows that have not been tampered with. And yet a man was killed in this room with all of these means of entry barred to his killer." I dusted my hands together and withdrew from the window.

Without rejoinder, he yanked his head out of the open window and abandoned this part of the room. He strode quickly across to the window opposite looking out on narrow Blandford Street. Holmes had set up his desk directly in front of this window. The top of said article of furniture was quickly vanishing under a spreading mound of papers of all kinds. To the left of this was the table for chemical experiments he had jammed in a corner and was the means for imprisoning us here. Various vials smoked even as we stood near the thing as Holmes contemplated how to get at the window his desk now blocked.

"Let us pull it back," he suggested after a moment's thought. "Pray gently Watson, my experiments are at a crucial stage and I should hate if we were to bump my lab table as we moved this one."

We did as he instructed and had his desk pulled from the window without so much as brushing against his precious experiments. Once the way was clear, Sherlock Holmes fairly leaped into the expanse we had created and, without laying so much as a finger on the closed windows, scrutinized them first with his keen eyes, then with the lens. Then a further test was made on the locking mechanisms and they were not found to be defective. Holmes stepped back for a moment and I saw his eyes take on that singular half-lidded expression with which I was becoming most familiar. He set the lens down and eased the window upwards. The outer storm window was closed and this, too, he swung out. The resulting invasion of street noise was much less audible than busy Baker Street, Blandford being a quiet avenue. The odd man or women strolled by on errands that were a mystery to all but them. The street lamp the newspaper had reported as defective in the days leading up the night of the murder stood some twenty feet from the window near the gutter and was the only one within two hundred feet of the building due to the mouth of the alley and a bend in the footpath. I had to half-turn to join my friend in his inspection as the window here was not so large as our bow-window and it was a tight squeeze for both of us to lean out at once.

"The workers Mrs. Hudson hired to re-tar her roof were uncommon sloppy, wouldn't you say?" asked Holmes.

"How's that?"

He looked down at the sill to direct my gaze. "The sill here bears the same spray of crusted pitch as the other."

As I at no time saw Holmes so much as glance at these droplets prior to his mentioning them, his statement surprised me.

"She strikes me as a woman of somewhat limited means. Perhaps she employed the best she could afford."

For an answer to this remark, Holmes bent low and studied the sill. Then he thrust his chin forward to gaze down at the outside wall. Aside from smooth brick, I noticed nothing. Pulling ourselves out of the window we stood side by side as the cool twilight air wafted in against our midsections. The storm window had been swung out, and Holmes closed it idly. Taking up his lens, Holmes bent to examine the entire frame, ending his inspection at the air holes at the base. The action struck me as petulant persistence. The room and, indeed, the building had not surrendered its secrets and the murder of Judson Farris was not to be solved so easily.

Holmes's stubborn inspection of the storm window seemed to me to be a flat refusal to admit defeat.

"Are you thinking fairies entered through these holes and did the deed?" I chided.

"They do bear more pitch." He poked at the middle one. "This one is almost clogged with the stuff." He shut the window with a bang which betrayed his frustration.

"We have covered every avenue of entry," I noted. "Where should we search next?"

"Although the mystery of how the murderer entered and exited has eluded us, it is safe to assume that he used the street to gain entry. I shall go down and investigate further."

"Investigate what, precisely? The crime was committed weeks ago. Thousands of pedestrians and carriages have passed by since. The Spring rains have washed the stones clear countless times. What could you possibly hope to find?"

Sherlock Holmes smiled enigmatically. "Perhaps I shall see the delivery man when he comes round. Either way I am going down and will return in a few minutes. Hold the fort, Watson!"

It was with a certain degree of mute wonderment that I watched as Holmes bustled into his frockcoat and plucked a deerstalker from a wall peg. Without so much as a backwards glance he exited our chambers. He was lost to my sight as he navigated his way around the building to take up position directly beneath the window we had just been examining. As my position afforded me a bird's eye view of Holmes at work, I leaned out on the sill with great curiosity for I was convinced that the deductive powers of my friend were about to be tested to the limit. After all, if the actual crime scene yielded nothing to his probing mind, what could he hope to uncover in the surrounding area of an urban thoroughfare? Holmes tilted his head back to stare up at me, his eyes shining in the dying light.

"The best of British luck," I offered by way of encouragement.

In reply to this, he displayed the briefest flicker of an enigmatic curl of the lips, then set about his work. I must admit that it was with more than a little mirth that I watched him on this task. He swung his head this way and that as he studied the pavement before undertaking a startling action. Ignoring the odd passers-by around him, Holmes, displaying a remarkable gymnastic ability I would not have thought him capable of, proceeded to shimmy his lanky frame up the pole of the street-lamp. I watched, astounded, as he secured his position by wrapping his feet around the pole and coiling one hand around the top in serpentine fashion while he used his free hand to gently open the small glass door in order to examine the inner workings of the lamp — all this while the few nearby pedestrians paused in their journey to gape at the spectacle. Before I could recover my senses sufficiently to hurl a comment of my friend's extraordinary behaviour, he shut the glass panel, dropped down to the cold stones and disappeared into the alley dividing this building from its immediate neighbour.

A semblance of calm had just been restored on the street below when suddenly there arose from the alley a tremendous noise and clatter as though someone were attempting to squeeze a coach and six through the slim expanse. Then Sherlock Holmes re-appeared, moving rapidly towards the front entrance. Surmising his search had been completed, I withdrew from the window and went to meet him as he came in.

"Ah, Watson!" he ejaculated as he moved past me to go and stand by the fire. "We are making some small headway, I assure you." He turned his tall frame this way and that before the blaze in the hearth. When he had warmed himself sufficiently, he lit a cigarette then spoke of his discoveries. "Nothing below the window revealed itself to me. However I was undaunted. Next I attempted to inspect the street-lamp that was reported as being out on the night of the murder."

"Yes, so much I observed," I interjected. "Whatever did you hope to find?"

"The point was moot, since the shining brass fittings gave mute testimony to Mrs. Hudson's claim that the light had been repaired since the time the crime took place. It was the alley which provided a most singular clue."

Leaving the warmth of the fire, Holmes stepped towards me as he fished into one of the pockets of his coat and withdrew what appeared to be filthy rags which he unceremoniously dumped into my lap.

"There!" said he in triumph. "What do you make of these?"

Overcoming my initial revulsion, I took up the dark, wadded mass and examined it. The clumps soon revealed themselves to be a pair of rough, soiled gloves, stiff with much wetting, drying and night frost. The gloves were of an ebony hue.

"It is a pair of old work gloves," I said at last.

"Precisely."

"But these prove nothing. Oh, perhaps I speak too hastily. You found them in the alley, you say?"

"Yes, behind a large, stubborn trash bin there which did not wish to be moved."

"All right, then I amend my previous statement. They prove that one of the workers Mrs. Hudson employed to repair the roof was a clumsy oaf who dropped the gloves off the roof after setting them down to free his hands to take a cup of tea or light a cigar. Certainly they can have no bearing on the case."

"You may be right, Watson, I daresay. Time will determine this. Do you not notice anything peculiar about the gloves?"

I looked them over again. "The elements have not been kind to them, I see. Understandably so after weeks of exposure. And they are stiff with black pitch from the roof. That is all I have to say about them."

"Nothing else catches your eye? No detail demands your attention?"

"None."

Sherlock Holmes extended a hand, and I gratefully placed the sodden gloves in his open palm. He kneaded the tangled mass apart and held the gloves up for me to look at.

"And now?"

At first I saw nothing unusual, then the obvious hit me like a thunderclap and I felt the proper dolt for not noticing it sooner. "By Jove! They are both left hand gloves. That is queer. What can this mean?"

"Perhaps nothing, perhaps everything," Holmes replied, cryptically. He set the gloves down on the side table and adjusted his coat on his wiry frame. "Well, Watson, I must take my leave of you for the moment. I should not be gone more than an hour. In which time, I hope the wretched deliverymen will have come and gone, leaving us both free to pursue this locked room murder."

"You are leaving? But your experiments..."

"They are almost completed. Some thirty minutes or so will ensure their success. At any rate, they are now beyond the reach of whatever clumsy oafs pay us a visit. However, that being said, I wonder if I might impose upon you to await my return here and so protect my lab table should the settee arrive this day. Will you do that?"

"You may count on me, sir. By the by, where are you going?"

"The Yard. I must discover why Judson Farris was in hiding on the night he was murdered. We begin this investigation with a serious handicap and shall have to work quickly to gain lost ground."

"You suspect Farris was in hiding because he knew his assailant? That the murderer was expected?"

"I suspect nothing. The newspaper account reveals these things."

"How so?"

At first I saw nothing unusual, then the obvious hit me like a thunderclap...

"Watson, it is quite elementary. Farris was in town from the country, presumably on business. Yet he did not book himself into one of the city's innumerable hotels. Rather, he came here to this nondescript flat and rented rooms. He had no luggage with him other than the mysterious portfolio. Also, on what was a chilly night in late March, every light was out, the drapes were drawn and there was no fire in the hearth. Clearly the man had gone to great lengths to conceal his presence in the room, thus fooling anyone watching the building into thinking that no one was at home."

"Why, of course, Holmes. I see it now that you have laid it out so plainly. And the logical next step must be the police. I shall await your return with eagerness."

Sherlock Holmes cocked his head to one side by means of farewell and stepped through the door on his way to the street.

Three-quarters of an hour after his departure, the street bell chimed and the deliverymen had come at last. Mrs. Hudson went down to see them in and I opened the inner door to make the delivery easier. Two burly men entered, bearing the new settee between them. Mrs. Hudson followed closely on their heels as they stepped across the threshold but stood near the doorway as if halted by phantoms of the past. As Holmes had predicted, the men barrelled about the room and almost succeeded in nudging his lab table. I was able to prevent this, but only just. Mrs. Hudson lingered behind after they had gone out, the worry in her eyes a mute question directed at myself.

"He is looking into the matter," was all I could say to the poor woman. She nodded her gratitude and returned to her room.

Some thirty minutes after this little scene played out, Sherlock Holmes returned. I heard his key in the outer door and went to the threshold of the inner door to greet him. I had busied myself with removing the wrappings around the settee during the intervening minutes, but, all the while, my mind raced with theories about what my friend had learned from the authorities.

"It has come, finally," he called up to me by way of greeting although how he could possibly know this while standing with the street door at his back I had no clue. He continued as if having read my thoughts. "The mud on the stairs and the eagerness to be off reflected in your features, Watson. I have a hansom waiting outside and was just stepping in to see if you were free to join me on the hunt. What say you?"

I had my coat on in a flash and settled my hat upon my head as I pounded down the stairs. I climbed into the hansom and waited expectantly as

Holmes bade the driver to be off. He joined me inside and I stared openly at my companion, my meaning plain.

"I shall explain all on the way, Watson. Have no fear."

The hansom jerked and we were away. We rode in silence for the first leg of the journey. After being cooped up awaiting the deliverymen, it was at first pleasing to merely drink in the sights and sounds of the city. The air had a reviving, early evening crispness to it and the clamour of the city invigorated me. The streets were clogged with drays, wagons, carts, cabs and omnibuses jammed in horrible confusion. Horses strained and slipped over slick rough cobbles, drivers vying with each other for position on the road. Here and there such spirited competition degenerated into bouts of fisticuffs eagerly witnessed by the porters and loafers who sneered and jeered the contest. Timid ladies withdrew behind the curtains of their broughams, peeking out discreetly at the action before them. Seeing all of this and more, I soon regained my vigour. Yet all the while I took these simple pleasures, my mind could not shake the case, and these pleasant diversions could not settle my thoughts.

"You might begin by telling me where we are going," I suggested.

"We are heading to 5186 Clanranald, the home of Mr. Everett Hopkins, Esquire."

"I see. And what is his connection to the case?"

"Ah, Watson, thereby hangs a tale."

"I beg you to commence."

"I met with Inspector Lestrade as he was leaving for the evening. At first he did not wish to delve into the matter. However when I mentioned that you and I were living at the crime scene, he could not resist what he referred to as a 'cosmic jest' and readily agreed to my request. He prefaced his statement with some remarks about the history of Judson Farris. With your indulgence, I shall relate them to you."

"By all means, Holmes. I am all ears."

Holmes continued. "Very well. The tale begins with the untimely death of one Edgar Hopkins of Castleford, a successful coal magnate. A consumptive, he left behind a wife, Lucilla, and one living son, Everett Hopkins by name. The older son, christened Lucius, had left home at an early age to make his fortune. He saw action in Afghanistan and was reported killed in that conflict. The two boys were fraternal twins."

The reference to Afghanistan struck home and conjured endless nightmares of the loss of life I had seen in my service to the Crown, I could not help but feel an immediate sympathy for the Hopkins family.

Holmes went on. "The loss of the Pater familias came at an unfortunate juncture in the history of the modest Hopkins fortune. Lestrade could not furnish all of the details save to add that several notes had come due which spelled disaster for the surviving members. Until, that is, Mr. Judson Farris appeared on the scene. A perfunctory courtship lead to his marrying the widowed Lucilla. A union of convenience? One cannot say at this stage of the investigation whether any tender feeling existed between the two parties, but the union was sanctified and the Hopkins interests were saved. And that is all Lestrade could tell me on the matter. As for the crime itself, he directed me to the case file and permitted me access to its pages. However, before leaving me to its study, he admitted to me quite candidly that they believe they have solved how the murder was committed though he confessed he could not officially lay the finger of blame on any one individual. Here are the facts of the case as he understands them: Lestrade is convinced that the killer entered through the hole in the ceiling of what is now my bedchamber. A ladder was found at the time in the same alley I investigated earlier today and he believes it was used to scale the building. Note that I say he believes this to be true. He cannot prove it. Also, as the official medical examination of the body confirms that Farris died of gas asphyxiation, the murderer's presence in the room takes on a singular meaning. And here is an unexpected twist: the ladder belonged to the Baker Street lamp-lighter who was found murdered that very night. A murder, I might add, that is also unsolved. Lestrade believes that the lamp-lighter was the killer's accomplice enlisted to ensure the light outside 221B was darkened to allow the killer to enter and leave under unobserved. Once the deed was done, the lamp-lighter became a liability and was murdered in turn."

"And what do you think?" I asked.

"The theory has its merits but is, ultimately, neither here nor there as it does not reveal a killer, a motive or even how the crime itself was carried out."

"I agree with you on the first two points," I said. "However, Lestrade's theory of how the crime was committed makes perfect sense. The murderer bribes the lamp-lighter to darken the street while he climbs atop the roof, enters through the hole in the ceiling and murders Judson Farris. As to the means of dispatching Farris, the killer need only have pressed Farris's face to an open gas jet in the room until his victim succumbed. Then he shuts off the gas and, with the windows curtained, easily makes his escape the way he came in, killing the lighter in the process to ensure his silence."

"And the lack of debris on the carpet?"

"The killer removed his shoes."

Holmes considered this for a moment in silence before speaking, "You and Lestrade clearly see eye to eye in this matter and it is possible you have hit the nail on the head. In which case, I commend you both. For myself, I believe more light needs to be shed on the matter." He leaned out the window and gazed ahead. "As I see the house of Everett Hopkins looms, perhaps now we will have some answers."

"Do you think Everett Hopkins will cooperate?"

"Hardly. He disappeared on the night of the murder and no one has seen him since." The hansom lurched to a stop. "Ah, we have arrived. Come, Watson. Let us see if we can untangle this knot."

We stepped down before a sprawling manor house bordered by a high hedge, and the cabman was directed to wait. We stopped a moment and looked over the place. Bristling Tudor chimneys stabbed at the sky, black smoke coiling out of their maws. The manor itself was blackened stone, stately, in a low key sort of way. The windows appeared draped however some warm light seeped through here and there. The gate squealed with rust as Holmes swung it open, and I noticed weeds poking out through the cracks in the walk and the patch to the coach house. Holmes used the chipped knocker and the sound reverberated within. He was about to knock again, when suddenly the door was opened by the butler. He was a tall, gaunt, hard-faced man I gauged to be five-and-sixty at minimum for he was slightly stooped and moved with some difficulty. His attire was immaculate however and I caught the smell of toilet water as I passed him in the doorway after he bade us enter. We were shown into a high-ceilinged foyer and two oak doors opened on to a sitting room on the left. The butler followed Holmes and myself into this room and closed the doors behind him. We went to the low fire in the hearth and warmed ourselves. It struck me as odd that the butler did not immediately inquire as to our business here. Rather, he stood stiffly awaiting this revelation.

"Is your master at home?" asked Holmes.

"No, sir."

"It has been many weeks since you've heard from him. Correct?"

The man seemed to wither at this. "That is so."

"What is your name?"

"Douglas Gavin, sir."

"And how long have you been in the employ of the Hopkins family?"

"All my life. And I thank you, sir, for using the proper family name."

"Really?" Holmes stared open-faced at the man. "I thought I might have spoken out of turn in not employing the Farris name."

Gavin shut his eyes as though a spasm of agony lanced through him. "Please do not speak that name in this house."

"Yes, I can see that it is unpleasant to you. Might I be so bold as to ask why?"

"He killed the mistress," Gavin whispered.

"I presume you mean Mrs. Lucilla Hopkins."

The butler nodded.

"As I am investigating the murder of Judson Farris, I wonder if you might be able to shed some light on his relationship to your mistress. Can you do that?"

A strange shadow seemed to pass over the man's features. It struck me that he did not wish to drum up unpleasant memories but felt he had no choice but to do so.

"Mrs. Lucilla Hopkins was an angel upon this earth," he began, his voice barely above a whisper. "Those who knew her well were aware of her pale, retiring nature, and the frail breath within her frame barely held strength enough to raise her voice above a whisper. But her heart was of the purest gold. Her first husband worshipped her, her sons doted on her and would deny her nothing." He paused and his eyes clouded. "When Mr. Edgar passed, it drained her life force and we feared for her. However, for all her frailty, she was made of sterner stuff than any could have imagined and rebounded. Then he came along. Judson Farris. At a time when fate seemed poised to destroy her. As indeed it did in the end. Farris took advantage of the mistress's state and took up the family business in one hand and her hand in marriage with the other. He was not worthy of her."

"You speak to his character...or is it to something else you refer?" Holmes asked, seeking clarification.

"Judson Farris married up. He came from Sussex, the son of a mill owner. He lived well but longed to make a show of it. Once he added the Hopkins fortune to that of his meagre holdings, he set about setting this right." Gavin wrung his hands as the memories clearly tormented him. "He spent the fortune liberally, while, and it pains me to say a word in his favour, expanding the Hopkins holdings. Mrs. Lucilla made no public complaint over the state of affairs and the semblance of bliss was believed to exist between them. That was not the case. Farris was crude in his attentions to her. She was a means to an end for him, said end being the use of her fortune without her continued presence."

"Are you accusing the man of killing Mrs. Hopkins?" Holmes asked.

"He did it. I make no accusation. I state a plain fact."

"If it is a plain fact, then why was he not taken into custody?"

"A serpent can wind its way out of most anything, I suppose. When Mrs. Lucilla began to weaken, as her life began to ebb away, it was first thought that she was consumptive as her first husband had been. This was not the case."

"Poison?" I prompted.

"Most assuredly. No trace was ever found, but I am certain of it. And there were grumblings in town. In her last days she was barely coherent. Under the guise of caring for her, he brought her papers to sign and she did so though she was beyond comprehending what they contained. Everett did what he could to prevent this, going back and forth between here and Castleford. He was unable to stop it in the end. He was in the process of bringing about an injunction to prevent Farris from seizing the family fortune, but was circumvented in this when Mrs. Lucilla signed it away in her delirium. Papers in his fist, Farris had what he wanted and fled here to London in order to oversee the transfer of all holdings to himself. It is only by a bold stroke of good fortune that he was prevented from doing so by the abrupt ending of his miserable existence. May he rot for all he has done."

"And what of your master?" Holmes asked. "Everett Hopkins."

"What of him?"

"Come now, don't be coy," cautioned Holmes. "He disappeared the very night Judson Farris was murdered. There is something to that."

Gavin suddenly flew into an indignant rage. "And what if there is? Would it be so terrible a thing to snuff out the existence of so foul a beast as Judson Farris, a murderer in his own right!"

"I am not prepared to comment on the matter as yet," replied Holmes. "I should like to know more about Everett. For instance, do you recall where he was on the night of the murder?"

"He was not at home on that night. There. It is said. It pains me to reveal it but I say what must be said. He left early that night and no one has seen him since. And that is all I will say on the matter."

"And what is the state of the house? Who is living in it?"

"Means have been secured to keep the household going. Only myself and the other servants live here. We keep it ready for the return of our master. If that will be all — "

Holmes ignored this request without expression or rejoinder, then, casting his glance about the room, said, "May I have a look around the house?"

"By all means. I beg your pardon, but I am not a young man anymore and these shadows of the past have sapped my strength. The house is yours to examine. There are no secrets here."

"Of course," replied Holmes. "Thank you for your cooperation. You have been most helpful."

The butler left us and Holmes prowled around the sitting room. The chair of Everett Hopkins drew his eye, and he spent some minutes examining the lamp next to it as well as the small end table with a book and coaster on it. I followed Holmes as he made a quick examination of the main floor. He poked around in a closet, inspecting coats belonging to the missing Everett Hopkins. Jackets, sweaters, caps, even the man's abandoned footwear seemed of interest to my friend.

Holmes led the way upstairs and the master bedroom was gone over. Our searching took place in the eerie quiet pervading the house. This keen silence and the dim lighting in every room gave the house a funereal air as if it harboured an invalid beyond the reach of science and the occupants could only await the inevitable outcome.

At last Sherlock Holmes seemed satisfied that his examination of the premises was complete. Gavin was nowhere to be seen, so we let ourselves out. My mind was in something of a quandary for I could not make heads nor tails out of what Holmes expected to find in his search. Perhaps this was due to my ire being up at how Judson Farris, who we believed to be an innocent victim, had now taken on the aspects of a despicable cad in my eyes and I found myself hoping Holmes would not bring the murderer to justice as I had a strong suspicion as to the identity of the guilty party after Gavin's revelations. This was a horrible conclusion, which plagued my mind, but there it is. Such were my thoughts as we left the house of Everett Hopkins and prowled briefly around the grounds.

What was going through the mind of my friend, I could not hazard a guess. We climbed back into the coach and were on our way without a word exchanged between us. Finally I could remain silent no longer and had to speak.

"Well, Holmes? What of it?"

"The mystery deepens, Watson. There is much to consider before I can render a conclusion."

"You can't be serious? Why, even someone of my limited deductive abilities can solve this case."

The eyebrows on Holmes's head arched expectantly. "Pray, do so."

"Everett Hopkins killed Judson Farris. That much is plain. He did it to avenge his mother's death at the hands of the scoundrel. And to keep Farris away from the family fortune."

"That is an interesting theory, Watson, and I agree with part of it. However, I must ask, to what end did Everett Hopkins do this? As the only surviving relative, all suspicion would naturally fall upon his shoulders. If he was prepared for this, and one is inclined to think he would be after taking such pains to arrange the murder in the first place, why did he not have an alibi prepared? Why was he not home to deflect the police inquiries? Taking flight on the very night of the killing only confirms his guilt in the eyes of many – and I include you among that number. Also, locked up or hanged for his crime, the family fortune would be of no use to him. No. It is too early to open avenues of thought along these lines. We haven't the facts on which to build. Circumstantial evidence, as damning as it is in this case, cannot completely point the finger of guilt."

"I must disagree. Who else would have reason to murder Farris? You cannot claim that Everett Hopkins did not have justification to break the law."

"I claim no such thing. I merely state that if he is guilty — and I'm not absolving him of any involvement — his behaviour can best be described as erratic. And, yet, the crime itself was committed with a degree of precision that has baffled police."

"Well, I say he is guilty. A case of justifiable homicide if ever there was one."

"Everett Hopkins is left-handed," Holmes revealed without provocation.

This statement took me aback for a moment before I realized what he alluded to. "Oh, the gloves you found? The left-handed gloves?"

"Yes."

"Ah, there you see. If you believe the gloves to be involved in the thing, then here is one more piece of evidence against him. Is this not so?"

"Perhaps. I mention the coincidence merely as an object of interest. Of course, two left gloves, not one, were found at the scene. Remember that. You don't propose that Everett Hopkins possessed two left hands, do you?"

"I suspect an investigation into the murdered lamp-lighter will uncover that he was left-handed as well."

"That is one of many possibilities."

Then something else occurred to me, "How in the deuce were you able to determine that Everett Hopkins was left-handed?"

"It was simplicity itself. The reading table with the book upon it was to the right of the chair but the lamp was on the left. One tends to hold a book in one's weaker hand, in this case the right hand, while leaving the stronger hand to manipulate the light on and off. Also, the man's shoes were more worn down on the left soles than the right as one tends to lead with the stronger leg while striding. Everett Hopkins was also not a robust man. All of his personal items were placed close to hand. For example the book upon his reading table was drawn from a nearby shelf set a short distance from the chair. The higher shelves were coated in dust indicating that the books on them are not regularly used."

"Holmes, you astound me. What do you make of this?"

He made no reply. I was growing accustomed to the peculiar habits of Sherlock Holmes and was learning that he preferred to make his disclosures at his own time and in his own way.

"What is our next move?" I asked.

"We have some time and shall make a quick stop at the lighting station to determine the handedness of the lamp-lighter. Then we shall delve deeper into the case. I suspect an end is in sight."

"An end for Everett Hopkins," I added.

Sherlock Holmes said nothing.

It is with some measure of guilt that I recount the unconscionable feeling of triumph I felt when our short stop at the gas works to inquire about the dead lamp-lighter revealed that Roddy Smyth, for that was the murdered boy's name, was, indeed, left-handed. I say I was plagued by guilt for in my moment of elation over my assumption being proved correct, I overlooked the sad end of young Smyth, who had been strangled and left for dead in a cold alley two blocks from the gas works. But this moment of conscience came later. In the heat of the moment, I glowed with success and had to bring the matter up as soon as Holmes and I were back on the road.

"You see," I crowed. "Everett Hopkins and poor Smyth were both left-handed. This accounts for the odd pair of gloves you found. That is, if we are to assume the import you place on them is justified."

"My, my, you are in high spirits, aren't you? Now you see the spice such investigations add to our mundane, workaday lives. I wonder, since you are so certain in your assessment of the gloves, if you could tell me how they factored in the murder? How were they used? Why were they discarded afterwards? Pray, tell me, for I am at a loss to explain them under your theory of the case."

And so dimmed my moment of elation, for I could not explain these things. In fact, I did not know how we were to proceed from here, so lost was I in the proving of this one detail. With some reluctance, I admitted this.

"Why, my dear Watson," Holmes announced with some energy. "I thought it plain. We must take the Underground to South Kensington Station to catch that butler, Gavin. We must do so in order for him to lead us to where Everett Hopkins is hiding."

My mind fairly reeled from this statement. I had no clue whatsoever as to how Holmes could have deduced this. Needless to say, my earlier glory left me and I was humbled at the capacious intellect of my friend and companion. I knew at some point he would reveal his reasoning to me and dared not ask as the hansom made its way to Baker Street Station.

"It is very simple," Holmes began, divining the source of my silent astonishment. "The ground leading to the coach house of the Hopkins House was unmarred by horse hooves or cart wheels. Also, man has domesticated the horse to his daily use and one encounters dozens of them on the streets and thus the odour of the equine passes unnoticed to the olfactory sense. Except in its absence – then the lack of it registers to one's mind. Think back, Watson, do you recall such an odour as we searched the grounds?"

"You are right, Holmes. I did not."

"There, you see, my conclusion that Hopkins House does not keep horses is an obvious one. So, proceeding from this conclusion, we turn our minds to other means of travel. Standing on a street corner flagging a hansom is not reliable. Mind, we are assuming a degree of stealth in the endeavour as well. Coachmen are inclined to take something against the chill associated with their occupation and, having once imbibed, are inclined to talk. That is point two. Now consider these two points together. The lack of personal transportation with a need to reach one's destination on the quiet leaves only one form of anonymous transport: the Underground. South Kensington Station lies within walking distance of Hopkins House. If you require further convincing, I peeked into the butler's closet, you might recall. A cursory examination of its contents told me all I wished to know. I detected the distinct odour of sulphur – an odour peculiar to underground railways due to low tunnel ceilings. The London Underground may be a technological wonder unmatched in the world. However ask any individual who uses it regularly and they will freely admit that the atmosphere within the tunnels and in the stations themselves is fairly dense with sulphurous clouds. It burns the eyes, stings the throat and impregnates all clothing. Thus its presence in the fibres of Gavin's outerwear leaves no other conclusion possible. He frequents the Underground. As I do not trust him, we shall follow him and discover where he goes."

"Holmes you are a marvel! But what of Gavin? He struck me as a man obliged by his nature to tell the truth."

"There is something to what you say. I first suspected something was up when first we spoke with the man. My inquiries carried the implication of guilt directed at his master. If Everett Hopkins was completely innocent in the matter, this was Gavin's time to make protestations of innocence. He made none. Rather he was evasive in speech and manner. Also, as a butler in search of his missing master whom no one has seen for weeks, Gavin should have been most eager to render whatever aid he could. Instead he was reticent with his information at best, only yielding crumbs of facts when called upon. This singular behaviour aroused my interest and, if you recall, I did not press him for answers. My intention was for him to think he had put one over on us and that our mere presence there would spur him to action. If my assumptions are correct, he will wait for full dark before he moves. And that time is soon upon us, Watson. Here is Baker Street station."

We alighted and entered the spacious station, passed quickly under its vaulted ceiling and paid our fare before proceeding to the lifts leading down to the train platform. As an infrequent rider, I was something of a novice with regards to the Underground and gazed around me with great interest. My initiation to this route known as the Inner Circle was a stark one. The atmosphere on the station platform consisted mostly of the sulphurous fumes Holmes had mentioned and breathing in the concoction was like the inhalation of gas preparatory to having a tooth drawn. In seconds one was coughing and spluttering like a boy with his first cigar. The lighting being dim in the foggy gloom, Holmes and I blended with the other spectral forms haunting the platform and awaited the train.

"The line is operated by use of an improved type of condensing steam engines that are supposed to consume their own smoke," said Holmes with some indignity. "To this end they burn coke and are fitted with condensing apparatus." He put his hand to his lips to stifle a cough. "It seems more work needs to go into the design. Let us hope the train can get us to our destination with some alacrity. As the motto runs: 'Swift and sure. The way through London'. Eh, Watson?"

At last the train chuffed its way through the mouth of the tunnel and the station was filled with clouds of billowing hot smoke. The twelve-coach train shuddered to a halt, belching steam from its undercarriage. I peered into the coach directly in front of us as we waited for the doors to be opened. Through the murky air, to my surprise, I beheld coaches of almost Pullman luxury. The doors parted and we stepped inside. The carriage was low-ceilinged and dim yet there were mirrors on the wall, a richly carpeted floor, what appeared to be comfortable seat cushions, hot-water bottles and oil lamps for each passenger though the coach as a whole was lit with coal gas if the long rubber bags I'd seen on the roofs were any indication. We bent low as we made our way up the length of the carriage, fairly bumping our heads against the roof with each step.

"It would be inadvisable to ride the line with a hat to which one attaches any particular value," observed Holmes.

"Or hobnail boots," I added, as I raised a hand to my head to steady my bowler.

We had barely taken our seats when the whistled shrieked and the train was underway. The four-wheeled coaches ran with a certain springless rigidity. Holmes had the slit of a window open for whatever breeze it might afford but all this frail wind accomplished was the extinguishing of our little oil lamp. The coach was terribly warm due to the gas lighting and every bend in the snaking black tunnel seemed laden with unknown, indefinite dangers. I judged the train to be making forty miles an hour, which would allow us to cover the circuitous journey in excellent time. Holmes seemed to grow more and more tense with expectation in his seat as the next station indicators were pulled and each name plate snapped up into place from its slot between the coaches.

At last the station indicator read South Kensington and Holmes proceeded to the doors in order to be amongst the first to alight. We exited and moved the rear of the platform as far from the stairs as was possible. Struggling to draw air, we dug in and awaited the arrival of Douglas Gavin. Thankfully, our wait was not overly long. It was Sherlock Holmes who spotted our quarry as Gavin stepped heavily down onto the boards after a train pulled out, casting his gaze this way and that to see if he was being followed. The next train pulled in and we climbed aboard after ensuring Gavin had already done so, for we could see him two cars up ahead scrutinizing his fellow passengers.

"Our work for the moment is completed," observed Holmes. "We shall let this man Gavin do the work and bring us to his master."

We settled in for the journey, which was a long one. The train rattled along the circumference of the Inner Circle. The stations came and went while we wilted in the oppressive heat. I found myself growing dizzy from lack of oxygen and too large a dose of the noxious soup that had replaced it. Holmes seemed to endure it better than I. His eyes never left Gavin's form. How he managed to see in the murk was a mystery to me.

"This is it, Watson," said he. "Mansion House station is the next in line. It is also the last station on the line as the Inner Circle is still under construction. Gavin must exit here and so shall we."

The station, small and unfinished, did not boast a lift so we followed Douglas Gavin up the stairs to street level. I, for one, was glad to leave the Underground behind and take the night air. I gulped great lungfuls of it when we were once again on its cobbled avenues. We kept Gavin in sight as he made his way to the river. Once there, our noses were assailed anew with the stink coming from the Thames and I groaned at this fresh assault. If it was Gavin's aim to shake pursuit by way of this olfactory assault, he had chosen the correct route, for only the most ardent of followers would continue the hunt under these conditions. Sherlock Holmes was such a hunter and he bade me follow. It was imperative that we give the man some room, since we could not be certain he was not in search of a boat to take him across and we risked stumbling into him if we stuck too close. Also, with the array of businesses, shops and serpentine byways the risk of losing him should we hang back was something else to be aware of. Gavin continued along the river's edge until he turned left up Beer Lane, then right to Tower Hill.

"It's to the Tower Subway that he is headed!" Holmes hissed, his eyes gleaming with excitement.

"Knowing his destination," I observed, for both Holmes and I were very familiar with the pedestrian walkway running under the Thames, "perhaps we can hang back and thus better avoid discovery."

Amidst the buildings and warehouses that separated the street from the river, we came upon an octagonal edifice of marble. Gavin entered one of the several great doors with Holmes and I hot on his heels. We found ourselves in a rotunda some fifty feet in diameter, the floor of which was laid in a mosaic of blue and white marble. Stuccoed walls surrounded stands for the sale of papers, pamphlets, books, confectioners and all manner of objects and there was a great din of business being transacted by throngs of shoppers even at this hour. Gavin passed these by with hardly a sidelong glance. He pushed through the teeming mass of humanity to the watch-house off to one side in which a fat publican kept a watchful eye on the throng. Before him stood a brass turnstile and, upon paying him a half-penny for a one-way trip of a full penny to make the return journey, pedestrians were permitted to enter the subway. Holmes noted that Gavin paid the full penny, and we did likewise when it was our turn to pass through.

We entered a large door and began to descend a very long flight of marble steps which came to a wide, marble platform from which could be heard the notes of a huge organ playing excellent music. From here, a second flight of steps descended ever downwards in the opposite direction. The walls of the shaft were circular, stuccoed in turn, and studded with paintings, statues and figures in plaster to engage your attention while one stopped to take some rest before resuming one's descent to the bottom of the shaft some eighty feet below. Once at the bottom, we found ourselves in a rotunda which was a mate to the one above. Alcoves in the walls were packed with contrivances aimed at picking your pocket, from Egyptian necromancers and fortune-tellers to dancing monkeys. The room, gas-lit, was bright and close.

The tunnel maws were before us. These consisted of two beautiful arches, extending to opposite sides of the river. Each contained pathways for pedestrians which ran along the gigantic iron tube undulating beneath the Thames like a great intestine in the enormous belly of the river. The inside of the tube presented a subterranean corridor, of which the end was invisible. Only three feet wide, it was something of a tight squeeze with foot traffic coming from both directions at once and the interspersed lights cast veiled illumination like lamps in a sepulchre. Gavin scurried up and onto the closest walkway. We followed close behind, attempting to keep a cluster of men, women and children between us and him. The tunnel appeared to be well-ventilated though the atmosphere was still foggy, perhaps from the exhalations of so many users. The walls sweated like those of an aqueduct and the floor moved under our feet like the deck of a vessel. Connecting partitions between the two arches allowed pedestrians to move from one to the other. As these short, joining corridors were jammed in turn with all manner of shops, kept principally by women, offering everything from toys to tapestries all decked out in the finest manner with marble counters and gilded shelves, they became a very labyrinth of places for Gavin to shake us off. Tall mirrors everywhere reflected light and faces and threatened to blind us or give us away at every turn. The gas burners lit the area as bright as the sun and we had a devil of a time keeping Gavin in sight without being discovered.

The chaotic throng soon gave way to a long stretch in the tunnel without so much as a soul in front or behind. Keeping an eye on Gavin, we had no choice but to withdraw and lengthen the gap between us. Around one slight bend in the tunnel, we lost sight of him completely and the ghostly voices and footsteps of the people coming the other way echoed with cavernous intensity until we lost the sound of Gavin's progress altogether. We sprang around this bend and could only see the shadowed figures of approaching men and women. Skinning our eyes, we caught of glimpse of Gavin's back up ahead as he passed beneath a lamp. We had not lost him! At the mid-point of the tunnel we could no longer see the end in either direction and the silence of a catacomb pervaded. A vague feeling of disquiet came over me. My mind was plagued with thoughts of the countless crushing tons of water above my head and the indeterminate length of tunnel which lay before us before we came to the end. If a crack should open in the wall, Holmes and I would not have the chance to commend our souls to God before the black tide with its drifting, bloated bodies of suicides poured in. Imagine my relief when Gavin halted his progress up the tunnel and produced a skeleton key from a pocket and doused the nearest lamp. Holmes yanked at my arm and we retreated back around the turn we had just made a split second before Gavin looked both ways to satisfy himself that he was alone for the moment.

"Watson, your pistol!" hissed Holmes. "Stand ready!"

The length of the tunnel had provided us excellent, though treacherous, means of pursuing Gavin. And yet, it was all for nought if he entered some unknown side tunnel before we could move against him. We heard the key rattle in the darkened passageway, the sound echoing along the close walls around us. A bolt turned like a thunderclap.

"Now, Watson! Seize him!"

We sprang forward as one. Gavin gave a start and dropped the key. We caught him between two avenues of flight. At first he made as if to dash up the tunnel, then he turned as if to pitch himself headlong through the door he'd just opened. Before he could make up his mind to do either, I was on him. Holmes drove a fist into the man's stomach and that knocked the fight out of him. Holmes seized him roughly to keep him from falling. I stuck the muzzle of my pistol to the side of Gavin's head.

"Quietly now, Gavin," said Holmes. "Lead us to your master."

The man slumped and he knew we had him. We did not let up our guard, however for feigning compliance is an old trick. For my part, I felt that not only the fight but the very life had fled out of the man. Gavin led us along the short passageway which resembled a crew worker's conduit. Our shoe heels rang loudly against the cold iron, but there was no preventing this. Water dripped as if the Thames itself was set to crash through and drown us. We came at last to a simple wooden door bearing the stains and gouges of rough use. The metal bands across it showed rust red where not slicked with moisture. Holmes held up the ring of keys Gavin had dropped and the lifeless, resigned butler indicated the key that was needed to unlock the door. He raised a trembling hand and stayed Holmes's arm.

"There is a coded knock," Gavin whispered reluctantly. "I must give it before we enter."

I pressed the pistol closer to his head and put my lips to his ear. "If you are lying, it will mean your life."

"My life is already forfeit," he said. "I speak the truth. Do what you will."

Holmes touched my shoulder. I turned to stare at him. He closed his eyes and nodded briefly. Then he turned his gaze on Gavin. "Proceed."

Gavin bunched one bony fist and proceeded to pound on the door in rhythmic fashion: four drawn out thumps like the tolling of a great bell. He did not await a reply. He merely stepped back. Sherlock Holmes turned the key. I pressed close to him so that we might squeeze through the low, narrow door and face what dangers lay on the other side together.

Bright light blinded us, and we had to squint and raise a hand against the glare. Sightless we stepped across the threshold. Our filthy shoes were suddenly silenced by soft carpeting. Our eyes, partially adjusted, beheld winking gas lights, gleaming white walls and crystal that took up the light and flung it over the fine furniture all around. I stared dumbfounded at an expansive drawing room more suited to receive royalty than a hole hollowed out beneath the river. I cannot say precisely what I had expected to find on this side of the door and could not speak for my esteemed colleague, but such opulence was never in my wildest imaginations.

"So you have come at last," a voice spoke. My eyes were too dazzled by the lights to see the speaker but he spoke with a cultured voice. Holmes revealed the identity of the speaker for me.

"Everett Hopkins," said he.

Gavin regained some of his earlier vigour at the sight of his master and sprang forward. "Forgive me, Evy!" he cried. "Forgive me!"

"There is nothing to forgive, my dear friend," said Hopkins. "You did what had to be done. You are blameless."

At last my eyes obeyed my brain and I could see once more. Before us, standing in the middle of the room, feet wide apart, was a man of medium height, no more than thirty years of age. His hair was grey and thinning and he was broad of face though this aspect was being tested by gauntness in the cheeks and neck. His large eyes were red-rimmed, slightly rheumy, which I chocked up to his prolonged abstinence from natural light. He wore dark tweed trousers and a semi-military smoking jacket over a white chemise. In his left hand he clutched a revolver.

"There is no escape for you," observed Holmes. "What purpose will shooting us serve?"

Hopkins jabbed the pistol at me. "Your weapon, sir. Toss it behind the settee if you please."

Holmes regarded Hopkins keenly, then said, "Better do as he says, Watson. Let us go where he seeks to lead us."

I complied. The pistol hit the settee cushion and bounced out of sight between the sofa and the hearth.

"We know you killed Judson Farris," I said, my temper kindled by being forced to disarm. "And the lamp-lighter as well. I suppose we are next."

"Not unless you give me provocation," said Hopkins mildly. "The pistol buys me your attention. I hope at the end of my sordid tale you will see things my way."

"Murder cannot be bargained for or explained away," said Holmes.

"No. However, it can be justified. Judson Farris was a monster!"

"He was your stepfather," said Holmes.

"Never! He was a villain who ensnared my blessed mother in order to get his filthy hands on the family fortune. When he had it at last, he murdered my mother!"

"So you claim. Have you any proof? If so, why did you not got to the authorities?"

"Proof! The proof lies in her grave. Farris skirted the law and no one could lay a hand on him."

"You did," Holmes countered. "Or, rather, you were an instrument of his demise."

"There is no shame in my actions," Hopkins insisted.

"And the method of dispatching Farris was most ingenious. Tell me, was it you or your accomplice that affixed the rubber tubing to the gas-light nozzle? And did the same man run the tube across to Farris's lodgings and insert the free end into the air hole at the base of the outer storm window?"

Hopkins could only stare open-mouthed in shock at the revelations Holmes had made. "How- How can you know this?"

"By merely observing. The police record states the room was sealed from the inside. The gas had been shut off. The doors and windows bear no marks of tampering. All was as it appeared to be. Or so it seemed at first. The only thing out of the ordinary was the defective street-lamp. And a lamp that has its flame doused still emits gas, does it not? A length of tubing would bridge the gap between lamp and building. One need only affix one end to the gas jet, close the seal with pitch, then mount a ladder at the side of the building and guide the free end of tubing, also blackened with pitch, into the air hole of the window thus allowing the free flow of gas into Farris's room which he had sealed himself. His own security measures so neatly turned against him. Is this not how it was done?"

"It was, but we covered our tracks. How could you — "

"Remnants of pitch were found on the sill and outside the air holes of the both outside window frames. Nothing could be made of these droplets for they meant nothing. But the *inside* of the middle air hole of the window looking out on Blanford Street is black with pitch – an impossibility unless something coated with the sticky substance had been inserted into the hole. I found your gloves as well, blackened with the stuff. It is quite understandable that you could not walk about with them on your hands or stuff them into your clothes where they would leave residue inside your pockets. So you discarded them at the scene along with the rubber tube and a small pitch pot once the deed was done. A handy trash barrel served this purpose. Only your aim was off, wasn't it? The tubing and pot went into the bin and were viewed, if they were examined at all, to be common trash, but you missed with the gloves and they tumbled behind the bin and lay trapped between the receptacle and the wall. Perhaps you did not give them a second thought while you went about deliberately placing the ladder in the alley as misdirection. How am I doing thus far?"

"You astonish me, sir!" confessed Hopkins. "It was as you say. All transpired in the manner you have outlined. I am at a loss to fathom how you reasoned it out. The fact that you did begs a question. If you will permit me. Are you Mr. Sherlock Holmes?"

"I am."

"The consulting detective written about in the papers?"

"At your service."

"Ah, now things are clear to me. I have been in this self-imposed exile since that faithful night. Douglas brings me papers and news when he can, but there are gaps."

"Mr. Hopkins," said Holmes, "We can discuss various matters until the end of time but it changes nothing. You are wanted for the murder of Judson Farris."

Hopkins grew incensed. "He deserved what he got! Where was the justice for my poor murdered mother? Tell me! I demand that you tell me! Were you aware that he had in his possession papers which he'd had my mother sign under duress? Papers that would transfer ownership of all Hopkins holdings to the Farris family? Papers he meant to file the instant the bank opened that morning. This could not be allowed to happen."

"I sympathize with your loss, I do. But what of the lamp-lighter that was killed? Does he not deserve justice? Would you have us believe that the taking of innocent life merely to cover one's flight is justified? If so, then you are a bigger scoundrel than I had imagined."

"The lamp-lighter was an unfortunate necessity," said Hopkins as though repeating something he'd memorized or had so often repeated to himself that he had convinced himself of its veracity.

"This debate has ended," stated Holmes. "You have played your hand and have come up short. Will you come along or won't you?"

"I do not wish to have more innocent blood on my hands so I will not shoot the two of you down in cold blood. Instead we will duel for my fate. If your companion will give me his solemn promise not to take up the pistol the instant I set it down, I shall speak for Douglas in this regard and I shall lay down my firearm so that we might have at it with blades, Mr. Holmes. Do you agree?"

"Very well," said Holmes without a moment's hesitation.

Gavin and I reluctantly stepped back as Sherlock Holmes and Everett Hopkins came forward to stand facing each other in the centre of the room. True to his word, Hopkins set the pistol on a side table much to my relief. He pulled a set of blades off the wall and offered both to Holmes for his selection. Holmes took the rapier and tested its strength. Hopkins took the other. They saluted each other and squared off. I expected Holmes to lay back and wait for Hopkins to make the first move as this ridiculous duel had been his idea in the first place. Yet once Hopkins was set, Holmes sprang forward and launched his attack. Hopkins fended off the assault deftly. Holmes was extraordinarily skilled with a blade and for Hopkins to hold his own was no mean feat. He followed this with a thrust which

Holmes just barely deflected and the tip of Hopkins's blade grazed my friend's left shoulder. Holmes ducked to one side, raising his own blade with sufficient force to almost strike the blade from his opponent's hand. For his part, Hopkins seemed to be suffering from waning strength. His countenance took on a sickly pallor and his breathing had become a ragged gasp. Holmes pressed his advantage and Hopkins was driven back. With his back almost to the far wall, he made one last advance but his entire frame was trembling now with fatigue. Holmes had to parry the attack none the less and nimbly sprang back a step. Hopkins seized this moment to kick back against the wall and a spring panel popped open. Clutching his sword now like a spear, he hurled it at Holmes, then disappeared through the hidden compartment.

I dashed forward to pursue. Holmes merely stood there, blade lowered, only slightly out of breath and made no move to follow Hopkins. "It is finished," he said. "You will find him in the passageway, Watson. Pray, bring him in. He is in need of some medical attention."

Gavin stepped forward. "I shall bring him back. Lay a hand on him and you'll answer to me for it."

Holmes allowed Gavin to fetch Hopkins. I stood in the doorway to make sure no desperate attempt at flight took place.

Hopkins was a sight when he returned. Breathing heavily, his skin ghostly white, the circumstances or his condition eluded me until I viewed him in a professional capacity and realized the man was consumptive as had been his long-dead father. Well it was a wonder he could draw breath at all, having lived so many weeks in the fetid air of the tunnel. My evaluation of Hopkins's medical condition was cut short when Holmes bade me track down one of the tunnel constables. This was done and once the officer got over his wonder at the incredible surroundings he'd been oblivious to on his beat, Hopkins was taken into custody and led away with Douglas Gavin, his ever faithful servant, following close behind.

++++

That should have been the end of the matter. Oh, Holmes kept an eye on the legal proceedings while he took up his usual pursuits. Curiosity got the better of me and I must confess to some degree of sympathy with Everett Hopkins. Judson Farris had used the family terribly, he had been on the brink of swindling the family fortune, he had placed Mother Hopkins in her grave. I could not help but concede some moral justification for the act

Hopkins committed, however heinous. I found myself silently hoping he might get off easier once the facts were known.

The news of a sentence of death by hanging was not well received when it reached 221B Baker Street. Mrs. Hudson still suffered some pangs of guilt at being the catalyst to the fate of Everett Hopkins and she admitted several times that she wished she had never mentioned the matter. Sherlock Holmes seemed possessed with a feeling of expectation throughout the speedy trial. He was all the more anxious after the sentence had come down.

Then on the morning of the day of the execution, I rose at my usual hour and had gone out to my breakfast when, lo and behold, before me sat Holmes gingerly dipping a crust of toast into his soft-boiled egg. As my companion was habitually a late riser, this singular behaviour piqued my interest. What added to my bewilderment at seeing him was that he was also fully dressed.

"Good morning, Watson," he greeted me cheerily. "You may want to eat quickly, then get dressed."

"We are expected somewhere?"

"Yes."

"Is there something what needs doing?"

Holmes dabbed at his lips with his napkin. "No. I suspect we will need to do nothing whatsoever. Ah, there's the bell."

A messenger appeared at our inner door and thrust a telegram at me before pounding down the stairs on his way to the street.

"Will you read it, Watson?"

I opened the missive and gave a start of surprise. "It's from Everett Hopkins!"

"Really?" asked Holmes, unsurprised. "What does it say?"

"He wishes to see us at Newgate Prison. Holmes, what can this mean?"

"What say you we go and find out?"

I threw my clothes on and we climbed into a hansom. Holmes did not make a sound the entire journey. We alighted and entered the prison. Once through the offices, we were shown down the dim, wretched corridors to the cell of Everett Hopkins. The guard unlocked the door for us and Holmes begged a private moment with the prisoner. The guard acquiesced and strode off. Alone, Holmes turned his attention to the prisoner. Hopkins did not rise up out of his bed to greet us for he could not. So sickly was he from the effects of consumption that I doubted he'd live out the hour, let alone have breath in his body to face his executioner. Whatever did he want from us in these his last moments on earth?

Holmes's usually stoic expression softened and he spoke gently. "Is there any way we might get word to your brother?"

The prisoner's eyes widened like saucers and I felt my own following suit. It had been established that Lucius Hopkins had been killed in Afghanistan years ago!

"So," Hopkins rasped. "I'm to be denied even in this? How long have you known?"

"Almost since the beginning" replied Holmes. "Our duel confirmed what until then I had only suspected."

"That Lucius committed the murders?" said Hopkins. "That I only assisted?"

"Precisely. In your consumptive state, and please forgive me for saying this, you are hardly sound enough to go shimmying up light poles on cold, damp nights and strangling lamp-lighters."

"Very well, you know all. How the deuce — "

"The two left gloves. Seventy percent of all fraternal twins are left-handed. That was the start of it. And murder is not entered into lightly. Thus it was unlikely a stranger would so endanger himself. Oh, a common ruffian for hire might take the job, but an upstanding lad of 19 with gainful employment as a lamp-lighter and no grudge against the victim? Unlikely. The only conclusion was that your accomplice had to be someone with a stake in the outcome and the physical means to carry out the deed. Who better than Lucius Hopkins met these requirements?"

"If you knew that Lucius was alive and in hiding, why did you not give us away?"

Holmes did not answer this question. Rather, he posed one of his own. "Why are you taking the punishment for his acts?"

"I love my brother as we both loved our mother. Does that answer your question?"

"It does. What became of the papers you killed Judson Farris over?"

"I do not know. I sent Douglas around the next morning to lay claim to whatever was in Farris's possession. The papers were not among these effects. Their whereabouts haunts me to this day. No one has come forward to use them against the family."

"I believe I know where they are, and they will be taken care of. You have my word on that."

Hopkins smiled weakly and closed his eyes and I, even in the state of shock that had possession of me, could see he had a great deal of trouble

Holmes's usually stoic expression softened and he spoke gently. "Is there any way we might get word to your brother?"

opening them. He was not long for this world.

"What will happen?" he said at last.

"Why, nothing. Nothing at all." Holmes replied, placing a hand on the man's bony shoulder. "A crime of murder has been committed and someone has paid for it. Justice is served all around."

"You- you would do this for us? After I called you here to gloat with my last breath on how we had beaten the great Sherlock Holmes!"

"No. Watson and I will remain silent because you loved your mother and there was no one to come to her aid in her desperate hour of need. God speed, Everett Hopkins."

We left him then and back in the cab we discussed the extraordinary events of the morning.

"If I may be so bold, Holmes. You mentioned your suppositions to the condemned, but how did you know Lucius Hopkins still lived?"

"I shall answer your question with some of my own. We came late to this affair, did we not?"

"We did."

"The police investigation had been stymied?"

"It had."

"Then why was Everett Hopkins still hidden away? He'd had ample time and opportunity to flee after the initial uproar had died down. Yet he spent his last weeks in a lavish drawing room under the river. Why is that?"

"I cannot hazard a guess."

"As a consumptive, what did Hopkins have to look forward to?"

"A slow cessation of breath in a sick bed or hospital ward," I replied.

"Would these accommodations be equal to the lair in which we discovered him?"

"Hardly."

"There you have it, Watson. It was understood between the two brothers from the beginning that Lucius would commit the crimes and the terminally ill Everett would face justice for them. To that end he was provided palatial accommodations where he had only wait to be discovered while wanting for nothing in his last days. The rest was all smoke and mirrors. His feeble attempt at flight when we'd caught him was orchestrated to cement his guilt in order for his brother to go free. Douglas Gavin's reluctant help was a ruse, but the best kind of ruse because it contained an element of truth. His part in the affair was to lead whoever came close to reasoning out the matter to his master. As he cares deeply for Hopkins, his hesitant Judas act came across as a reluctance to implicate his master and was utterly convincing. For my part, I was the final instrument in which the master plan was carried out. Everett Hopkins aimed my intellect at his breast as one would aim a pistol. And the plan succeeded. That is what he brought us to Newgate to witness. Everett has been convicted and Lucius is a free man. I must confess that this Lucius Hopkins strikes me as a fascinating fellow and I confess to some curiosity concerning his past actions. Perhaps our paths will cross one day. There is still the murder of the lamp-lighter he must answer for."

"Well, Everett Hopkins has beaten the hangman's noose," I offered. "He'll be dead within the hour, I'm sure of it."

"There, you see, Watson" said Holmes, his manner brightening. "He did outsmart someone after all. Now let us swing round to the second hand shop. I believe they have a settee, recently delivered, containing concealed documents which require our immediate attention."

Holmes is Where the Heart Is

W hen Ron invited me to contribute a tale to this first of what I hope are many Sherlock Holmes anthologies by Airship 27, I was excited and more than a little apprehensive. You see I wasn't a fan of the adventures of Holmes and Watson. I know that's hard to fathom since you've just read my Holmes tale, but that was how things stood when I got the call. Now I had nothing against the two intrepid Victorian investigators. Quite the contrary. The opportunity to write two of the most popular characters in all of fiction was just too good to pass up. And, of course, like anyone who has picked up a book or watched a movie in the last century, I was somewhat familiar with the characters. I'd read a couple of the novels and dabbled in the some of the movies, television series, even comics featuring the great sleuth over the decades, but the original works of Arthur Conan Doyle were something of a mystery to me. The original yarns seemed destined to stay on the "someday" corner of my bookshelf.

Then, out of the blue came the chance to write a Holmes tale! How could I say no? I readily agreed to try and then sat back and wondered how the heck I was going to do justice to these immortal characters of whom I knew so little.

My first idea was to base the tone and feel of my tale solely on the original stories. I marched to that dusty corner of my shelf and took down a whopping 900+ page collection of the stories and novels, cracked the cover and immersed myself in Victorian London. It was research born of necessity but I found myself enjoying the tales. Holmes and Watson captivated me and kept me turning the pages.

Early on I decided that my tale should be set in the early days of the duo, shortly after having first met in *A Study In Scarlet*. This, I felt, would free me up from the mountain of clichés which has been heaped on the characters through the various mediums over the decades.

From there I hit on the idea of an old murder having taken place in their new lodgings at 221b Baker Street and couldn't resist indulging in one of my favorite mystery settings: the locked room. The idea of 221b as a crime scene seemed an obvious choice to me and I couldn't help but wonder if another writer had done such a tale. Or even if Doyle himself and given it a go. I must say that once this plot idea was germinating in my gray cells, I began reading each tale hesitantly, dreading coming across a Doyle yarn dealing with the plot I'd hit upon. Nine hundred pages later, I had not come across the plot and felt ready to tread the foggy London streets of the 1880s.

Next came what I refer to as A Study In Style. I do my best in all my pulp tales to capture the voice of the original source material as best I can. It has always seemed to me that the ghost writers of the 1930's who stepped in to aid Walter Gibson, Lester Dent and all the other pulp giants had the task of writing yarns which the casual reader could not distinguish from the ones written by the main contributors to the various series. I like to carry on this tradition of trying to make my tales fit the classic continuity and I've done my best with my Jim Anthony and Secret Agent X efforts. I certainly wanted to do the same with Sherlock Holmes.

However, there was nothing elementary about this undertaking. Doyle's style is typical of the time: verbose, flowery yet he does not waste words. His Holmes tales move quickly and he throws facts and clues at you with some regularity, though there is not a lot of action in the early stories. It was going to be quite a challenge to forgo the choppy pulp racheting up of action and indulge in Doyle-like lengthy paragraphs and the wonderful language of the Victorian period.

Luckily, I'm a fan of the literature of this time and have read my Dickens and Hardy, so I was not a complete novice. Maybe it was due to my British heritage, I don't know, but the style came relatively easy to me and, if anything, I had to pay particular attention to Doyle's great knack of presenting the speech patterns of the street and not come across as too hoity-toity. I also couldn't resist adding a nod to said British roots by referring to Castleford, my mother's home town in Yorkshire. I'd also like to express my thanks to my friend, Doug Gavin, a Holmes enthusiast. His passion for the Doyle tales kept this newcomer focused and dedicated to getting the feel of my story right. You might notice that Everett Hopkins's butler bears his name.

Well, you've read the result and I hope you've enjoyed it. It was a fun challenge conjuring up a murder which Holmes couldn't solve without getting up out of his chair by the fire, and the process made me a fan of the original tales. I hope my story kept you guessing right up until the end and that the ending satisfied. It was a privilege to play around in the incredible world Arthur Conan Doyle created all those years ago, and I hope to be invited to do so again.

Tally ho!

Andrew Salmon

Ellis Award nominee **Andrew Salmon** lives and writes in Vancouver, BC. His work has appeared in numerous magazines, including *Storyteller, Parsec, TBT* and *Thirteen Stories.* He also writes reviews for *The Comicshopper* and is creating a superhero serial novel currently running in *A Thousand Faces Magazine.*

He has published eight books to date: *The Forty Club* (which Midwest Book Reviews calls "a good solid little tale you will definitely carry with you for the rest of your life"), *The Dark Land* ("a straight out science-fiction thriller that fires on all cylinders" – Pulp Fiction Reviews), *The Light Of Men*, his first work for Airship 27/Cornerstone, which has been called "a book of such immense significance that it is not only meant to be read, but also to be experienced... a work of grim power" – C. Saunders. *Secret Agent X: Volume One* and *Three, Ghost Squad#1: Rise of the Black Legion* (with Ron Fortier), *Jim Anthony Super Detective* and *Sherlock Holmes* constitute his pulp fiction work for Airship27/Cornerstone to date.

Andrew's work will appear in the forthcoming *Mars McCoy* anthology. He is also preparing *Wandering Webber*, his first children's book, for publication.

To learn more about his work check out the Airship27/Cornerstone store (http://stores.lulu.com/airship27) and the following links: www.lulu.com/AndrewSalmon and www.lulu.com/thousand-faces.

SHERLOCK HOLMES
CONSULTING DETECTIVE

"The Adventure
of the
Tuvan Delegate"

by Van Allen Plexico

It was my privilege and honor from time to time during the years of my association with the noted consulting detective, Sherlock Holmes, to work on cases of particular import to the very safety and security of our nation and its people. Two of these cases are still classified by Her Majesty's Government and consequently I cannot write of them in any detail. (When the time at last arrives that I can divulge what I know of them, I shall likely call them "The Incident of the Blue Algerian" and "The Mystery of the Left-Handed Assassin.")

A third case, however, turned out to involve matters so specific and isolated that to lay them before the public today can cause no harm whatsoever to anyone—save to the guilty parties themselves, of course. I later had cause to name that case "The Adventure of the Tuvan Delegate."

The matter began simply enough, as such things often seem to do. It was a cool autumn evening of a time well into my association with the Great Detective. Mrs. Hudson had just announced me at the door of 221-B Baker Street, and Holmes had called for me to enter. His voice sounded muffled, as if he were calling from another room entirely; it also carried an air of weariness, and this concerned me greatly. A slight tinge of fear came over me as I pondered the possibility that Holmes had once again slipped into his occasional cocaine habit. The drug provided, as he saw it, the only release for his vast mental faculties when no complex and challenging criminal cases presented themselves. Thus I understood why he would from time to time indulge in the practice. Yet the destructive potential of the drug weighed heavily upon my mind, and as usual I found myself fretting over various possible lines of argument that might persuade him to give up the practice once and for all.

And yet all my worry turned out to be for naught. For, as it turned out, Holmes was already at work on a modest case, and would shortly be drawn into another—one which turned out to pose numerous challenges for him.

I thanked the good Mrs. Hudson for announcing me and stepped inside Holmes's apartment. I could not help but notice the expression of disgust on the face of the good lady as she turned to go, and I wondered precisely what Holmes had done to offend her this time.

One glance around the room told the tale of her oppression in full: The place was an absolute disaster. While never the most tidy of men myself, my time campaigning with the Army had forced upon me a certain base level of cleanliness and orderliness that had stuck with me in later life. Holmes, of course, shared this attribute not at all.

Stacks of papers and documents reached up above the furniture, tottering and threatening to collapse with enough force to injure a small child, should one be foolish enough to venture inside. The old jackknife still held Holmes's unanswered correspondence skewered securely to the mantle. In one corner lay a veritable laboratory of bottles and pipes and tubes—and it was behind this that I spotted my old friend and companion, hard at work on some chemistry experiment or another.

"Good day, Watson," he called, scarcely looking up from his work. This greeting was followed not two seconds later by a second glance, and then, "So I assume you've come for your checkbook."

"Yes," I replied, not terribly surprised that my friend should have guessed this. I'd thought I must have left it here a few days before, and he had to know I'd come back for it immediately upon noting its absence from my pocket.

"It is stored securely in my safe," he announced. "But—are you absolutely certain you wish to invest your funds in as risky a venture as Norwich Rail?"

"I think it's a safe enough investment," I replied automatically, somewhat miffed at him for sticking his nose into my private financial business.

"Perhaps," he countered. "But I would not trust any advice received from Joseph Corran, were I you."

"Really, that's not your concern," I began. Then I paused and blinked several times as I came to realize what he had just said. "Holmes—how could you possibly know that I was thinking of investing in Norwich Rail? Or that Joseph Corran suggested it to me?"

He glanced up again from his work, smiling slightly.

"Simplicity, Watson. You have chalk on your left thumb and forefinger."

My eyebrows rising by themselves, I looked down at my left hand. Sure enough, a bit of blue chalk was smeared across those fingers.

"So I do. But—but how could that lead you to—?"

"You have been playing at billiards. I know very well that you only play at the Aubrey Club, and that Joseph Corran is often your partner for these contests."

"Just so, but—"

"Corran is known to have an interest in the Norwich Rail. He very much needs for the venture to succeed, in order to retain the considerable sum he has invested in it. Therefore he has been pressing his many acquaintances to jump into it with him." He smiled again. "I would advise against it. But it is, of course, your money."

He had opened his small safe and removed my checkbook, handing it to me. I stared down at it for a few moments, considering... and then placed it in my coat pocket, buttoning the cover securely. I would not be writing any checks today, after all.

Mrs. Hudson reappeared at that point with tea, and Holmes and I sat and sipped in peace for a few minutes. Then our reverie was shattered by the clattering of feet on the stairs outside. The landlady reappeared at the door, announcing our harried visitor and his associates.

"Inspector Bradstreet," Holmes said, greeting our old acquaintance as he stepped through the doorway. "What brings you here with such haste?"

"It's this gentleman here, Mr. Holmes," the tall, stout inspector replied, and I became aware of two uniformed policemen behind the inspector, the two of them standing on either side of a fourth man—whose appearance admittedly startled me.

"Well, well—what have we here?" Holmes asked, rounding the sofa and approaching the group. I could see that Bradstreet's charge had Holmes's full attention now—my friend could sense an interesting case in the offing.

"We found him wandering the streets a bit earlier today," the inspector replied, a look of puzzlement creeping across his face.

"Did you?"

Holmes and I both studied the man. I at least bowed and smiled, while Holmes ignored all social pleasantries entirely and regarded him as though he were a specimen on a table. The man was little more than five feet tall and of East Asian origins. His face reflected some of that same confusion so prominent on Bradstreet's face, but perhaps to an even greater degree. He wore a shirt and pants that obviously had been borrowed, as they were a few sizes too large for him.

"He speaks no English," Bradstreet went on. "And get this, Mr. Holmes—to top it all off, he was naked! Running through the streets, frantic as anything—and wearing no clothes at all."

"Indeed?"

Holmes nodded respectfully to the poor man, who continued to regard all of us with what looked to be puzzled suspicion and confusion.

"And why have you brought him to me, then?"

"Well, sir, we were hoping you might help us determine exactly who he is, and where he comes from—and why he was running around London in his birthday suit, if you follow me."

Holmes regarded the gentleman once more, then spoke a few words in a language I had never heard before. There was no obvious reaction. Holmes tried a few more phrases, none of which provoked the slightest response. Finally the Asian man shook his head and launched into a brief but sharp oration in a language I had never encountered before.

Holmes listened carefully, then turned to Bradstreet, his lips pursed.

"I am afraid I will not be quite so much help in this manner as you might have hoped, Inspector," he said flatly.

"I can't imagine that's the case," Bradstreet said, frowning.

"I'm simply not familiar with this man's language."

The inspector frowned, appearing quite forlorn.

"However."

At that one word, the inspector perked up a bit.

Holmes absently ran his right index finger along his chin, looking the man over once more. "It is true that a few things do rather jump out at me," he conceded. "For example, the man is educated, and was probably kidnapped and has escaped his captors. It is also extremely likely that someone is impersonating him, even now."

Bradstreet's mouth opened and closed soundlessly. "That's a good deal more than we knew before," he finally managed.

"Beyond that, Inspector, I simply lack sufficient data from which to draw conclusions with any degree of confidence." Holmes smiled. "However, I do find the matter intriguing in the extreme. Perhaps I know of someone who can shed more light on the situation."

"More than you could? Well, sir—I'm all for that, though I have to add that I'll believe such a thing when I've seen it."

"You flatter me, Inspector," Holmes replied. Fetching his coat and hat, Holmes gestured for the officers to lead the man down the stairs, then turned to me.

"I presume you will be joining us, Watson?"

"I wouldn't miss it, Holmes, for all the tea in Ch—um, I wouldn't miss it."

And with that, we took our leave.

++++

In retrospect, I should not have been surprised that the person my friend had in mind was none other than his older brother, Mycroft Holmes. I realized this to be the case not because Holmes so much as told any of us where we were going—he is wont to keep such information to himself until the last possible moment—but when the carriage we were riding in pulled up in front of the Diogenes Club, his brother's favored recreational institution.

"He's not here?" Holmes gasped when told by the secretary at the front desk that Mycroft was nowhere to be found. He turned to me, frowning deeply now. "Not here..."

This was shocking news indeed, for surely few individuals in all of London—in all of the Empire itself—stuck with such rigorous regularity to a set schedule, day after day. For Mycroft not to be at his club during his regular hours portended grave doings indeed.

"Something is most definitely afoot," Holmes muttered to me as he turned and walked back outside.

But no sooner had the last of us cleared the doorway and made our way out onto the street than none other than our quarry, Mycroft Holmes himself, strode up, breathing heavily. His large frame was somewhat disheveled as from hurrying at great haste across the city, and sweat trailed down the sides of his broad face—a face so like his younger brother's, and yet both larger and somehow even more inscrutable.

"Sherlock. Well. I expected you would be looking for me by now." He glanced quickly at the Asian man in his borrowed clothing next to the

Our quarry, Mycroft Holmes himself, strode up, breathing heavily.

inspector and nodded to himself. "Ah. Yes. Things are becoming still more complex—just as I anticipated."

My friend bowed to his brother, a tiny degree of relief now evident upon his face. Holmes's words of reply, however, surprised me greatly.

"So, brother, will we avoid war between Russia and China?"

While I'm sure I must have gaped, Mycroft Holmes merely gave his brother a circumspect glance.

"You have deduced, then, that those two powers are meeting at a peace conference here in London."

"Of course."

Mycroft nodded. "I would expect no less of you. The clues were obvious in the extreme."

"To say the least," Holmes agreed. "So—you've been looking for me, as well. What's happened?"

"A murder. A diplomat at the conference. We've kept it all quiet so far, so as not to disrupt the delicate proceedings, but..."

"Yes," Holmes replied, "I quite understand."

"And seeing this gentleman with you now," Mycroft added, motioning with his great head toward the Asian man standing with the policemen, "I am sensing a larger pattern at work here, behind the scenes. Larger even than I had first suspected."

Holmes's smile then struck me as quite needlessly cold-blooded, and yet I could not help but feel some degree of relief for my friend. Truly he was never so alive as when a difficult and complex case presented itself.

Instantly the two men turned and began striding rapidly and purposefully along the sidewalk. I paused a moment, looking from their departing figures to the group of policemen who still stood near me, clearly as confused as I had become. I started to ask the inspector a question, when Holmes turned back and shouted, "Well, come along then, Watson—and bring the Inspector and his charge with you!"

++++

"Russia and China? Avoiding war?"

"Yes, Watson?" Holmes asked, as we all raced along the street, toward a destination I could hardly guess as of yet.

"How could you possibly know that?"

"Simplicity itself," he replied, aiming a look of mild disappointment my way. "Mycroft never varies from his daily routine. Only the most unusual and extreme circumstances would keep him away from the Diogenes Club during his regular hours. Given his line of work—" And at that point Holmes gave me a knowing look, reminding me that while I'd never determined Mycroft's precise occupation, I was quite well aware that he held some sort of supremely important but unnamed position with Her Majesty's Government. "Given his line of work," Holmes went on, "I knew that most likely a matter of international importance had diverted him." He nodded toward the Asian man, who was still accompanied by the officers. "And with our foreign visitor being from a country so tiny and, dare I say, insignificant, but yet situated strategically between those two giants..."

"A tiny country? So you have discovered where this man is from, then?" I interrupted, surprised.

"Not the specific country," Holmes answered, "but it must be one of several very small kingdoms situated along the Sino-Russian borderlands, who have also been invited to the conference, given their location and proximity to the major parties. I can deduce that much from what little I have seen and heard so far."

I accepted this—his explanations always seemed so logical in retrospect—but did not drop the matter quite yet.

"I still don't understand how knowing the approximate location of this man's native land causes you to understand why Mycroft was not at his club, nor why you suspect a war brewing."

Holmes shrugged. "Only a matter of international import that involved those two Great Powers would have resulted in a representative of a tiny and probably remote state making his way to London at no doubt great expense—or in his being invited here in the first place, I imagine. And given my brother's heavy and constant involvement in international affairs, it was reasonable to conclude that he had been called away from his club and his normal daily routine to deal with the situation."

I could not argue with any of that; and yet, as always, I felt my head spinning at the mere prospect that Holmes had worked it all out so rapidly and so completely.

"Wait a moment," I said then, as something else clicked within my mind. "Mycroft is wearing a lapel pin—the Union Jack, flanked by the flags of Russia and China!"

Holmes's smile was wry indeed.

"Yes, my old friend—there was that clue, as well."

++++

As we hurried along, I sought to summarize within my mind what we believed we knew thus far:

A foreign man, apparently from a small country in East Asia, probably situated between China and Russia, had been found wandering the streets of London earlier in the day, unclothed, and speaking no understandable language. A peace conference was being held between those same two Powers, here in London, involving Mycroft Holmes. It all made little sense to me at this point. Of course, as one might expect, circumstances were about to get even more complex before they could be unraveled.

After a short walk we all arrived at a tall, looming edifice that flew the Union Jack on either side of its front entrance and bore Government emblems on the glass. Mycroft led us briskly inside and then he and his brother moved around to where they could peer through the front windows at the building across the street. I stepped next to them and saw that they were staring at the Blackmoor Hotel—one of London's finest such facilities.

Mycroft was quite out of breath at first, but his brother scarcely gave him time to recover.

"The dead man. Asian, yes?"

"Of course," Mycroft gasped.

"When did the conference begin?"

"Two days ago." Mycroft had bent forward and placed his hands on his thighs, struggling to catch his breath. "All of the delegations had arrived by then." Straightening at last, he regarded the mystery man once more. Nodding slowly, he glanced at his brother.

"I believe we must determine just which delegation this man belongs to, and we must do it very, very quickly," he growled. "I believe it is a matter of considerable urgency, far beyond a simple murder."

"Without question," Holmes replied.

"So you believe he is part of a delegation?" I began, but then realized how obvious that must be. Changing tack, I asked them what seemed to me a much more intelligent question: "Could we not simply return him to the conference and let him find his own party?"

The two brothers regarded my suggestion with such disapproving looks that I felt embarrassed to have offered it—though I scarcely could have said why that should be so.

"We believe this man was kidnapped at some point within the past two days and a cuckoo—a doppelganger—put in his place, Watson," my friend took great pains to explain to me. "We know not for what reason, but the perpetrators cannot be up to anything good. The gentleman's sudden reappearance at the conference could throw things into chaos—certainly it would tip our hand to our unknown adversaries, who may not yet know that he is free. There may come a time when such a development—surprise, confusion—would work to our advantage. But that time is not yet."

"Certainly not," Mycroft agreed.

I nodded to myself, then grew puzzled again.

"Where are we now?" I asked, glancing around the interior of the building at the subdued setting of plain gray walls and, beyond the reception area, the rows of wooden desks stretching into the distance.

"It is part of the Foreign Ministry—the international conference is taking place just across the street," Holmes replied and, before I could ask how he had seemingly known this from the moment we arrived, he anticipated my question and pointed across the way. "One of the finest hotels in London. Conspicuous presence of plainclothes officers. Conspicuous lack of the pedestrian and carriage traffic normal to this part of the city. The conference has to be there—in the hotel."

I was glancing across the street at the elegant façade of the Blackmoor Hotel, when suddenly its front doors burst open and a young man in suit and tie came racing through, running headlong across the street. He flung the doors to our building open and looked around frantically, then spotted Mycroft Holmes and ran to him.

"Mr. Holmes, sir—there's been another murder. Three of them, in fact!"

"And so we see the events begin to unfold," Sherlock Holmes muttered to himself.

"The Russians or the Chinese?" both Holmes brothers asked the young man at once.

The man opened and closed his mouth in surprise, then answered, "The Russians, sir. Three of their delegation—killed!"

"And I'm certain the evidence implicates the Chinese," Sherlock Holmes stated to no one in particular.

"Evidence, sir? It's only just happened!"

"Nevertheless…"

Before any of us could react further, there came the blinding flash and deafening roar of a massive explosion. The windows in front of us rattled and shook as we all instinctively ducked and cringed.

Recovering as quickly as anyone—I had, after all, endured shelling from enemy forces more than once during the Afghan Campaign—I stared in shock out across the street. From the upper floors of the hotel rained down rubble and debris, while smoke poured through gaps in the ruptured wall.

"Good heavens," I managed to mutter, even as the officers leapt up from around me and raced out the doors. The Holmes brothers and I followed on their heels, and within seconds we were in the street and surrounded by coughing, soot-covered men and women who were emerging, shell-shocked, from the Blackmoor.

Holmes took in the scene in an instant and whirled on Inspector Bradstreet.

"Round them all up, Inspector! Let no one leave!"

"Yes—yes, of course!"

Bradstreet barked orders at his uniformed officers, who were joined now by a dozen more who had converged on the hotel from either direction of the street at the sound of the explosion.

"We cannot keep them in the hotel under these conditions," I said to Holmes. "I understand the importance of your investigation, but—just look! This building might collapse at any moment! It must be evacuated at once."

"Of course, of course," Holmes agreed, his voice troubled and his eyes darting here and there, watching as the officers obeyed Bradstreet's commands to prevent anyone from leaving the scene. "But we must have them all together somewhere."

"There is a large conference room on the fourth floor of the building we occupied moments ago," Mycroft suggested. "It is fully the size of a small ballroom."

"Excellent. Bring them all there." He glared at Bradstreet. "All of them, Inspector."

"We cannot keep them restrained for very long at all, of course," Mycroft pointed out, his face deeply lined. "They are all foreign dignitaries with diplomatic immunity."

"Yes, I understand," he replied, beginning toward the hotel entrance even as shocked and disheveled statesmen and their ladies continued to stagger out. Some of them held bits of cloth up to their faces, attempting to block out the heavy black smoke that filled the air. "Give me only a few moments to confirm what I already suspect, and then I will meet you in the conference room."

I stood there in the middle of the street, a distraught Mycroft Holmes on one side of me and Sherlock Holmes on the other, clearly lost in deep thought. Then, without warning, Holmes was off, racing through the front entrance of the damaged hotel. I considered for only an instant, then ran headlong after him.

I caught up to him in a heavily damaged suite on the third floor. He held a handkerchief over his mouth with one hand as he carefully sifted through debris with a thin knife held daintily in the other.

"This is not a safe place for you to be at the moment, Watson," he said to me without looking up as he continued to work, his voice muffled by the cloth.

"It isn't safe for you, either, yet here you are. And you may need help."

"True enough," he replied. "I will not argue the point further. I—Ah, yes!"

He lifted two small objects from the rug, studied them for a long moment, and pocketed them. Then he stood and looked around, his keen eyes peering along his hawklike nose at the scene of devastation that surrounded us. I understood instantly from my years of watching him work that he was seeing things amidst the chaos that scarcely anyone else would perceive. Nevertheless, I feared for his safety—and for my own!— the longer we remained in the shattered hotel.

At that moment there came a shout from the hallway. It was a uniformed policeman—one of Bradstreet's men.

"Mr. Holmes, sir!" he cried, nearly out of breath and his face a mask of panic. "Over here, sir! There's another bomb!"

++++

Holmes did the opposite of what most men would have done under similar circumstances. He grinned savagely and ran—ran toward the bomb!

For my part, I considered fleeing the premises immediately…but then I reasoned that I had already followed my friend into a building that had been bombed once and was presently on fire. What was another bomb, more or less? Insane to hear such reasoning related calmly now, I realize;

but, at the time, it seemed to me to make some measure of sense.

Thus I raced after him, and seconds later we both stood before the infernal device that had been exposed by one of the officers where it lay concealed in a clothes closet. It consisted of two parts—a stack of bound explosives, most likely dynamite, resting on the floor, and a cylinder about a foot tall, standing on one end, sitting atop it. A small door in the center of the cylinder was closed.

"Our explosives man is on the way now, Mr. Holmes," the officer informed us breathlessly, "but I don't know how long it will take him to—"

"Move aside," Holmes commanded. "If I have judged correctly, Watson," he said to me as he kneeled before the device, "we should encounter a set of red and blue wires, with red being the critical color." Deftly he popped the latch and swung the little door open, staring inside.

He gasped in surprise—a sound that I must admit disturbed me far more profoundly than any of the carnage around us.

All of the wires were white.

"Holmes," I managed after a moment's shock. "What—?"

He made no reply. Instead he pulled some of the wires out through the little door, careful to leave them attached but out of the way. Then he leaned in closer, his eyes flickering from one component to another in rapid fashion.

Looking over his shoulder, I could see that beyond the coils of wires lay more sticks of dynamite, surrounding a small clock at the center, effectively sealed away behind a piece of glass. As I peered at its face, cold fear gripped my heart: It was set to detonate in mere seconds.

"Holmes, the timer—"

"Silence!"

Deftly he turned the device all the way around once, studying it from every angle.

The clock continued to tick, a half-revolution of the second hand all that lay between us and annihilation.

"Even more diabolical than I had imagined," he was muttering. I missed the next few words, and then, "...expected me to anticipate the blue ones, but..." The rest of his monologue was lost to me; and, truth be told, I was far more concerned with the ticking timer than with his self-reproach at the moment.

Turning the cylinder back around to the front again, Holmes raised one hand, hovered it near the wires—then drew it back again sharply, stroking his chin.

"No, no...precisely what he expected..."

The clock ticked on, the second hand sweeping upwards, now at the "8" mark on the face and climbing.

"Holmes—"

"Can't be the one," he was muttering now, "but in fact it *must* be the case that..." his words trailed off at that point, and he merely stared at the coils of white wires. Meanwhile, sweat ran down my back in rivulets.

The second hand had passed the "9" and approached the "10."

Holmes's slender fingers shot out and grasped the entire mass of white wires, snatching them loose.

The second hand kept moving, crossing in front of the "10."

"Ah!" he cried—and I could see that the white wires had lay in front of two more, much smaller and shorter wires, one red and one blue, that connected directly to the explosives.

The second hand was nearly at the "11" now, and moving relentlessly, remorselessly toward the "12."

"So we are back to our original problem, then," he growled softly, staring at the red and the blue wires.

The second hand was a mere inch away from the "12"—now a half inch—now a—

"HOLMES!"

His hand darted forward, slender fingers deftly grasping the blue wire. He yanked it free.

The second hand swept past "12."

The bomb did not, in fact, explode.

I dropped nervelessly back onto my haunches, sweating profusely.

Holmes stood and dusted himself off.

"Devilishly clever of him," he muttered to himself. "One would naturally imagine the red wire would be the correct choice. But of course last time it was the blue. Were it not that I understood his mind as well as I do, surely I would have chosen incorrectly."

I mopped at my brow with a handkerchief.

"So you worked out a rationale for why the blue wire was the correct one?" I managed to ask, curious now that my fear was receding.

"For once, my friend, my deductive powers were of no use," he replied to my great surprise. "For, given a red wire and a blue one, and seeking to work out whether my foe would repeat his previous choice of blue or switch to red, I found my reasoning spiraling down into an endless loop. He knew that I knew he had used red last time. But I knew that he knew this—and he knew that I knew it! And so on." He flashed a smile at me. "You perceive the problem, Watson?"

I struggled to follow this.

"You—you are saying, then, that you chose which wire to disconnect purely by using random chance? A mere flip of a coin, so to speak?"

"Would it trouble your spirit less to believe otherwise? To believe I managed to discern some hidden clue that revealed without any doubt the correct choice, an instant before I disconnected the blue wire?" He laughed softly. "It matters not. We survive. And the game is still afoot."

I lowered myself carefully to the floor, not trusting my suddenly wobbly knees to hold me up for the moment. Meanwhile, Holmes caught the attention of the equally drained police officer who'd been watching from behind us and pointed to the bomb.

"Secure that device immediately. Let no one tamper with it. I shall need to study it in greater detail later."

The officer gasped an acknowledgement, though he didn't seem particularly happy to be spending any more time around the bomb.

"Well, Watson—are you going to sit around all day, or are you going to help me to catch the villain responsible for this?"

And as Holmes strode from the suite, I bit my tongue and climbed to my feet, following him.

++++

"Holmes—from what you were saying just now, I take it you know who constructed the bombs?"

"Oh indeed, Watson," he replied with confidence as we crossed the street to the Government building. "I know such work intimately well."

"So it was not the Chinese, then?"

He regarded me with a sort of disdain.

We climbed the stairs up to the fourth floor, where Inspector Bradstreet and Mycroft Holmes had gathered everyone from the Russia-China Peace Conference. The room was large; as big as a government conference room might reasonably be, with a high, vaulted ceiling and three large windows looking out over the street far below.

As might be suspected, no one was happy with the arrangement. The two men were being bombarded by protests in a dozen languages from twice as many individuals.

"I have told them they are being kept here for their own protection—which is true enough. But some are asserting their right to go free under diplomatic law," Mycroft informed Holmes as we entered. "And some wish to cable their superiors back home."

"You have not allowed them under any circumstances to do so, I trust?"

"Certainly not," Mycroft replied.

"Good."

"Others," Mycroft went on, "simply fear being held together here alongside the likely perpetrator."

"I can imagine they would feel that way," Holmes replied. "But I believe we can bring this matter to a speedy enough conclusion now."

This was of course news to me, and I stood to one side, observing carefully.

"You have the Asian gentleman who was kidnapped?"

"We've kept him secured on the third floor," Mycroft replied.

"I believe this would be a fine time to re-introduce him to his party," Holmes said flatly.

Mycroft issued orders and an officer went off to fetch the man.

"Now—if I might?"

Holmes strode across to the front of the room and looked out over the crowd. Between forty and fifty men in soot-stained finery and a dozen or so ladies in equally despoiled dresses stood looking back at him. Some were European in appearance, others Asian, but all wore expressions of shock and outrage. A few of them still held bits of cloth up to their faces, as though struggling to breathe after the smoke exposure.

Holmes introduced himself formally and then explained that he had just defused a second bomb—much to the surprise and discomfort of all present.

"This bomb, I can assure you, was of neither Chinese nor Russian manufacture. Indeed, I believe that it was built and planted by an old acquaintance of mine. A gentleman who is neither Chinese nor Russian, and cares for the advancement of neither of your countries, gentlemen, I assure you—nor of his own, truth be told. All that matters to him is his own self-aggrandizement."

I had my suspicions as to whom Holmes alluded, but kept my own council for the moment.

"That second bomb, in its style of design and in its array of components, is quite familiar to me. The surviving components of the first bomb, which I was fortunate to find scattered about, match perfectly with the second. The same party is responsible for both bombs."

"The Chinese!" screamed one of the Russian delegates. "These dogs tried to kill us all! It will be war between us—I assure you of that!"

"It was not us," cried the Chinese chief delegate. "These are all baseless lies. I believe the Russians—these criminals!—bombed their own suite, in order to fabricate these charges and unfairly blame us for war!"

"Outrageous!" the Russian chief delegate shouted back.

"Look at their delegation," the Chinese chief asserted. "They are all present! No one was killed! What are the odds that—"

"Perhaps God is on our side," the Russian replied. "This proves nothing!"

"Criminals are indeed at work," Holmes interjected, raising a hand and managing to quiet both sides for the moment. "And indeed there was an attempt here to place the blame for the bombings unfairly—at both your feet."

The Russians and the Chinese eyed one another warily but with new suspicion, and then turned and began looking around at the other delegates filling the room. Those men and women from the smaller countries which lay between Russia and China all reflected in their faces sudden surprise and concern, and some of them stepped backwards warily.

"But the true culprits can be smoked out easily enough," Holmes continued. "We simply must discover to which delegation this man belongs."

At that, a police officer led the mysterious Asian man in through the side doorway and around to the front of the crowd, next to Holmes.

Judging by their reactions, many of those present recognized him, though no one at first spoke.

I glanced at Holmes in concern, but he was focused intently on the crowd, his sharp eyes darting from one face to the other as those diplomats beheld the mystery man. Still no one spoke.

"His delegation may have consisted only of him, alone," Mycroft whispered. "Yet surely someone—*someone* here remembers him…"

"Solchak!"

"Toka!"

A voice from within the crowd had called the first name, and our man had responded with the second, in an excited tone. It was the first time I had observed any positive emotion from the man since he'd first been brought to Holmes's apartment.

Another Asian diplomat—the man who had spoken up—rushed forward and grasped our man, and they embraced warmly.

"What are you doing here? I was told you were not coming on this mission!" And then, realizing his friend did not speak English, the diplomat repeated himself in a language unfamiliar to me—the one our man had spoken earlier.

"Quickly, quickly," Holmes hissed, intruding on their obviously happy reunion, "for time is absolutely of the essence. Which country is this man from?"

"From—from Tuva," replied the diplomat, eyes wide. "He is from the Kingdom of Tannu-Tuva!"

Mycroft blanched.

"But—the Tuvan delegate is that man there!"

All eyes followed Mycroft Holmes's pointing finger to where a man in black jacket and tie stood, a handkerchief still pressed to his face. Instantly the man began to back away from the others, until he stood alone against the three massive windows that looked out over the street.

"Arrest that man!" came the booming voice of Bradstreet.

The policemen raced towards him. He spun this way and that, like the trapped animal he had become, and then whirled about.

"Stop him!" shouted Holmes—but too late.

With a blood-curdling cry, the man launched himself forward into the great windows. As the dignitaries looked on in horror, the fugitive smashed his way through the glass, out into the thin evening air—and then down, down, all the way down to the unyielding surface of the street four stories below.

++++

Of course Holmes had concluded that none other than his old adversary, Professor Moriarty, lay behind the entire episode. Upon hearing his rationale, I concluded that this was not an unreasonable assumption.

"It is not an assumption at all, my dear Watson," Holmes stated as we made our way back to Baker Street. "The evidence is as plain as if Moriarty had himself been caught wearing the fire-damaged disguise, rather than his henchman."

"Whatever could he have sought to gain?" I asked. "To the best of my understanding, the only outcome of his actions would have been a war between China and Russia."

"Quite so," Holmes replied, nodding sagely. "And where can a sly and opportunistic man—a conscienceless man—reap greater profits than from a war—particularly a large and savage one? No doubt Moriarty stood poised to sell armaments to both sides…to work out high-interest loans to factions in both governments… to provide mercenary forces to both… and so on."

"I will take your word for all that, Holmes," I replied. "And yet I find that a few points of interest in the case remain somewhat obscure to me. Should I ever be allowed to write this matter up for public consumption—"

"Where you will, no doubt, once again fill the tale with far too much excitement and bravado and far too little of the scientific method of investigative practices."

"—Yes, yes," I nodded, letting the remark pass. "But should Her Majesty's Government ever allow the tale to be told, I require clarification on a few certain points."

"Pray proceed," Holmes replied.

"In no particular order," I said, "we can start with the bombs. You knew them to be Moriarty's devices, rather than belonging to either Great Power delegation."

Holmes nodded.

"The bomb I defused was virtually identical to at least two other such devices I have encountered in the past two years, both of which were parts of investigations that led directly to Moriarty's doorstep. And neither used components common to Chinese or Russian munitions of that type."

"But the Russians or the Chinese could have purchased or stolen the components for the bombs after they arrived in London," I countered. "Perhaps from Moriarty himself."

Holmes shrugged. "Possible, yes, but the window of time for such activities was exceedingly small. Why seek out someone like Moriarty and attempt to work a deal with him, when you could simply bring the devices with you from the home country? While not air-tight in and of itself, this point lent support to my theories."

"Very well," I replied, "but what about the three bodies that were found murdered? I never heard any more about them."

"We were not supposed to hear about them at all, Watson," Holmes replied. "The same is true of the first murdered man, which sent Mycroft after me in the first place. While we cannot be sure, Moriarty's henchman must have murdered them when they discovered his identity. He could not have kept himself hidden from all prying eyes for the entire two days of the conference, and surely some of the other delegates knew the Tuvan by appearance. The henchman must have believed the bodies would be caught in the explosion and that the authorities would chalk up their deaths to the blast."

"I see—yes, that fits."

"And now that our friend from Tuva has been able to tell his tale via translator, we know that indeed he was kidnapped shortly after disembarking from his ship. Moriarty's men held him for more than a day before he managed to free himself through a fortunate oversight on the part of his guards—who were not, apparently, of the usual quality employed by the Napoleon of Crime."

"Fortunate for him," I noted, "and for the rest of us, as well."

"Quite so. But of course the poor man was tired, hungry, and completely disoriented, not to mention naked, as the criminals had taken his clothes and given them to his double."

"Perhaps Her Majesty's Government will do something for him, to make up for all of this hardship he has borne since arriving on our shores?"

"I do not doubt it," Holmes replied. "And with my brother now shepherding the reconvened conference in a new and secret location, I rest assured that a major global conflict has been averted—at least for the nonce."

"Thank heavens for that," I replied. "The last thing I would ever want to contemplate would be a world-wide war."

++++

And so as I conclude my account of the Adventure of the Tuvan Delegate, I cannot help but think back to that moment when our immediate opponent—the man who had taken the Tuvan delegate's place at the conference—plunged through the windows and to his death on the street. And as I think of that moment, I likewise cannot help but imagine Holmes's great adversary, the puppet-master Moriarty himself, pulling that poor doomed soul's strings all along, lurking in the safety of the shadows nearby and watching.

In my mind's eye, I can see the Professor waiting for his second bomb to explode—for the two Great Powers to launch into a catastrophic war, and perhaps for the Great Detective to be slain in the explosion, as well.

And then I think of his weathered, wrinkled, sour face as he witnesses his plans undone and his schemes shattered into ruins. I think of that face as the second bomb fails to explode and Holmes—his great foe—emerges unscathed from the hotel. And I think of it as his henchman crashes through the windows and tumbles to his death. And thus, despite all the dangers we faced in this case, not to mention the great danger of a Great War that might have engulfed the globe as a consequence... Despite all of it, I think of Moriarty's face at the climactic, decisive moment, and I cannot help but smile.

The Making of "The Adventure of the Tuvan Delegate"

By Van Allen Plexico

My first story having clocked in at half the size expected, I was asked to create a second, similar one to make up the difference. I was thrilled at the chance to do it all again, but I knew this one needed to be different enough from the "Stanford Bridge" story to be worth the time and effort of myself and the readers. I knew from the start that this story would be a somewhat "bigger" tale, and would include Moriarty (at least peripherally) as well as Mycroft Holmes—two colorful and very important characters I had intentionally omitted from the first tale, in order to strip it down to the bare minimum necessary. So, in the case of this story, the characters came first, and I had to find a plot that would fit around them.

Naturally, if Mycroft were involved, it might include government activities and foreign intrigue. But what countries would be involved? I'd recently happened to stumble across some of my old notes about physicist Richard Feynman and his love of the "lost country" of Tuva (or Tannu Tuva), a country he remembered hearing about as a child but was unable to find on the map during the 1980s. As it turned out, the Soviet Union had absorbed the little kingdom. Years before, however, it had been ruled by the Chinese. Foreign intrigue indeed! With such thoughts bouncing around inside my head, the story began to write itself.

What of Moriarty? Naturally, he would wish to stir up trouble between those two Great Powers, Russia and China, in order to profit from the conflict. By having them send delegates to meet in London (where naturally Mycroft would be involved), Holmes and Watson could be pulled directly into the situation. The image of a Tuvan diplomat, disoriented and naked, lost in the back streets of London—and speaking a language no one understood!—completed the picture. I chose Bradstreet as my inspector for this one since I'd used the much better known Lestrade in the first. Unlike Lestrade, the inspector here did not have to be a rival to Holmes; he merely had to admire the detective and be willing to follow his orders when necessary. Bradstreet, who had appeared in one or two of Doyle's stories, served admirably.

I think the two stories share a common interpretation and dramatization of Holmes and Watson, in terms of their personalities and speech. I hope the two stories are different enough that the reader will feel each was worth his or her time to read.

Van Allen Plexico

Van Allen Plexico is a political science professor and a freelance writer/ editor. He has lived in Atlanta, Singapore, Alabama, and Washington, DC, and now resides in the St. Louis area. He writes for Airship 27, White Rocket Books, and Swarm Press, among others, and created the long-running and popular *AvengersAssemble!* Web site, located at avengersassemble.net.

SHERLOCK HOLMES
CONSULTING DETECTIVE

"Dead Man's Manuscript"

by I. A. Watson

I hadn't seen Lumley since the Battle of Maiwand[1] ten years earlier. Just seeing him brought back the sights and sounds – and smells – of that terrible occasion; the clamour of the men and the scream of horses and the stink of split bodies on the ground. I could almost hear the cries of Ayub Khan's mad Afghans as I'd heard them before passing out from loss of blood as the front ranks broke and the tribesmen fell on us.

And here was Lumley, entering my very own surgery room, large as life. "My dear chap!" I cried, rising from my desk to greet him. Despite the unwelcome memories of my departure from Afghanistan and the service of the Berkshires it was always a pleasure to see an old comrade.

"Watson!" Lumley called, taking my hand and gripping it tightly. "The years have treated you well." His gaze took in my Paddington practice, my expanding waistline, the daguerreotype of Mary on the side-table. "Better than me, I fear."

I apprehended then that this was not a social visit. "Lumley, old fellow! Is there something wrong? Have you sought me out in a medical capacity?"

I shepherded my visitor to a seat and he dropped into it gratefully. "A medical capacity, yes," he confirmed. "I've got… a problem, and there's no other man in London I'd confide it to."

A medical practitioner with experience of the world learns not to be

---

1 On 27th July 1880, General Burrows took heavy casualties at the Battle of Maiwand, a key defeat for the British in the Second Afghan War. Amongst those injured in the retreat was John H. Watson MD, as described in *A Study in Scarlet.*

"Lumley, old fellow! Is there something wrong? Have you sought me out in a medical capacity?"

shocked by the problems brought before him even by old friends. "You know I'll do what I can, Lumley. Be absolutely frank with me."

Lumley accepted a glass of tonic water. I noticed his hand was shaking.

"Nerves," he said, following my gaze to his trembles. "Ever since Maiwand, and that stand amongst the Grenadiers."

I'd heard something about Lumley's injuries, that he'd been discharged as I had. "It was a beastly business and a terrible waste," I noted. "Your nerves are troubling you now?"

Lumley let out a short snort. "Nerves? Oh, I've got nerve problems all right." He leaned over the desk to confide in me. "Doctor Watson… John… do you believe that a man can speak with the ghost of his father?"

I blinked in surprise. That hasn't been a question I'd anticipated. "Well, Lumley, I've seen some queer things in my time, but I don't know if…"

"Watson, either my father is cursed to walk the earth as a phantasm or I am losing my mind!" His eyes rolled wildly.

"Calm down, old chap. There's clearly a lot you have to tell me. Just take a deep breath and start at the beginning."

Lumley accepted my advice. He closed his eyes for a moment and then told his troubles.

"It's fantastic, I know, but I have no other explanation for what has happened. How else can a man interpret the spectre of his father appearing to him by night in a sealed chamber, showing incontrovertible knowledge of my intimate past that only a parent might know and leaving behind ineluctable physical proof of his passing?"

I stifled a sceptical response but reached for a long cigar.

Lumley must have read my face. "I'll swear an oath, Watson. I saw my father, large as life – and he spoke to me! The things he told me…! The things I have had to do…!"

"From the beginning, old chap," I urged. "You must explain in order. What happened? When? How did you come to this… extraordinary experience?"

Lumley drew a deep breath. "Of course," he shuddered. "I'm sorry, Watson. I'm a bag of nerves at the best of times these days, and all of this, well it's not the best of times. I'll try and tell the tale properly. It began when I came to London three days ago, for the first time since my illness, for the reading of my father's will…"

When he'd finished I knew that Henry Lumley would need to repeat it again to Mr. Sherlock Holmes.

I was about to suggest that we retire to a friend's rooms at 221B Baker

Street when there was a commotion in the waiting room outside. Mary's familiar knock sounded on my door, then her sweet face appeared around the lintel. "John, I'm sorry to interrupt but there are two constables here. They're looking for your visitor."

The door opened wider. Now I could see the bulky shapes of two officers of the law. The sergeant was bristling at the implication he was a mere constable. Behind them my receptionist and the couple of waiting patients stared in amazement as the drama unfolded.

"We're sorry to interrupt, sir," the sergeant told me, advancing past Mary into my surgery. "We are looking for Mr. Henry Lumley."

I glanced across at my guest. He stood up and faced the policemen. "I'm Lumley," he told them in a resigned, defeated tone.

"Well then, Mr. Lumley, I am placing you under arrest, on the charge of destroying a rare and historical document at the Cresswell Museum."

++++

Holmes and I were no strangers to the detention cells under Bow Street Magistrates Court, to the shallow steps under the brick arches and the gloomy corridors where the duty sergeant with his huge bunch of keys sits at a battered old teak desk. On this occasion however, as we visited my old comrade Henry Lumley, the sights and sounds made a deeper impression upon me: the flickering light from the gas mantles painting the old whitewashed walls, the peculiar echoes from the street outside, the familiar smells of boiled food and bleach. I shuddered.

We were expected, of course. When I had sent off a runner to summon Holmes, I had also contacted the Clerk of the Court to let him know we'd be coming. The officers at the door knew Holmes and I well and there was no trouble gaining admission to the newest prisoner.

"'E's an unusual one, awlright," the duty sergeant admitted as he set down his tin mug of hot sweet tea and rose to take us to Lumley's cell. "Quiet as a mouse an' startles like one too. Doesn't want a brief and confessed straight up wot he burned that old bit o' paper."

"We'll need to see him right away," I answered.

As we were speaking, a well-dressed man in a smart morning coat was being let out of the cell corridor. He apprehended that we had come for Lumley and deigned to stop and speak with us. "You're here for Lumley's defence?" he asked. "I'm very much afraid you are wasting your time."

"And who are you, sir?" I demanded, offended by this stranger's haughty manner.

"Oh come now, Watson," Holmes interjected, "this can only be Sir Tarrant Besting, the new assistant crown prosecutor. Note the pristine white collar-bands hardly out of their tissue-paper wrappings, the flecks of alluvial soil on the boots from the road-workings outside the Prosecution Service offices, the tell-tale bulge of briefing notes on legal foolscap hastily crammed to an inner pocket – and of course the calling card which Sir Tarrant has left on the sergeant's desk as warrant of his identity."

The assistant crown prosecutor looked over at Holmes, disconcerted and suddenly unsure of himself; as Holmes had no doubt intended. Then he rallied himself. "You are Lumley's defenders, then?" he demanded.

"We are his friends," I chimed in. "Mr. Sherlock Holmes and Dr. John H. Watson."

Sir Tarrant's face assumed a knowing sneer. "The enquiry agent," he recognised.

"The consulting detective," Holmes responded.

"Well, Holmes, you are wasting your time here. A full dozen people, visitors and guards alike, saw Lumley enter the Cresswell gallery at eleven fifteen this morning. He was recognised by the curator, Forsythe. Four witnesses saw him shatter the case protecting a valuable historic manuscript, lift the document clear, then touch it with the corner of his cigar to set the paper alight. Before anything could be done the manuscript was ashes. Lumley shook off the guards, shouting nonsense, and raced away. I have testimonies aplenty and a full confession from the man himself."

"And did he tell you why he had behaved in this extraordinary manner?" I demanded.

Sir Tarrant snorted. "He claims he was instructed to this act of vandalism by his dead father. *I* say that a court will not accept such a defence from your client any more than they would have from the Prince of Denmark from whose account Lumley has clearly concocted his eccentric story."

Sir Tarrant glanced at the wall-clock. "I have other business," he told us, "rather more important than your client's vandalism. I will bid you good day."

Holmes and I watched the strutting young prosecutor mount the steps up from the cellars two at a time. "Well!" I snorted as he vanished from sight. "What do you make of that, Holmes?"

"'What a piece of work is a man!'" replied my friend. "Come, Watson, let us speak with Captain Lumley."

++++

T he duty sergeant led us to one of the cell gates and opened it. The lock-ups at Bow Street are small, intended only to hold prisoners before they are taken before the Bench, and Holmes and I quite crowded Lumley as we pressed inside. The stricken man glanced once at us with a lack of comprehension then turned his face back to the wall.

"Captain Henry Lumley, may I present Mr. Sherlock Holmes?" I began.

The formalities of introduction somehow penetrated Lumley's miseries. A lifetime of gentleman's habits stirred him from his lethargy and forced him to make some mumbled response.

Holmes took charge. "You have presented a pretty problem, Captain Lumley. If what my good friend Watson here reports is true then you have had a singular set of experiences."

Lumley winced. "I regret nothing," he declared. "My father's soul is worth more than every penny I have, and if I must be bankrupted and imprisoned for what I have done then I shall count it worth the cost."

"Your father's soul?" I responded, but Holmes held up a finger to cut me short.

"You will understand, Captain Lumley, that many questions will be asked of you regarding your curious behaviour and the extraordinary motivations which you claim. It will be of singular helpfulness if you would trouble to answer these questions in a clear and logical way. Indeed it might help to clear up a few points which will otherwise muddy your actions in the most regrettable manner."

"Holmes is the friend I told you about," I explained as Lumley considered. "You may speak to him as you would to me, with the same confidence."

For a moment I feared that the arrested man would draw back into that baffled haze where he had previously been lost, but at last he seemed to rouse himself and reach a decision. He sat up straighter, tightened his collar, and looked us in the eyes. "I am ready. But there is no earthly explanation for the events that have destroyed me, Mr. Holmes. I have been sucked from the world of the mundane into a place of dark shadows and darker evils. I shall never be free from it again."

"Lumley saw his father's spirit," I explained again to move the conversation forward. "It came to him last night."

"Indeed?" Holmes asked, curiously. "How so, Captain Lumley?"

Lumley glanced at both of us as if deciding whether to confess all. Doubtless the reaction he'd had from Sir Tarrant Besting had soured his taste for self-revelation. "Last night I was roused from a troubled sleep by someone calling my name. As I awoke, I saw the ghost of my father, standing across the room from me. It spoke in a whisper but it said such things as could only be known by my father. It gave me proof, physical proof which I touched and tested in the morning. Mr. Holmes, I know this is an impossible story, that my nerves are shot and that I might be considered hysterical, even mad, but I swear to you…"

"Do not trouble yourself," Holmes assured him. "Merely describe your experiences as you perceived them and leave the interpretation to others."

Lumley shivered. The Bow Street cells are never warm in the first place, although I noticed the sergeant had provided the prisoner with a mug of his thick sweet tea. The enamel cup sat untouched on the bench beside the prisoner.

"My father appeared as I had known him in my youth," Lumley told us, "attired in his Indian rig and…"

"Hold," Holmes interrupted, lifting a hand. "Kindly unfold your case to us from the beginning," Holmes commanded. "The background is as important as the events. The smallest detail can be the key to unlocking the puzzle. Spare no detail, no matter how trivial."

My old comrade nodded and began again. "I am Henry William Lumley, sole surviving son of Colonel Sir Derrington Lumley, the explorer and writer. Both my brothers also served in the army, the one lost against the Boers, the other the Zulus. We are an old military family, but we seem to have a genius for finding battles that go badly. In my father's case, it was the Sepoy Mutiny."

I'd heard that old Colonel Lumley had been in the thick of it back in '57 when the trouble had reached Meerut. He'd later been decorated for his part in the campaign when Sir Hugh Rose led his forces against the Rani of Jhansi[2]. From the stories, he'd been an adventurous young soldier in his day, but I only knew him from his son's comments about a sick and peevish old man.

Lumley went on. "In my case the fateful battle was Maiwand. In that same conflict where Watson found the wrong end of a Jezail bullet I, too was wounded. Separated from my company by those murderous Ghazis I found myself captured by hill-bandits and held for some months before I was finally ransomed back. I was not treated well by those savage cruel brutes, and thereafter my general health has not been good and my nerves

---

2 *The Indian Rebellion began on 10th May 1857 and spread across the upper Gangetic plain and central India. The Rani Lakshmi Bai, who had been dispossessed of her lands at Jhansi by British policy, rose to leadership of the rebels and fought bravely at their head until her eventual death at the Siege of Gwalior.*

have been less than they were."

"You have confined yourself of late to a rustic existence," Holmes deduced, glancing at the cut of my friend's clothing, at the scratches on the soles and rims of his boots, on the tiny burr still caught on one cuff of his trousers, on the calluses showing the regular use of a walking stick. "Until your father's recent passing." Even I could have interpreted the significance of the black mourning armband.

"Until then, sir," Lumley agreed. "My father was a man of variable temperament and he did not prize the company of others, even his surviving son. When I returned from Afghanistan it became clear that we could not equitably live together in the family seat. I therefore leased a small lodge in Hertfordshire where I could have the quiet existence I now craved. My father and I corresponded from time to time, but he did not visit me nor I him."

"You did not see him before his passing?" I asked, a little shocked.

"I had no indication of his deterioration," Lumley mourned. "If he had let me know, if his friend Cayden had written to tell me... but Cayden's letter was to inform me of my father's death, not of his illness."

"And Cayden is...?" enquired Holmes.

"My father's oldest friend. They served together in India and have remained close these three decades since. Cayden's house is only half an hour's ride from my father's. Apart from Cayden and Dr. Moore the family physician, my father rarely had visitors."

"You came to London for the reading of the will, Captain," Holmes prompted.

"Two days since, yes. I arrived the evening before that, of course, to settle in and accustom myself to the row of the city once more. I confess I found it quite disturbing. Loud noises leave me nervous these days."

I could see Lumley becoming agitated so I clapped him on the shoulder. "Can't be helped, old fellow. Lots of chaps came home startling at carriages and the like."

"Cayden knew of my difficulties, of course, and he was most helpful. He recommended a small hotel away from the main concourses where I might find a little quiet and solitude."

"The name of the establishment?" Holmes demanded.

"The Hanley," Lumley answered, "on Clarges Street, down from the Piccadilly Hotel. They found me a quiet room in their furthest corner from the road."

Holmes gestured for Lumley to proceed, so he did. "I slept badly that first night, troubled by the journey, the city, the noise. Eventually I managed a couple of hours of sleep before I was woken for breakfast. I spent the next day quietly recovering from my travels but lay awake again most of the night. Yesterday, I proceeded to the chambers of my father's man of business, Mr. Goodge of Dreyden and Cole."

"I am aware of the firm," Holmes confirmed. "Who was present at the reading of your father's will?"

"Not many people. Cayden, of course – that is Charles Cayden, my father's old comrade from his soldiering days, the only old contact he'd maintained during his long confinement; Dr. Moore, my father's physician; two distant cousins of mine; and there was Dr. Forsythe, from the Cresswell Museum, whom I'd not met before we were introduced."

"The terms of the will?" Holmes probed.

"Nothing remarkable," Lumley answered. "I inherited the bulk of father's estate. He spoke quite kindly of me in his last will and testament, kinder than he ever did in life. Cayden was bequeathed some of my father's books. He and father spent many hours in father's library, have always shared a love of old tomes, and Cayden will find better use for them than I ever did. There were small sums for my cousins, along with a trust that will give them modest incomes, and a pair of hunting pistols and some oil miniatures for Moore."

"And Dr. Forsythe?" I wondered. I remembered that the Cresswell Museum seemed to figure large in Leyden's current situation.

"The museum received ownership of the Jhansi Manuscript," explained Lumley. "My father had loaned the document to the Cresswell during his lifetime. On his death he passed it to them absolutely."

"This is the manuscript you are accused of destroying?" I checked.

Holmes interrupted me. "Watson, you are running ahead of our narrative. Captain Lumley, pray explain the background and significance of this Jhansi document."

"Of course," agreed Lumley. "It was that document which blighted my father's life and it is the cause of my ruin today."

"The facts," insisted Holmes.

"Very well. In March 1857, my father was an officer of the British East India Company, serving as a patroller leading a company of Indian troops based out of Meerut. When the great mutiny erupted, his men remained loyal to the crown and made their escape to join with other forces heading north to Jhansi. At that time the Rani Lakhsmi Bai had negotiated safe passage for British civilians from the besieged fortress of Jhansi, but had then turned on them and had them massacred. A punitive force was sent into her lands to rout her and regain control of those territories, and Colonel Derrington Lumley was amongst those on the expedition."

"That was the occasion for which he was made a knight," I recalled.

"It was a bloody, vengeful foray," Lumley admitted. "Neither side gave quarter and few prisoners were taken. My father never spoke in detail of those weeks, but I gather he was detailed to clear some hill forts of mutineers and sympathisers, and he finally captured one Satim Bey, a Marathi rebel who was some kind of local prince related to the Rani herself; or perhaps he was one of her lovers. Bey bargained for his life by revealing a hoard of the Rani's treasure, and that is how my father became a rich man."

"The Rani had no more need of it after Gwalior," I noted. That was the battle in June of that bloody year where Lakhsmi Bay and her rebels had finally fallen before the 8th Hussars.

Lumley looked a little uncomfortable. "Amongst that hoard of gold and gems was a document, an ancient parchment that Bey claimed was more valuable than everything else added together. He begged to be allowed to keep the Manuscript in exchange for giving my father all the other treasure. My father refused to negotiate and had Satim Bey taken outside and shot."

Holmes made no comment when Lumley looked across at him for reaction. If he disapproved of the Colonel's betrayal or approved of his dispatch of a traitor and a rebel he gave no sign.

"I have heard from Cayden, who had it from my father himself, that Bey died cursing English treachery. Bey swore that the manuscript would bring my father nothing but sorrow and ill-luck and that one day it would be the destruction of everything he held dear."

"What kind of document was this manuscript?" I wondered. "Some kind of holy tome? Some kind of literary work?"

"I do not know," Lumley confessed. "No-one knows. It is a single sheet of extremely thin parchment, decorated in a script unknown to civilised scholarship. The inks are faded now but different parts of the text are written in green, red, and brown. Both sides of the document are covered in it. It is considered a rare find and was valued for insurance purposes at some forty thousand guineas."

My eyes widened a little. If Lumley had indeed destroyed that document and the Cresswell Museum sought compensation for their losses, then my old comrade might be bankrupted indeed.

Holmes leaned forward, his forefingers pressed to the sides of his hawk-nose as he focussed his full attention on the problem. "What happened to the scroll when Sir Derrington brought it home?"

"The manuscript was loaned to the Cresswell," Lumley replied. "There was some scholarly investigation made to interpret the meaning of the text, but after a while interest waned and it has remained on display there ever since – until my father's ghost demanded that it be destroyed."

Lumley paused as if unsure what our reaction might be to his fantastic claim. I glanced across at Holmes, but for now my friend seemed content to let me take the lead in our hunt for information. "Lumley, as a sensible man you must be aware that your experience sounds a little odd," I suggested. "Tell us now about events last night that have so upset you."

"I have already told you – my father's ghost visited me and warned me of the Jhansi curse!"

"The facts," Holmes commanded. "Leave the interpretations for later. We must have facts."

Lumley was defiant. "Very well, sir. The facts. I retired early, upset by the day's proceedings and exhausted from lack of sleep the previous nights. Around eight forty-five, with a cup of warmed milk. Fact. As I am a nervous traveller these days I did what I always do in a strange venue and placed a chair under the knob of my door to prevent anyone entering – foolish, I know, but a habit that suits me when my nerves are bad. This is how I know that no mortal being could have entered my chambers."

"That does rather rule out a hotel servant with a pass-key or the like, Holmes," I admitted.

"Having chosen a quiet back room on the second floor, as far as possible from the road's noise, my chambers were small. There was only the bedroom itself and a tiny connected dressing room with no exit to the corridor. I entered the dressing room as I folded away my clothes into the wardrobe and can attest that there was nowhere a person might hide."

"What about the windows?" I wondered.

"Second floor windows fastened shut on the insides with good strong screw-down Brighton sash fasteners," Lumley replied. "Do you not think I made the most careful check myself this morning, Watson?"

"All must be checked again," Holmes insisted. "Proceed with your account, Captain."

"I retired to bed. I was cold so I drew the extra blanket from beneath the bedstead. In that way I know there was no-one and nothing concealed down there. I read Thomas Hardy for a short while but could not settle to

"The facts. We must have facts."

it, so I blew out my light and managed to settle into a fitful doze."

Lumley leaned forward and lowered his voice. "I was disturbed by a whisper and jarred awake by the light, sirs. It was the middle of the night, although I did not have the wits to check my pocketwatch as to exactly when. The curtains at the foot of my bed were open, although I had shut them when I retired. I apprehended a dim flicker of greenish-yellow on the wall opposite, the wall with the outer door. The glow was bright enough that I could see the door and the chair still wedged against it. And then I heard the whisper again, a distant calling of my own name."

"By what name did it call you?" Holmes enquired.

"Henry," replied Lumley, "the name by which my father addressed me. I tried to get up and see what was happening, but it was as if a great weight had been laid across my legs. I could not stir. The whispering continued."

"Did you reply to the calls?" I wondered.

"Not then. As I watched, the glow seemed to focus. Then the shape of a man appeared. It was pale and unearthly, as if drawn from some distant netherworld. It was the spectre of my father."

"A description, please, Captain Lumley," Holmes urged.

"My father appeared as I remember him from my youth, clad in the uniform he wore during his military service. He was indistinct, transparent, and he moved little, but I knew it to be him. I called to him then, 'Father!' and he whispered his reply to me: 'Son'."

Holmes nodded. I could tell from the gleam in his eyes that he was appreciating this bizarre account. "Was this figure with whom you communicated stood beside the bed or nearer to the door? Could you see the whole body right to his feet?"

Lumley considered this. "He was by the door. I could see most of him, albeit indistinctly for he was somewhat translucent, but because I was laid in bed and could not rise his lower legs were concealed by the foot of the bed-frame. I cannot say more; the whole encounter had a dream-like quality that makes it hard to recall details."

"This spectre had more to say to you, though?" I urged him.

"He said, 'Henry, I am damned. My soul stands in peril because of that Jhansi Manuscript. I am cursed and can never rest unless the document is destroyed.'"

"Remarkable. Did you put this spirit to the test with questions? You seem convinced that this apparition was indeed your father."

"I asked whom he was, and how came he there. He replied in terms which no other man could have: 'I am your father, who nurtured you in the cradle; who played soldiers with you on the nursery floor and retrieved the cannon from under the chest of drawers; who bandaged your knee when you fell from your first horse; who forbade you to see that gamekeeper's girl again when you would make a damned fool of yourself at Oxford; whom you brought an Afghan scarf when you returned from service. I am your father who wept alone with you when your mother died, who gave you your brother's watch as a token of remembrance, who expressed disappointment and disapproval when we argued in the library after you surrendered your commission. I am your father, and I am damned unless you are my true and loyal son at the last.'"

Lumley fell silent, staring at the wall, sucked back into the dark fears of his recent experience. I had to keep him talking. "How much of what the spirit spoke was private between you and Sir Derrington?"

"Much of it," Lumley replied. "But some of it – Ida the gamekeeper's daughter, and after mother's funeral, and our argument in the library when I invalided out of the Berkshires, those things were known only to the two of us and no other."

Holmes made a noise that might have been disapproval or merely fascination.

"I don't recall all that my father told me," Lumley admitted. "I was drifting in and out of consciousness, as if the spectre was drawing strength from me that he might manifest in this mortal world. I am tired even now. What I do remember, however, is the clear and repeated command that I must go to the Cresswell and immediately destroy the Jhansi Manuscript by fire."

"And your evidence that this was not all merely a vivid dream?" challenged Holmes.

Lumley pointed back to the general area where the duty sergeant sat. "They took it," he told us. "They made me empty my pockets, so it'll be wherever they put my watch and note-case. When I awoke this morning I found a paper weighted beneath my fob-watch beside my bed. It was a note from my father, in his unmistakable handwriting: a note from a ghost!"

"And the content of this missive?"

"The words are engraved on my mind," Lumley replied fervently. "It was that message which sent me down to the Cresswell Museum on my holy quest, and I am not ashamed of my deeds for I have surely saved my father from damnation. The note was brief but said: '*Time is short. Pay no heed to Forsythe or any other. Go to the Manuscript and do what must be done. I must be freed from this torment or I shall have no rest.'"*

I confess to a sudden chill at hearing that message from the dead.

"What happened then, Captain?" Holmes pressed on, secure in his intellect, immune from the terrors of the night. "How did this phantasm disappear from sight, and what did you do then?"

"I... I do not recall it vanishing," Lumley admitted. "I rather think I must have passed out. When I next awoke, it was morning. Light was coming into the room from behind the curtains. I remembered the events of the night before and startled awake. That was when I saw the note in my father's hand."

"You checked your rooms too," I remembered.

"Most carefully," Lumley assented. "The windows were fastened tight. The chair was wedged in place. There was nothing in the wardrobe or beneath my bed. No mortal agent could have entered my room since the evening before. And then I knew what I had to do."

"You went to the Cresswell."

"I did. What of the consequences? My father's soul was in peril. What if I am hurled in prison or condemned to Bedlam? A man has a duty to his kin. I have done mine."

"You have done what you considered right and moral," Holmes told him, rising suddenly, "and now it is for others to untangle whatever lies behind this murky affair. Rest assured, Captain Lumley, that you will not be abandoned to the darkness which surrounds you. The light of reason and truth shall shine again."

I made my goodbyes when Holmes swept out and followed him to the sergeant's desk.

Sir Tarrant had already taken the note from Lumley's father.

++++

The Cresswell Museum was located in one of those large rambling row-houses off Cavendish Square. It was a bequest from the late Sir Charles Cresswell, who had served in India and Egypt and had left his collections and fortune to a private trust for the edification of the public. This much Holmes was able to tell me as we walked to the museum's blocky façade, and I was once again astonished with my companion's intimate knowledge of the city of London.

"The Cresswell is small but of good reputation," Holmes told me. "It collaborates with the British Museum on questions of provenance of items from India and is often called upon by the auction houses and insurance firms to offer valuations of objects of art or historical interest."

We reached the steps up to the museum's doorway but to my surprise Holmes did not turn towards the porch. Instead he kept straight on, talking animatedly about the work of the Cresswell. "The foundation is particularly known for its collection of Taprobane pottery and for some tapestries and images from the Indian Mughal dynasty. It also has some early works on the sons of Aryas and some erotic carvings from ruins outside Lucknow. Keep walking, Watson, and show no indication that we are being observed from that carriage at the corner of Wigmore Street. The Cresswell is of course a likely place for an item like the Jhansi manuscript to be examined and displayed."

I tried not to break my stride or to turn and look in the direction that Holmes had warned me about. "Watched?" I asked. "By whom, and for what purpose?"

"It is too early to draw a conclusion," answered my friend as we rounded the garden in the centre of the square and continued our circuit. "However, we can say that the carriage is privately hired from Schott and Sons of Stamford Street and that it was waiting there keeping the front entrance of the museum in view before we came along. The accumulation of mud-splashes on the streetward side of the coach suggests that it has been parked for some time. The watcher is a somewhat inexperienced sentinel, having twitched the curtain behind which he is concealed when he observed us moving towards the entrance."

"Shall we then confront the spy?" I suggested.

"For now we have no verification of the observer's nature," Holmes replied. "It is no crime to stand a carriage on a public street nor to covertly observe passers-by. Better that we complete our constitutional and go into the Cresswell, and hope for more and better data to piece together the observer's intent."

So we turned at last through the entrance to the museum and left the mysterious coach behind.

++++

D r. Hogan Forsythe turned out to be a balding, fretting man with a shiny domed forehead and thick prescription spectacles. He hurried out to us from behind a roped-off room that exuded the stench of burning paper. "I'm sorry, sirs," he told us, "but the museum is closed."

"We are well aware of it," Holmes assured the curator. "We have just come from Bow Street Magistrates where we have interviewed Captain Lumley about the events of this morning. I would now like to question you and other staff on the matter and to observe the place where the incident took place."

Forsythe blinked in surprise. "A... policeman?" he asked, taking in Holmes's morning suit and my own tweeds and not quite matching us to his expectations.

"An enquiry agent," Holmes replied. He did not say for whom he was working and Forsythe didn't know enough to ask. "Please allow us access to the room where the vandalism took place. While I examine the scene perhaps you would be so good as to explain to Dr. Watson here what you observed?"

Forsythe automatically stood aside as Holmes swept past him into the display room. The interior of the townhouse had been divided up into various sections, each chamber devoted to a different aspect of the Indian and Ceylonese collections that gave the Cresswell its reputation. The room we entered was a well-lit chamber lined with glass-fronted cabinets containing scrolls and fragments from the Indian sub-continent. Neat cards labelled the exhibits and said something of their nature and origin.

Pride of place was given to a tall lectern standing alone in the centre of the room. It, too had been topped by glass, but now museum staff were sweeping up the debris where the case had been broken open. I half-expected Holmes to object to the people swarming over the crime scene and destroying evidence, but my friend ignored them and looked at the damaged cabinet itself. He particularly examined the keyhole of the lock which held down the glass top of the display lectern.

"Could you describe to us what happened?" I asked Dr. Forsythe. "I know you must have been asked about this several times by now, but..."

"It was a little after ten," the curator answered. "I was in the back office going through the second post. Mr. Reed was walking the halls. Mr. Shawdene was in the Ceylon Room. Mrs. Dawlish was at the desk by the main door. Sergeant Potter here was out back, shifting the dustbins."

An elderly man in livery saluted with remembered military precision. "This is their day to be collected and they always leaves a mess," he explained.

"No other staff were present?" I asked.

"We are a small establishment," Forsythe replied. "We have two students interning with us and a number of fellows who work here occasionally but we are not a well resourced foundation, for all the generosity of our original benefactor and the support of men like Sir Darrington Lumley."

"Sir Darrington was generous towards your institution," Holmes prompted from beneath the display lectern. He was examining the joints of the varnished wood case.

"Sir Darrington was a great benefactor," Forsythe admitted. He signalled his distress by wringing his handkerchief in his hands. "It makes the perfidy of his son that much more terrible!"

I knew that Holmes would want a clear account of events so I was about to draw the curator back to the events of that morning when my friend interjected again. "How did Sir Darrington come to place the Manuscript into your care, Dr. Forsythe?"

"How? Oh, through the auction house. The Cresswell was invited to assay a value for the artefacts from India that Sir Darrington returned with. Evidently Sir Darrington had done rather well out of an expedition against the Rani of Jhansi and had wisely selected his share of the bounty from that adventure. He brought home a number of nice pieces of jewelry from some of the minor dynasties, the sale of which set him up comfortably for life. He was most generous in his appreciation for the museum's assistance."

"He also brought home the Jhansi Manuscript," I noted.

Forsythe winced. "A unique piece! Lost! When I think of how happy I was that the museum could examine it at last..."

"Please offer your narrative in a chronological fashion," Holmes chided him. The great detective was prowling the room now, examining chimney and windows and the other cases around the walls. "How did Sir Darrington come to lodge the Manuscript here?"

"It was my suggestion," Dr. Forsythe confessed. "So delicate a parchment requires special care and handling, storage in a certain light, preserved under glass. I persuaded Sir Darrington that we could best care for the Manuscript, that our scholarship offered the best chance of interpreting its meaning."

"The Manuscript has remained here in all the intervening years?" I asked.

"It has never left this building," the curator promised, "and rarely left this room. We were very aware that it was a very valuable and sought-after item."

"That's why I was always keeping a special eye on it, sirs," interjected the ancient Sergeant Potter. "So as no foreign blighter would be 'aving away with it."

"Foreign blighter?" I echoed.

Forsythe sighed. "On three or four occasions we have had some unpleasantness with a person of Indian origin who came here seeking to acquire the Manuscript. He claimed it had been stolen from his people and demanded its return. At first he seemed to believe we would give it to him for the asking. Later he offered money or threats. He was shown out of the building."

"Describe this man," Holmes demanded.

Forsythe wasn't very good at descriptions. He offered a generic summary of a young Indian man dressed in English clothes and speaking with very little trace of an accent. Holmes was not impressed.

"That was the only interest in the Manuscript?" I inquired before Holmes could launch into a catalogue of Forsythe's observational shortcomings.

"There have been offers from private collectors, of course. The antiquarian Hector Dorner, for example, offered Sir Derrington a very handsome sum for it, even above the valuation the Cresswell had made. But then, Mr. Dorner is very rich. And of course there are many other academic institutions that would love to examine the Jhansi Manuscript." His face fell. "Would have loved to examine it."

"Criminal, what that man did," Sgt Potter interjected, putting down his bucket of broken glass and approaching us. "'Oo'd have believed it of 'im? Just marches in, bold as brass, says good morning to Sybil – Mrs. Dawlish, that is, who recognises him o' course and condoles on the death o' 'is pore father – then into the room and... smash!"

"Later," Holmes instructed the old soldier. "I'll have the account from someone who observed it at first hand."

The sergeant seemed a little put out. I moved the interview along. "The Jhansi Manuscript was unusual, and of significant interest to scholars?"

"Most unusual," Dr. Forsythe answered, "and of singular interest to a small select group of scholars with a particular interest in Indian affairs."

Holmes had found a ledger beneath the pedestal and now flicked through it. "A good number of academics came to examine the document it its early months here," he observed from the guest-book, "but interest later waned."

"Waned is not the right word," objected the curator. "Say rather that when it became apparent that the Manuscript would only reward prolonged and diligent research only a few dedicated souls continued to persevere."

"I observe that the last two times the document was removed from the case by a visitor it was Sir Derrington's friend and companion Mr. Cayden."

Forsythe sniffed. "Mr. Cayden is hardly a scholar. A dilettante, perhaps, with pretensions at being lettered. However, in those visits some three months back, Mr. Cayden was acting on behalf of Sir Derrington, who was then too feeble to make the journey up to London. It was some trivial insurance quibble, the company wishing to have an updated authentication of the Manuscript. They used Dansen of Cambridge and he was quite satisfied with both provenance and valuation."

"This Dansen could comment on the nature of the Manuscript?" I offered.

The curator bristled. "Dr. Watson, I can speak to the nature of the Manuscript. I have studied it these thirty-two years. It is my life's work."

"Then kindly summarise for us," Holmes instructed.

Forsythe clutched the lapels of his jacket pedantically. "The parchment was most unusual, being so thin as to be almost translucent. The script was in a cursive alphabet with similarities to several aboriginal Indian languages but not the same as any of them. Some colleagues were sure that the different colours of letters held a particular significance. There was little agreement about the Manuscript and much more to be learned."

"There are accurate copies of the inscriptions?" asked my friend.

Dr. Forsythe sent an assistant scurrying across the display chamber to bring hand-coloured photo-plates off the wall. He laid them out on one of the glass side-tables by the window where we could appreciate them in good light. "As you can see, the script is somewhat reminiscent of the early Aryan character-sets, but contains several unique glyphs which have not been observed elsewhere. The use of the three different pigments…"

Holmes interrupted Forsythe before he could turn the visit into a lecture. "The use of the characters and the gaps between them is very suggestive," he observed. "The thinness of the original parchment is also significant. You have failed, Dr. Forsythe, to see the wood for the trees."

The curator did not like being chided in his own museum. "Sir, the finest linguistic scholars in England have studied these plates."

"Then the wrong men were looking at them," retorted my friend.

"What do you mean, Holmes?" I asked. It seems to be my destiny.

Holmes flicked a glance over at Forsythe. "I mean that the display of the Jhansi Manuscript was of key importance, Watson. The parchment was positioned there in its protective case, one side up and one side down. I presume it was the more ornate side, that most would judge to be the transverse, which you displayed, Dr. Forsythe?"

"That is correct," agreed the curator. "I fail to see…"

"You do indeed," agreed my friend.

I examined the copies more closely. The script had that curling, flowing font so characteristic of the Indian sub-continent, but none of the letters were joined together. There were only a small number of characters, unless their colours were significant. Most of the lettering was brown, but other seemingly-random letters were picked out in red and green. There were spaces between groups of letters like the breaks between words. Each side of the parchment carried around eight hundred characters. It was a most unusual document.

"These facsimile plates are most helpful," Holmes said, "but there are several things which could only be determined by the original Manuscript. Has any test been done to determine the age of the paper or the constituent components of the various pigments on it?"

"Sir Derrington was reluctant to risk the document in that way," Forsythe admitted. "It was a point of contention between us." He cringed again and mopped his brow. "And to think it was lost to us just at the moment when we might have some answers!"

Holmes looked up sharply. "How so?" he demanded.

"Why, the Manuscript was willed to the Cresswell," Forsythe replied. "Whilst we displayed it for Sir Darrington it remained his property and he superstitiously refused to allow any kind of testing upon it. There are various chemical operations which could help us fathom the age of the parchment and the composition of the inks, clever tests which…"

"Yes, I am familiar with the mechanisms," Holmes answered dismissively. "So you now planned a range of investigations which the Colonel had previously refused? Interesting."

"Until this morning's disaster," the curator moaned. "The insurance company will reimburse us for the financial value of the item, of course, but its loss to scholarship in incalculable. And the insurers will surely seek to recoup their losses with a suit against Captain Henry Lumley, which will ruin the son of our benefactor."

"And ruined 'ee should be!" opined Sergeant Potter, still outraged at the assault upon his museum. "Such wilful damage and then to blame it on 'is poor sainted father!"

"So Lumley tried to explain his reasoning here?" I realised.

Now Holmes wanted a full description of the morning's events from those who had witnessed them. A half dozen people had been visiting the museum at the time, and two had even been in the Manuscript Room when Lumley had strode in and shattered the glass. The security men

Reed and Shawdene had been too late to prevent Lumley from igniting the document, but had been able to tackle him to the ground for a moment. Then he'd thrown them off and raced out of the museum, leaving them to cope with the aftermath of his visit.

"Shouted 'is dead father 'ad told him to do it!" repeated Potter disgustedly as he recalled his own late entrance into the confused scrum.

"There was no doubt that it was Captain Lumley," confirmed Forsythe ruefully.

"But still a question about his dead father," answered Holmes pensively.

++++

Mrs. Lobb's description of Sir Tarrant Besting was far from complimentary but easily identifiable. It was clear that the crown prosecutor was taking a special interest in the case of Captain Lumley and that he had been to Hanley's Hotel on Clarges Street before us.

"It matters not, Watson," Holmes assured me. "Either what we wish to see is still here for us to observe as much as Sir Tarrant, or it is not."

Mrs. Lobb was not best pleased at yet more people tramping through her rooms and was quick to say so. In the end I tipped her a half-crown to go away and leave us to our investigations. She led us through a maze of corridors and small stairwells and left us at the door to room 113 with a disdainful sniff. "Don't you go and be making a mess," she warned us as she departed.

Holmes examined the outside of the door and its lock before entering.

"Has the lock been tampered with?" I wondered. There were a good number of scratches and scuffs on the lock-plate.

"It has seen a deal of rough use," answered Holmes, "as one might expect in a lodging house where different men make use of the room each night. There is nothing to help us here. Let us go inside."

The bedroom itself was uninspiring, a dull dark chamber whose light was restricted by the shadows from adjoining properties. The canopied bed was oak and well-polished. The room was clean and tidy, but it had a gloomy air. The wallpaper was a dismal midnight-blue and had seen better days. I quickly recognised the layout that Lumley had described, with the entrance door on the opposite wall to the bed and a connecting door to a small dressing room on the side opposite the window.

I checked the window locks but could see no sign of tampering.

"I see you are putting your experiences to good use, Watson," Holmes chuckled. "What do you observe about these windows, then?"

I renewed my examination. "They are regular sash windows," I noted. "The lower half slides upwards but the upper half has been painted shut. They are secured by Bristol catches, these metal pins affixed to the upper casement that drop into a clasp atop of the lower sash. The knob on the end of the pin screws down to fix the pin in place and secure the window closed. The windows here and in the dressing room are sealed tight."

"And?" Holmes prompted.

"There is no sign of a hidden catch that might spring the window open and allow entry or exit. The frame is not secretly hinged." I hesitated, unsure of what else to say.

"The windows are well cleaned, inside and out," Holmes supplied.

"I fail to see the relevance of that, Holmes."

"Later, then, Watson. Instead consider these indentations in the carpet here by the door."

I looked over Holmes's shoulder. "Surely these two imprints are where Lumley wedged a chair under the door handle as he told us?" I judged.

"Indeed they are," Holmes affirmed. "That chair there, from its dimensions and the shape of its feet." He crouched down on all fours and examined the nap of the carpet most carefully with his eyeglass. Then he lifted the chair over and positioned it as Lumley must have done. I tested for myself how impossible it would have been for anyone to enter the room while that furniture was wedged in place without creating a huge row and probably breaking the chair.

Holmes's search took him to the window of the dressing room. He unscrewed the sash and threw it up to peer outside, above and below. He opened the built-in wardrobe and cupboards that lined two sides of that tiny room. He noted that the dressing room door opened inwards.

"I don't suppose you would care to explain to me what you are looking for?" I ventured.

"Verification, Watson," Holmes answered. "We are seeing how much of the Captain's tale we can bear out. For example, you will observe the marks upon the polish of the side-table beside the bed indicating where Lumley set down his evening drink, that mug of cocoa he mentioned. The dour Mrs. Lobb has cleaned away the cup but has not yet had the opportunity to polish the table, due no doubt to incessant visits from officers of the law, from a certain crown prosecutor, and from ourselves."

"About Sir Tarrant, Holmes," I wondered, "Surely it's unusual for a legal man to involve himself like this?"

"Sir Tarrant is making a name for himself," my friend replied. "His interest in this case waxed when he learned of my interest in it."

"Then he seeks to set himself against you?" I realised.

"He is welcome to seek the truth," Holmes answered, "so long as he does not obscure the facts." I realised that Holmes was still sour that he had not been able to examine the remarkable paper that Sir Derrington's ghost had left behind for his son. "I trust that when Sir Tarrant visited here he noted the slight scuff marks in the wardrobe, that the cocoa mug was shifted slightly after its contents had cooled, that Lumley shed a button from his nightgown as he searched beneath the bed, and that the place where the ghost appeared, beside the door to the corridor, was highly suggestive."

"If he did then he's a better man than I," I confessed. As always, Holmes observations seemed elementary after he had made them.

"A more observant man, perhaps," Holmes said, clapping me on the shoulder, "but hardly a better one." He opened the door to the corridor suddenly and caught Mrs. Lobb with her ear to the door.

"You're not with the police force," she accused us, electing accusation to cover her blatant eavesdropping.

"We're assisting with enquiries," I answered the old besom. "If you know anything then you'd better come clean before it's the worse for you!"

"I already told them I know nothing! I don't hold with ghosts and I don't want them in my 'otel. Nor you either, I'm thinking! So out! Out! Out!"

We soon found ourselves on the doorstep in the street, with the door slammed shut behind us. "Well!" I snorted, angry at our treatment when we had been trying to solve a puzzle that might cost a man his fortune and his freedom.

Holmes looked up at the four storeys of the Hanley, his eyes narrowing and his expression grave. "Ghosts," he muttered. "Ghosts indeed."

Behind us the carriage from Wigmore Street rolled away.

++++

From Hanley's we retreated to the nearest post office. Holmes spent the better part of half an hour sending a series of curious telegrams: to the insurance agency that had underwritten the Manuscript; to the public registrar of wills and oaths; to the British Museum; and to his brother in Whitehall regarding port immigration records. Then he set the street rascals he used as an irregular research resource to race round the carters and hauliers that plied their trade west of Waterloo Bridge.

I was dispatched to the Cresswell again to beg copies of the Jhansi manuscript while Holmes hurried off on some urgent mission of his own.

The gas-lamps were lit by the time we made our way back to the familiar surroundings of Baker Street. I'd sent word on to Mary that I would be spending the night at my former lodgings. My wife knew that I sometimes yearned for the adventure of my bachelor existence, and having become my bride as a direct consequence of one such foray she was kind and sweet enough not to begrudge me to Holmes when the game was afoot.[3]

Young Wiggins was waiting anxiously on the step to pass Holmes a note and receive five shillings in his palm for the work done by Holmes's street lads. My friend pocketed the information without troubling to read it.

A visitor was waiting for us in Mrs. Hudson's drawing room, and according to Holmes's landlady he had been waiting anxiously for some time. "This gentleman is…" Mrs.. Hudson began, but Holmes was already ahead of her.

"Mr. Charles Cayden," he deduced. "Pray do not be startled, sir. The mourning band on the hat on the hall-stand, the bulge of a foolscap legal document inside your jacket, your bearing as a man formerly under military habit, the condition of your boots which betray a largely rural existence, the ruddy air of a man who enjoys brisk walks in the fresh air, the calluses and ink-stains indicating extensive if eclectic scholarly habits; all elementary indicators. And who else of that description would seek us out on the day that Henry Lumley was arrested than his father's lifelong friend?"

"As you say, Mr. Holmes," Cayden agreed, shrugging off in his distraction this demonstration of my friend's acumen. "It is about Henry that I have come." He glanced at me also. "You are Dr. Watson, the medical practitioner to whom Henry appealed this morning?"

"I am Watson," I agreed. "I served with Lumley."

"Very good," Cayden replied. "Very, very good. I have been to see him. He is not well. Not well at all. The police have refused to allow him to leave

---

3 *Most scholars of Dr. Watson's accounts agree with W.S. Baring-Gould's famous 1962 biography that John H. Watson MD wedded Miss Mary Morstan, daughter of the late Captain Charles Morstan of the 34th Bombay Infantry, probably on the first of May 1889 at St Mark's Church, Camberwell. Mrs. Cecil Forrester was matron of honour, Mr. Sherlock Holmes the best man. Watson's meeting with Miss Morstan is described by him in* **The Sign of Four.**

on bond. He is spending a miserable night in the cells."

"That is not good," I frowned. "What does Lumley's legal man have to say about that?"

"Mr. Goodge is of the opinion that the prosecutor in the case is unlikely to be lenient," Cayden answered. "Indeed, given Henry's remarkable story and his claimed motivations, Goodge has asked me to enquire of Dr. Watson's medical opinion on the subject of Henry's... sanity."

"A defence of insanity," snorted Holmes, "and a lifetime in some benevolent institution."

"I would gladly fund Henry's care," Cayden promised, "should the legal claims upon his estate exceed his own resources."

"That's all well and good," I objected, "but it rather assumes that Lumley is mad!"

Cayden smiled sadly at me. "Come now, Dr. Watson. This is 1891. This is the age of science. Surely you are not one of those superstitious table-tappers that believes the dead can speak?"

"There may be other explanations that do not defy the laws of Newton," Holmes suggested. "Since you have helpfully presented yourself to assist Colonel Lumley perhaps you would be able to answer me some questions, Mr. Cayden?"

"I should be pleased to assist," Sir Derrington's friend assured us. "But I will tell you frankly that I believe Henry's nerve condition has overcome his sensibilities and that his actions are those of a hero pushed beyond his measure into the realms of unreason."

"The Manuscript," began Holmes. "You were present when it was first discovered?"

Cayden shook his head. "Lumley – that is Derrington Lumley – had taken a squad of men up into the passes to cut off the Rani's retreat. I was with the horse who took the low road. By the time we caught up with Lumley he'd already captured that Marathi, Satim Bey, and got him to show them the Rani's hidden hoard. I did help bag the treasure and get it on the horses back down to camp."

"Did you ever speak to this Satim Bey?"

"No. I heard from some of the troopers that he pleaded for his life, weeping on bended knee, but he was a murderous rebel and Lumley had him shot."

"These men also told you about the supposed curse he placed upon the Manuscript?"

Cayden frowned. "It was clear that the Manuscript had been important to him. He'd seemed more upset about its discovery and loss than about all the jewels of the Rani's horde. Lumley and I pored over it for many an hour, trying to make sense of what it was."

"Not a language that anybody understood," I ventured.

"Not a language at all, in my view," Cayden snorted. "What language has only thirteen characters, Mr. Holmes?"

"A code, then?" Holmes suggested. "Something based upon the placement of the characters and the colour of the ink. Fascinating." He pulled himself back to Cayden. "So Colonel Lumley came home a rich man."

"He came home a sour man. We all did, those of us that had lived through the mutiny. India lost its lustre to us when we saw it for what it was, that brutal savage vicious place, like a rabid dog waiting to bite the hand of its master."

"And Sir Derrington placed the Manuscript in the care of the Cresswell."

Cayden snorted. "That Dr. Forsythe, so certain that his scholarship could unlock the secrets of the Manuscript, so fervent in convincing Lumley to vest it with him! And yet all these years later what has Forsythe to show for his theories and musings and research? Ashes!" Cayden thought again. "Ashes and a large insurance settlement which will maintain his living for many years to come."

"You are suggesting that Forsythe will benefit from the destruction of the Manuscript?" I asked.

"How can he not?" demanded Cayden. "First he inveigles a fortune by bequest from Sir Derrington, and then not a day later the Manuscript which the museum could never sell while keeping its reputation is destroyed in a way which brings it a fortune in insurance."

Holmes stuffed his pipe and continued with his questions. "You were the last man outside the museum to handle the parchment," he noted.

"Was I?" Cayden shrugged. "That would be three months past now. My friend was passing sick and not likely to recover, and he was being plagued by some officious little man from the insurance company about the authenticity of the Manuscript. It seemed they'd had information that the scroll was not genuine or had been substituted or some such. I went down there to the Cresswell – twice, in fact – and met with the pre-eminent man in the field, some Cambridge chap who looked at the Manuscript in my presence and proclaimed it the real thing. Forsythe was livid at even the suggestion that it was a forgery."

"Others had shown an interest in the Manuscript, too," Holmes noted.

"You mean Mr. Hector Dorner?" Cayden suggested. "I know for a fact that he offered Lumley fifty thousand for it. Lumley would never budge. He was convinced to his dying day that the scroll contained some secret far greater than its value on the market. Or are you thinking about that blasted Indian who kept writing, demanding that the Manuscript be returned to the people of Jhansi?"

"An Indian?" I asked, perking up. "Is this the same fellow who made a commotion down at the Cresswell?"

"I have no idea," shrugged Cayden. "All I know is that the man plagued my friend with letters, even with calls to the house. In the end Lumley set the dogs on him."

"You do not recall his name, or any way in which he might be traced?"

"I do not." Cayden glanced at Mrs. Hudson's mantel-clock. "I fear the hour grows late, gentlemen. If Dr. Watson is unwilling to assist in young Henry's defence with a medical opinion…? No? Then I'm afraid I must arrange for some specialists to listen to Henry's story on the morrow. I'll keep you from your supper no longer and bid you good day."

"I'm eager to enjoy my meal," Holmes agreed as Cayden made his departures. "First I must locate a little pepper."

I was at a loss to understand Cayden's reaction to so innocent a remark.

++++

One of Holmes's eccentricities which a friend must learn to bear is that sudden frenetic mood which comes upon him from time to time, and the demands he makes of those around him to move at his pace and with the same efficiency he would expect of himself. Such a turn came upon my friend then. Dinner was abandoned despite Mrs. Hudson's dismay and I found myself hailing a cab and heading off to do the impossible. Holmes left the flat at the same time I did and strode away in the opposite direction.

My task was a difficult one, and I did not relish it. I travelled to the address Holmes had supplied and interrupted the supper of Assistant Crown Prosecutor Sir Tarrant Besting. He was not pleased to be bearded at home, and less pleased still that I came with a challenge from Holmes to the prosecution's case against Henry Lumley.

"Dash it, man, you're expected to seek out the truth!" I exclaimed as

Sir Tarrant threatened to have me ejected by the servants. "Are you so afraid of being wrong that you'd let an innocent man be convicted? And how foolish do you think you'll look when Holmes proves his innocence despite your best efforts?"

"Lumley committed his crime in front of many witnesses," Sir Tarrant argued. "Some saw him break the glass of the display case. Others came running in time to see him burn the Manuscript."

I had to admit that the case did seem fairly watertight, but I had faith in my friend's abilities. "Holmes has invited you to find out what really happened," I persisted. "He asks you to move quickly as time in now of the essence, and he recommends that you bring some uniformed officers."

Either my indignation or my resoluteness worked their way with Sir Tarrant. The crown prosecutor sighed heavily and abandoned his meal. We took the carriage to Bow Street, where we picked up Captain Lumley and two uniformed constables as Holmes had requested.

By the time we got back to Clarges Street the city's clocks were chiming ten. Holmes was waiting for us outside the Hanley. Sir Tarrant was in a foul mood.

"It is only my respect for your reputation that has convinced me to endure this folly, sir," he warned Holmes. "I will hear no more special pleading on Lumley's behalf from you than I did from that friend of his father's. I have witnesses and the accused's own confession."

Lumley nodded. "I did it. I would do it again. I have told you why."

"Captain Lumley has spoken the truth as he knows it," Holmes owned, "as did those people who observed his behaviour in the Cresswell Museum. However, none of them has full possession of the facts and therefore none of them can draw the appropriate conclusions."

"Why are we here?" Lumley shuddered, looking up at the bleak façade of Hanley's Hotel. The first wisps of fog were curling up from the Thames and the night was becoming cold.

"We will shortly be going inside," Holmes told them. "I trust you brought the appropriate paperwork, Sir Tarrant? First we will wait for another member of our party to arrive."

The prosecutor frowned. "Another member?"

Holmes held up one finger for silence and cocked his ear. We could all hear a Hansom approaching. Shortly the cab turned the corner and pulled to a halt outside the Hanley.

There was a fierce shouting from inside the carriage. Holmes darted round to the other side of the cab and intercepted the man who flung open the far door to make his getaway.

"Not yet, Satim Bey," Holmes told the bearded, turbaned Indian who tried to leap for freedom. The two constables, sensing a felon fleeing, quickly pounced upon the man.

"Satim Bey?" I recognised the name. "Wasn't he shot dead by Sir Derrington Lumley over thirty years ago?"

This Bey wasn't much over thirty years old. He struggled in the policemen's grasp but they held him firm, curious as to what was going on. "Just keep still, Johnny Foreigner," one of them warned the Indian.

"I think you'll find, Watson, that this Satim Bey has another name just like his forebear did," Holmes told me. "Satim Bey isn't a real name at all. It's the sort of Indian-sounding cognomen one might adopt if being roughly questioned by British troops intent on torturing secret treasures out of one."

"The Indian who made a nuisance of himself at the Cresswell and had to be ejected!" I recalled.

Sir Tarrant wasn't following this and didn't like the fact. "Just who is this person, Holmes?" he demanded. "What does he have to do with anything, and why is he being detained by my officers?"

"And why did he simply drive up to us, then try to run away?" I added, puzzled along with Besting.

Holmes smiled thinly. "As to why detain him, Sir Tarrant, I'd suggest you direct your constables to the bulge in Satim Bey's left coat pocket, which by the shape of it appears to be a four shot Derringer. Carrying concealed firearms on the streets of our capital is something I'd expect a crown prosecutor to discourage."

Satim Bey struggled again, speaking rapidly in some Indian dialect I couldn't follow. The constables wrestled him down with considerable efficiency, removed his firearm, and handcuffed him.

In answer to my question Holmes moved over to the driver of the Hansom that Bey had arrived in. He handed a generous tip up to the cabbie and said, "Thank your supervisor for me, Shedlow. Tell Mr. Schott that your help was most appreciated."

"You visited the cab company," I realised. "You observed the cab that watched us this afternoon and traced it back to its stables, then arranged that if the passenger used it again - as well he might go to the same company another time—"

"Then instead of remaining concealed in an adjacent street where we could be watched, the cabbie would drive his passenger straight to me," Holmes completed my deduction. "Indeed. I don't suppose Mr. Bey would care to tell us why he was watching the Hanley?"

The Indian spoke a few words in his own tongue then fell silent.

"'Ee can speak the Queen's English," Shedlow told us. "'Ee knew enough to tell me where to park and when to move on."

Lumley looked closely at Satim Bey. "This is a fellow who plagued me about the Manuscript a few months back," he declared. "Wanted me to convince father to return it to Jhansi. I sent him packing."

"Doubtless he was also the Indian who was reported to have troubled Sir Derrington and the museum," intervened Sir Tarrant, determined not to be left behind. He turned to Bey. "You will tell me now why you are here and what you know of this case."

Satim Bey spat on the ground.

"According to the Port Authorities a man called Satim Bey with an Indian passport disembarked in Bristol three days ago," Holmes supplied. "He had visited England before, but this time it was news of Sir Derrington's death that brought him here. He was keen to know the fate of the Jhansi Manuscript." Holmes turned his hawk-eyes on the Indian. "Were you not?"

Satim Bey shrugged. "It was stolen from my people," he answered at last. "To my family's shame my father lost it to your English plunderers. I have tried to regain my family's honour by retrieving it and restoring it to its rightful place."

Holmes seemed to lose interest in Bey. "Come inside now," he invited us. "Present your credentials to the formidable Mrs. Lobb, Sir Tarrant, and let us revisit the haunting of Captain Lumley."

++++

Holmes insisted that the constables remain in the hotel foyer with Satim Bey. The rest of us made for the stairs with Mrs. Lobb complaining in our wake. Her objections became shriller and more urgent as Holmes ignored the door from the first floor landing and continued his way up to the second floor of the hotel.

"Room 113's this way, sirs!" Mrs. Lobb shrieked.

"I am aware of that," Holmes replied. "However I am now interested in examining room 213, the site of the apparition."

Lumley frowned. "213? I was in 113, Holmes," he objected.

"You went to sleep in 113, certainly," Holmes agreed, "and you awoke there in the morning. There are traces to prove it, of the chair you positioned to block the door, of the drugged drink you took which rendered you insensate so you could be moved. But both were positioned twice, as if they had been shifted then replaced."

Mrs. Lobb fell suddenly silent.

"Other traces are missing, however," Holmes noted, "and the summoning of your father's ghost would require rather more preparation than could easily be tidied away without leaving signs of it in the morning."

"Are you suggesting, Holmes, that Captain Lumley really did see an apparition?" objected Sir Tarrant.

"I'll wager a guinea that he did," my friend replied.

Lumley shook his head. "I couldn't have been moved from my room. I had wedged the door. Nobody could enter."

Holmes had the answer, of course. "If you re-examine the dressing room of 113, you will notice the indentation marks at the rear of the wardrobe which indicate the former presence of a false back. Concealed as it was behind your hanging clothing, it would not be immediately obvious by candlelight. A man could hide there and emerge once you had entered your drugged repose, then easily transport you to the chamber we go to examine now."

"But Holmes," I said, "even if that was so, Lumley searched his room thoroughly in the morning. The chair was wedged in place, which could not have been done unless someone was in the room to do it. Any false back to the wardrobe would surely have been detected then and any one concealed within it discovered."

"I'm certain I would have seen such a thing if it had been there," Lumley agreed. "I searched very thoroughly when I awoke."

"By then the partition was long gone," Holmes agreed. "And so was the man who had reset the chair in place."

"Then how?" I asked.

Holmes paused as we reached the top landing. "Come now, Watson, you observed it yourself. The windows were clean."

Mrs. Lobb twitched a little. "I keeps a clean house," she muttered defiantly.

"The upper sashes are painted shut," Holmes reminded me. "The only way to clean the outside of the lower sashes, which slide inside the upper ones, is to wash them from the outside using a ladder. Access to the windows is therefore commonly gained with such a ladder."

"But the windows were sealed," Lumley objected. "I checked them."

"The windows have Bristol catches, Captain Lumley. A thin cotton thread looped around one would be sufficient to drop it down from outside. Once is place the catch would prevent the sash from opening even though the screw-end was not as tight as it could be. The thread itself could be broken and yanked away. What is suggestive is that between your check and ours the screw-knobs were undoubtedly tightened to conceal the effect."

"This is all supposition, Holmes," growled Sir Tarrant. "Nor does showing how a thing could be done prove that it was done."

Holmes snorted. "Proof? Step this way then, Sir Tarrant, and let us find some."

He led the way to room 213. The upper floor perfectly mirrored the layout below and 213 was directly above 113. Mrs. Lobb claimed not to have the key until she was hectored and threatened by the judicial majesty of Sir Tarrant Besting.

Lumley exclaimed in amazement as we entered the room. "Why this room is almost identical to my own!"

"It would be identical in every way once the wall-paintings were exchanged," Holmes argued. "But we shall find a difference on the carpet, I believe."

I looked to the floor. "More indentations where a chair has been placed under the doorknob!" I exclaimed.

"Naturally," Holmes replied. "But what of this line here, would you say? This long thin line where the nap of the carpet has been depressed, indicating that something quite heavy stood here for quite some time?"

"A suitcase?" I ventured. But there was only one line, not the imprint of four. Then I noticed the pairs of screw-holes that had punctured the carpet along the line of the impression.

"Something was installed here," Sir Tarrant reasoned, "Something fastened to the floor."

Holmes moved over to the doorway that led to the dressing room and examined the floor beyond with special interest. "The angle of that carpet mark is at forty-five degrees to this doorway?" he checked. He moved into the antechamber. "And I am out of sight here, as is the doorway, when the curtains are closed around the bed except for those at the foot?"

Lumley sat upon the bed and verified it. "Mr. Holmes, I confess that I am at something of a loss. I saw my father's spirit, but now you say I was drugged and brought to this chamber for my vision? But that visitation included information only my father might know and left behind tangible proof of his presence in the form of the letter that Sir Tarrant confiscated."

"It's time to explain, Holmes," I advised my friend.

"It is," he agreed. "Captain Lumley, you have been made the scapegoat in a venal plot which has cruelly exploited your weak nerves and your filial loyalty. This is what took place: On falling asleep you were brought to this room, which in the drug-induced haze of your half-lucid midnight awakening would not appear any different from the chamber you thought it to be."

Mrs. Lobb made to sidle to the door. I closed it and stood in front of it.

"Here, where this long mark mars the carpet, was a plain glass panel some six feet square, connected to the floor by a wooden frame. It would be invisible in a dim light, but moreover it would reflect any brightly lit image coming from the dressing room beyond. This illusion was first used on stage back in '62 and is named after Professor John Henry Pepper, the man who popularised it as a means of causing Hamlet's father and Banquo's spectre to appear on stage – Pepper's Ghost[4]."

"Why, I've seen that effect!" I cried. "At a performance of Dickens's *The Haunted Man*."

"It's a simple illusion," Holmes replied. "Anyone looking out from a lit room into a dark night who has seen their own reflection has seen the basis for it. The angled mirror allows for an actor offstage to appear as a transparent spectre onstage."

"But I saw my father," Lumley objected. "And he spoke to me."

"He whispered to you," Holmes corrected him. "It was easier to conceal that it was not your father's voice that way. As for his appearance, anyone with a daguerreotype or tintype or other old photographic image could use a magnifying lens and project Sir Derrinton's phantom into the room. With your faculties clouded by the substance that had drugged you, the same substance that made it impossible for you to rise from your bed, the effect must have been quite convincing."

"You checked the hauliers," I remembered, "because the glass is not here now. It must have been delivered and hauled away by some tradesman."

"Back to the Travoli Theatre," Holmes supplied. "I have from Wiggins the name of the stagehand who abstracted it and brought it here and back."

Sir Tarrant was not ready to concede Holmes's thesis yet. "But the knowledge that Lumley claims the spectre had?" he demanded. "And this letter?"

"Ah, the letter," Holmes responded. "In confiscating that key piece of

4 *Pepper revised a mirror illusion invention developed in 1862 by inventor Henry Dircks so it could be used in theatrical productions at reasonable cost. It debuted in the Dickens **Dr. Amatisation** to which Dr. Watson alludes.*

evidence you very nearly thwarted the very proof you demand." He took the paper from the crown prosecutor and held it up to the light. "You will notice that the ink is somewhat faded, the handwriting that of an elderly man in poor health."

"I would know my father's hand anywhere," Lumley asserted.

Holmes thrust the note back at Sir Tarrant. "It is the writing of Colonel Sir Derrington Lumley," he confirmed. "However this letter was written months ago. It is an instruction, a plea for help in dealing with a problem that the reclusive old man was troubled by. Read the message again, but this time consider that Sir Derrington was contacted three months ago by a concerned insurance firm that had doubts about the authenticity of the Manuscript. After due enquiry today I can tell you that those doubts were raised by an Indian gentleman who called at their offices. The insurers insisted on a new authentication and were being rather persistent."

"*Time is short,*" read Sir Tarrant. "*Pay no heed to Forsythe or any other. Go to the Manuscript and do what must be done. I must be freed from this torment or I shall have no rest.*'"

"A letter to an old friend," I ventured, "asking Charles Cayden to go down to London of Sir Derrington's behalf and see to the Manuscript's provenance."

"It's possible," admitted Lumley, "but how came it here?"

"How came the ghost by his remarkable knowledge of your childhood affairs and youthful improprieties?" retorted Holmes. "You took it as knowledge only a father might have. I took it to mean that only one who had regular access to your father's library and papers, to his journals and diaries, to his personal confidences, might know such things."

"Cayden!" I concluded. "It was he who recommended the Hanley!"

"Cayden?" yelped Sir Tarrant. "But why?"

"I suggest we ask him," Sherlock Holmes told us all. "He is, after all, concealed in this very hotel. Lead us to your employer, Mrs. Lobb, and then all shall be revealed."

"I don't know what you're talking about," denied the vicious old lady, her beady eyes darting between Holmes and Sir Tarrant and back to the door I was guarding. "I don't know no Cayden."

"You may not know him by that name," Holmes agreed. "Perhaps then you would recognise him in person?" He strode back into the changing room, opened the wardrobe, and hammered on the back-board. "You can come out now, Mr. Cayden. You are discovered!"

++++

"I knew Cayden would hurry here after I made my pepper reference," Holmes explained as Sir Derrington's old friend was escorted down to the lobby to join the rest of us. "There were still traces of the ghost illusion to be dealt with; the mirror to be returned, the magic lantern that magnified an old photograph of Sir Derrington to be dismantled. I calculated that if we arrived here at the correct time, we might corner him in the act and force him to make use of another of Mrs. Lobb's curious wardrobes. You may speculate what nefarious purposes to which such concealments might ordinarily be put."

"I have done nothing," denied Charles Cayden. "I was here examining the case for my old friend's son and concealed myself out of embarrassment when I heard others coming."

"You'll get your chance to state your defence in due course, Cayden," Sir Tarrant told him as we met with the constables in the foyer. The crown prosecutor had the worried frown of a man who has strayed well beyond the usual bounds of his professional experience.

"You!" shouted Satim Bey as he saw the man we were escorting, and loosed a torrent of Indian vituperation at Cayden.

"What now?" demanded Sir Tarrant.

"I 'ad nothin' to do with it," Mrs. Lobb snivelled. "I just gave 'im his drink at bedtime, that's all, an' left 'em to it."

"I think you will find that Satim Bey once expected Mr. Cayden's aid in returning the Jhansi Manuscript," Holmes suggested. "Doubtless, money passed hands for Cayden's promised assistance. When no manuscript appeared, then Sir Derrington passed away, and especially after the mysterious destruction of the document in the museum, our mysterious Indian decided to investigate. Watching the Cresswell led Bey to us, then to the Hanley, and now to Cayden."

"I have rights," Charles Cayden insisted. "I have the right to silence."

"But not to my silence," Holmes told him. "Sir Tarrant wondered why you would want to provoke Captain Lumley to destroy the Manuscript. I discovered earlier that Sir Derrinton changed his will to bequeath the document to the Museum only a few weeks before his death. Dr. Forsythe was overjoyed at the possibility of chemically testing the Manuscript and conducting other examinations previously forbidden by its owner."

Lumley was still baffled. "So?"

"Such examination would have quickly determined that the manuscript in the Cresswell was a forgery," Holmes answered. "It was genuine when examined by the expert from Cambridge, but you will recall that Cayden was the last and only person to handle the document thereafter before it was sealed in the cabinet."

Despite his previous proclamation Cayden couldn't resist a retort. "This is ridiculous. How could I forge a document like that?"

"I gave you the forgery!" blurted the man calling himself Satim Bey. "You sent me to those insurers to start those rumours, you took the copy from me that my people made, you took our money, and then you gave me nothing!"

"He said it was just a prank, him and them stagehands," Mrs. Lobb cut in, shouting her own case over the rantings of the Indian.

"I have nothing to regret," Cayden growled. "Derrington betrayed me at the last when he did not will the Manuscript to me with his other books and documents. For years I watched him wallow in the wealth of his Indian adventure, denied any reward because I had been sent on a different mission by nothing more than chance. You think the great Colonel Sir Derrington Lumley would deign to pass on any of his great fortune to his dearest friend? No. I was snubbed in Jhansi and again when he rewrote his will."

"You thought of the plan!" accused Satim Bey. "After the old man threw me out, you contacted me!"

"I'm just a poor old woman makin' her way in the world as best she can," sniffed Mrs. Lobb. "I don't know nothin' about big mirrors and secret compartments, on my life I don't!"

"What did the Cresswell ever do to deserve the Manuscript?" demanded Cayden. "Forsythe is a fool who cares only for prestige. He deserves the ignominy of his loss,"

"You used my relationship with my father against me!" Henry Lumley accused his father's friend. "You made me your tool of revenge in the most wicked way imaginable. You almost cost me my sanity!"

The scene descended into a loud chaos of recriminations and excuses.

Holmes remained above the furore he had caused. He took Sir Tarrant Besting aside and gestured to the little knot of malefactors rowing with each other. "And that is why you cannot prosecute Captain Henry Lumley for the destruction of the Jhansi Manuscript," he told Sir Tarrant. "Despite Lumley's confession, despite all the witnesses, the Jhansi Manuscript was not destroyed. It had already been stolen months before, by Charles Cayden."

++++

I t was two weeks before the ructions and ramifications of Holmes's revelation died down. After legal advice Cayden broke down and identified
the new owner of the Jhansi Manuscript as rich collector Hector Dorner.
During a dawn raid officers from Scotland Yard retrieved the document
from Mr. Dorner's Mayfair house and returned it to the Cresswell. After
much debate and discussion, Dansen and Forsythe accepted its authenticity.

Sir Tarrant Besting was much praised for his incisiveness and initiative
in uncovering the strange plot behind the dead man's manuscript.

Lumley remained in London until Mr. Goodge assured him that all
charges against him had been dismissed. On his final night in the city, he
joined Mary and I for dinner at our home, and Holmes attended, too.

"I have just seen off the esteemed Satim Bey," Holmes told us as we
settled down with our cigarettes after an excellent meal. "He has been
escorted to the boat-train and is no longer welcome in Her Majesty's
Kingdom of Great Britain and Ireland."

"He was lucky just to be deported," I snorted. "The man conspired to
steal a valuable artefact from a respected London museum."

"I understand that the local authorities in Jhansi will deal with him,"
Holmes replied. "They were less impressed with his noble quest to
retrieve the document his father lost. They view him as an opportunist
and a treasure-hunter."

"My father already found the Rani's treasure," Lumley pointed out.

"Your father found a hastily-concealed cache," Holmes corrected him.
"The Rani of Jhansi's fabled wealth was greater by far. The Koh-I-Noor
diamond that was presented to Her Majesty Queen Victoria was but a
plaything bauble in Jhansi's sparkling court[5]. The man naming himself
Satim Bey believed that far greater wealth remained yet uncovered from
the ancient days of Uttar Pradesh. He was eager to retrieve the Manuscript
that he believed was the key to discovering its whereabouts."

"The Manuscript describes where the Rani's secret horde is hidden?"
Lumley asked, taking another sip of his brandy to steady himself.

Holmes snorted. "Bey believed there must be invisible writing on

_____

5 *At 105 carats the Koh-I-Noor (Mountain of Light) was then the largest known
diamond in the world. It became the property of Queen Victoria when she was
proclaimed Empress of India in 1877.*

the parchment and so the original must be retrieved – but a man able to prepare so accurate a forgery actually already possessed the information he needed to solve the puzzle."

He reached into his jacket pocket and removed two wispy slips of tracing paper. I recognised the characters from the facsimile Manuscript I had begged from Forsythe two weeks earlier. Holmes had transcribed an exact coloured copy onto the sheets. "The fundamental error that the scholars made was in assuming that this was a language at all," my friend revealed. "They were consulting linguists when they should have called upon cartographers."

"Cartographers?" Lumley echoed. "How so?"

Holmes held up the transverse side of the manuscript. "Imagine that these are not words at all, but rather sigils indicating terrain. A simple map done like this in English might grid a landscape and place a single character in every significant square: an A for an ash, a B for a beech tree, O for an oak, W for water, R for a prominent rock. The remaining spaces might be filled in with any random letter so long as the significant ones were picked out in a different hue. Two additional colours might be necessary if the field contained both ashes and alders."

"The Jhansi Manuscript is a treasure map!" I exclaimed. A new thought occurred to me. "Yet it was on public display. Satim Bey the younger had only to visit the museum and make a copy of it."

"Except that only one side was visible," Holmes observed. "Even the framed copies available on the wall could not be held like this." He lifted up the two squares of tracing paper and positioned them back to back, then held them to the gas mantel so we could see both sides of the inscription at once. I recalled that the Manuscript itself was said to be translucent.

"Why, the coloured characters on each side fit perfectly with the gaps between words on the opposite side!" gasped Lumley. "The map is only complete if viewed like this."

"Just so," Holmes agreed. "Cayden had no idea of the real value of the document when he sold it to his unscrupulous antiquarian. Dr. Shadwell misinterpreted the significance of a document hastily concealed in the Rani's temporary treasure cache. Satim Bey knew something of its nature as a clue to treasure from hints in his father's papers but never understood the actual mechanism. Hector Dorner merely wanted to own a unique piece with that fanaticism that sometimes robs collectors of their good sense and morals."

"But with this we could find the treasure!" Lumley cried, rising from

He reached into his jacket pocket and removed two wispy slips of tracing paper.

his chair.

Holmes shook his head. "Calm yourself, Captain. With the help of the excellent maps of the Royal Ordinance Survey I have saved us a long and tedious trip to the Indian subcontinent. You will perhaps be disappointed to learn that on the 13th December of 1858, a great hoard was uncovered at the very spot denoted on this Manuscript. The treasure was divided between the crown and the ruling Maharaja of Gwalior in whose territory Jhansi then fell."

"I'm sorry, old chap," I told my army comrade.

Lumley took his disappointment with good grace. He sipped his brandy again and managed a smile. "I've inherited my father's fortune intact. I've been pulled back from the maw of madness, from ruin and imprisonment, my friends. I have even freed my father's spirit from immortal torment, at least in the sense that an awful burden has been lifted from *my* soul. No gem or gold chain could replace what you have given me."

"I am glad to have been of service to your father's ghost," Holmes told him. "And now as the hour is growing late and Mrs. Watson must be missing her husband's company, I propose to depart." He passed the traced sides of the Jhansi Manuscript to me. "Another item for your collection, Watson."

He strode away to hail a cab.

++++

I never expected to write a Sherlock Holmes story

by I. A. Watson

After all, detective stories are a very specialised genre. They demand a particular kind of plotting, a peculiar sort of pacing to unfold the mystery, a twist at the end to offer that final kick. They need to seed clues so the reader can "play the game" along with the story's hero. And when it comes to detective stories, Sherlock Holmes sets the bar.

Also factor in that Holmes was active in the last decades of the nineteenth century, and his original canon was written not as historical but contemporary fiction. The backgrounds, attitudes, dialogue, and motives were all drawn from what was then the modern day. When Holmes expressed views on politics, on science, on women, on Americans, he was echoing the authentic views of his fellow Victorians. Any new Holmes material, written over a century later, has to grapple with the tension between capturing the setting of the original stories versus the understandings and sensibilities of a readership for which 1891 is only something seen in movies.

As it happens though, I was invited to offer a contribution to a new Holmes anthology by fellow author Van Allen Plexico, and so I obliged.

I'm old school when it comes to mystery tales. The audience has to have a chance to solve the problem, so the writer has to play fair and slip the clues in somewhere; but it's also fair game to misdirect, to use the characters to deceive, to choose one's words very carefully indeed, and to do everything in one's power to leave the reader slapping their forehead at the end and saying "But of course, that's obvious!"

I also think it's best to start with the most impossible event one could conceive and then show why it wasn't really impossible after all. I've got another Holmes story I'd love to tell, the ultimate locked room mystery, but unfortunately I haven't yet figured out how to get the corpse inside the box.

I was surprised as I wrote *Dead Man's Manuscript* – and its predecessor *The Western Mail*, which wasn't included in the anthology because it was too short – to learn two things about Conan Doyle's creations. The first is that Watson's narration allows for a whole range of writer-tricks to shorthand the storyline, to mislead the reader, to quickly vignette characters, and to convey the feel of his era. He's a real boon to an author trying to keep to a word count. The second is that Holmes is a wonderful aid to information-dumping. Holmes can rattle off necessary plot information, descriptions of crime scenes, summaries of developments, all in his impatient, eclectic, brilliant manner, and because it's the Great Detective we just let his eccentric revelations wash over us and we don't complain. I found I had to use Holmes sparingly as I wrote; a little of his genius goes a long way. Watson buffers us.

For research I turned to W.S. Baring-Gould's excellent biography of Sherlock Holmes, itself now almost fifty years old but still the best and most readable extrapolated account of Holmes's career. I'd recommend it to all students of Holmesiana, especially if they are interested in Holmes's doings during his missing years after Reichenback, the further exploits of Irene Adler— *the* woman, and the mystery of the third Mrs. Watson.

I considered rereading the Holmes canon, at least in part, to remind me of the language and rhythms. Then I decided not to. That way would draw me to pastiche, to a stilted narrative that wasn't truly Conan Doyle in his authentic contemporary Victorian setting and wasn't a tale I wanted to tell. Instead I wrote the story in the style I remembered from the impressions I'd retained from earlier reading. That helped me find a comfortable blend between a modern narrative and one that could hopefully sit alongside Holmes's original accounts without embarrassing itself too badly. I unlocked my vocabulary and emphasized formal English. I spent a little more time describing Victoriana than Watson might have done under

Conan Doyle's guidance, simply because modern readers aren't as familiar with the setting as the original ones were.

Mostly I had fun, learned how clever Conan Doyle was in setting up his characters the way he did in the format he did, got to play with his toys for a while, and spent a week afterwards unintentionally sounding like John H. Watson.

I.A. Watson

I.A. Watson is a mild-mannered director of a counselling charity by day, a management development troubleshooter on his days off because he needs the money, and by night he would fight crime if only he wasn't writing stories. He's been an award-winning writer since the age of 11 (thank you Ilkley Literature Festival for your generous book token). He's done a lot of non-fiction writing, including a long-running newspaper column. Most recently, his articles on the Avengers comic series have been collected in *Assembled* and *Assembled 2*. His strangest published credit is probably getting a poem in the *Lewis Carroll Society of Canada Centenary Book* (or whatever it was) but until this year, he's always resisted turning his fiction-writing hobby into a paying job. Now he'll need to get a new hobby, so there'll be no excuse not to sneak out after darkness falls to battle crime.

THE GAME IS AFOOT
by Ron Fortier

I f you look at only the facts, they in themselves are awfully dry and boring. Sherlock Holmes is a fictional character of the late nineteenth and early twentieth centuries who first appeared in publication in 1887. He is the creation of Scottish-born author and physician, Arthur Conan Doyle. A brilliant London-based "consulting detective," Holmes is famous for his intellectual prowess, and is renowned for his skillful use of astute observation, deductive reasoning and inference to solve difficult cases.

The above data was taken from an entry in a popular encyclopedia. It goes on to add that Conan Doyle wrote four novels and fifty-six short stories that feature Holmes. The first two stories, short novels, appeared in *Beeton's Christmas Annual* for 1887 and *Lippincott's Monthly Magazine* in 1890, respectively. The character grew tremendous in popularity with the beginning of the first series of short stories in *The Strand Magazine* in 1891; further series of short stories and two serialized novels appeared until 1927. The stories cover a period from around 1875 up to 1907, with a final case in 1914.

All but four stories are narrated by Holmes's friend and biographer, Dr. John H. Watson; two are narrated by Sherlock Holmes himself, and two others are written in third person.

Conan Doyle said that the character of Holmes was inspired by

Dr.Joseph Bell, for whom Dolye had worked as a clerk at the Edinburgh Royal Infirmary. Like Sherlock Holmes, Bell was noted for drawing large conclusions from the smallest observations.

Perhaps one of the most blatant understatements ever is the line, "The character grew in tremendous popularity..." I would happily argue that Sherlock Holmes is the greatest fictional character ever created. His impact on English society goes beyond literature to actually have impacted twentieth century culture on so many levels. From the forensic sciences to criminal psychology and investigation, Holmes has left his mark. His name and his exploits are recognized around the world and there are Sherlock Holmes clubs in countries from Japan to South Africa.

Every minutiae of his life has been studied in infinite detail and his adventures have leapt off the printed page to every conceivable electronic communication media known to man. He first appeared in the flesh on the English stage. From there it was a short leap to radio and then movies which made him an international phenomena. And with each new adaptation, his original stories continued to be reprinted and translated throughout the world. Long before George Lucas amazed the world with his merchandise genius concerning his Star Wars franchise, there were Sherlock Holmes lunch buckets, Halloween costumes, wristwatches, briar pipes, statues and chess sets. Anywhere his name or image could be stamped, the Great Detective was represented.

With the advent of cinema, dozens of actors have portrayed the Baker Street hero from the silent shorts to the blockbusters of today. Gifted thespians such as Arthur Wotner, Basil Rathbone, Peter Cushing, Christopher Lee, John Neville, Robert Stephens, Nicol Williamson and Christopher Plummer all took on the role for the silver screen, while on the smaller television tube, actors such as Ronald Howard, Stewart Granger, Roger Moore and Jeremy Brett all put their on stamp on this classic icon. And there seems to be no letting up here in the Twenty-First Century as Robert Downey Jr. is set to appear in the much cherished role come Christmas, 2009 in as yet another interpretation simply labeled, *SHERLOCK HOLMES.*

And if Holmes's electronic cases seem vast, they are minimal in comparison to his ever expanding literary adventures. Even with the death of his distinguished creator in 1930, the public continued to demand more Sherlock Holmes stories and there was never a shortage of willing writers to pick up the hunt, starting with Doyle's own son. As the years passed, writers from every genre affixed their by-lines to the Great Detective to include such notables as mystery pro Ellery Queen and the Master of Macabre himself, Stephen King. The ranks of Holmes writers became legion as have the new stories.

Sherlock Holmes has found himself in every corner of the globe fighting all brand of villainy from the supernatural in Dracula and the Invisible Man to the Martian aliens of H.G.Well's classic, *WAR OF THE WORLDS*. One particular fanciful novel had him as a modern day detective put on the case of solving the assassination of President John F.Kennedy. There are obviously no limits to the imaginary worlds new writers are willing to take Holmes and Watson. And as silly, outlandish and awful most of these are, Holmes's army of loyal fans have stayed the course, remaining true through thick and thin.

And if you still do not comprehend just how popular this fictional character is, then let me appraise you of another fact. Fans will go out of their way to support even the minor players in the Holmes Canon. There have been entire book series starring Mycroft Holmes, Sherlock's older brother; the Baker Street Irregulars, a bunch of street urchins Holmes employs to gather information; Irene Adler, the actress who once bested Holmes in a battle of wits. Even Mrs.Hudson, Holmes's sweet, loveable landlady has appeared in her own stories. Adding to this endless list of related tales, Airship 27 Prod. will soon be releasing *A SEASON OF MADNESS*, a Victorian mystery written by Aaron Smith and starring Doctor Watson as he teams up with Dr. Seward of the *DRACULA* novel by Bram Stoker.

Which is as good a point as any to explain this volume from Airship 27 Productions. It was only inevitable that we would one day get around to doing a series based on one of the most successful pulp heroes ever. And yes, I do consider Sherlock Holmes a pulp hero. We have always considered popular fiction written to entertain the public at large to be pulp fiction and no other series has ever been as entertaining as that of Sherlock Holmes. It has been both our joy and honor to put this book, the first in a series, together. We make no boastful claims that it is any better (or worse) then the hundreds of such Holmes anthologies that have come before us. But we will tell you this: our writers approached writing their Holmes stories with both great enthusiasm and respect for the character and his history. You will find no aliens in this collection, nor cowboys or demons, but straightforward mysteries set down in the same tradition of Conan Doyle's original tales. We believe we have done right by him and all who love this character so dearly. But that is for you, dear reader, to decide.

As always, we thank you for your continued support. All our titles may be found at our on-line shop (http://stores.lulu.com/airship27) where they may be purchased at a discounted price. We sincerely appreciate your feedback and suggestions. Our goal remains our motto, *Pulp fiction for a new generation.*

Ron Fortier
6 June 2009
Somersworth, N.H
(www.Airship27.com)
(Airship27@comcast.net)

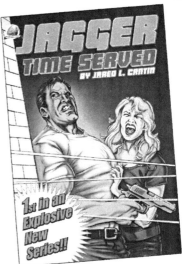

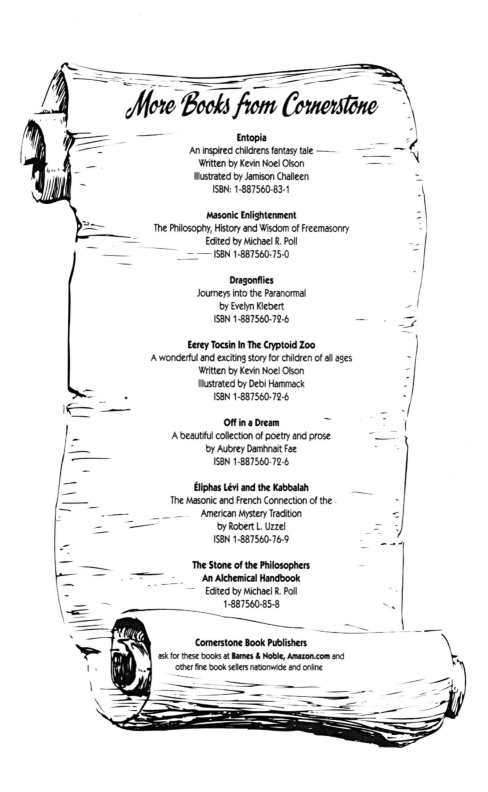

More Books from Cornerstone

Entopia
An inspired childrens fantasy tale
Written by Kevin Noel Olson
Illustrated by Jamison Challeen
ISBN: 1-887560-83-1

Masonic Enlightenment
The Philosophy, History and Wisdom of Freemasonry
Edited by Michael R. Poll
ISBN 1-887560-75-0

Dragonflies
Journeys into the Paranormal
by Evelyn Klebert
ISBN 1-887560-72-6

Eerey Tocsin In The Cryptoid Zoo
A wonderful and exciting story for children of all ages
Written by Kevin Noel Olson
Illustrated by Debi Hammack
ISBN 1-887560-72-6

Off in a Dream
A beautiful collection of poetry and prose
by Aubrey Damhnait Fae
ISBN 1-887560-72-6

Éliphas Lévi and the Kabbalah
The Masonic and French Connection of the
American Mystery Tradition
by Robert L. Uzzel
ISBN 1-887560-76-9

The Stone of the Philosophers
An Alchemical Handbook
Edited by Michael R. Poll
1-887560-85-8

Cornerstone Book Publishers
ask for these books at **Barnes & Noble, Amazon.com** and
other fine book sellers nationwide and online

Printed in the United States
221087BV00001B/30/P

9 781934 935507